MARKED

BOOK ONE:

SHADOWED SERIES

Alyson Dawn

Marked

Copyright © 2025 by Alyson Dawn

This book is a work of fiction. Any references to historical events, people, media, or incidents are the product of the author's imagination or used fictitiously.

Book Cover design/Map Illustration by Donnie Neuber

This book is dedicated to the readers

who have shadows inside of them.

Let them empower you.

Prologue

Four figures stood at the heart of the catacombs, ringed by a pool of living shadows that writhed like a starless void. Flickering torchlight danced across their faces, faces marked by the same silver sigils that bound them together, the first Shadowborn of Myrth.

Kyron rested a hand on the polished statue next to him, his stocky form demanding space in the small room. His voice was low, almost reluctant. "We were born of necessity, bound to shadows to protect our world. But it needs to end with us."

Celeste laughed in response, her straight black hair falling off her shoulder as she whipped her head to face him. "End? You speak as though evil will just vanish. Like they won't start a war again?" She stepped closer, towering over him with her height. "Our power needs to spread, or the world will be covered in darkness, and it won't be ours. Or do you mean to leave our people without the power to defend themselves?"

Idris, who had kept his distance, stepped forward then, his Healer's robes whispering against the floor. "It is not a curse, but if used wisely, a gift. I agree with Celeste. We need to find a way to preserve our shadows."

Muriel closed her eyes, feeling the shadow pulse at the edge of her vision. "People have already tried to recreate what we can do. We're the only ones who can fight back."

Kyron's shoulders stiffened. "I have seen children taken, families torn apart for mere gold, wars that arose over claiming land. If anyone knew we could pass on our power-"

Celeste's eyes glowed with inner fire. "There will always be innocents and tyrants. We can't control that, but we can control how our descendants will live and their chances at life. We have to fortify our kind. If we don't do this, the Shadowborn will end with us."

Idris thoughtfully dipped his chin as shadows flickered across his stoic face. "What if we find a way to seal our power? Let it reemerge when necessary?"

Muriel opened her eyes, exposing the tears that rimmed them. "And what if it fails? What will happen when the shadows reject and attack from the inside? That's a risk we have to consider."

A hush fell, and the four leaders looked at each other, assessing their options.

Kyron broke the silence. "Then we create something to hold our power, a vessel to stay hidden until the time is right." His gaze drifted to a slender blade draped across the altar. It was a dagger forged from dark steel. The light glinted off the sigil of Myrth, which was carved into its blade.

Kyron picked it up, eyeing the dull jewel set in the hilt. Turning it, he showcased the blade to everyone in the room.

Celeste reached out, fingertips brushing its surface. "Perhaps we use this to hold our power? Then, when it is time, we use it to find worthy people to preserve Shadowborn?"

Kyron nodded. "We pour our essence into the steel."

Muriel took a step closer, her voice soft. "If we choose this, to bind our shadows here, we free ourselves from them and offer hope to the next generation." She closed her eyes and whispered a word in the old tongue.

One by one, four trembling hands were placed upon the pommel. A purple diamond illuminated along the back of their hands as they touched. With a collective intake of breath, they released their power.

A wave of darkness erupted, spiraling from their bodies into the blade, coiling around its steel core. The darkness swirled there, engraving a pattern along the hilt and blade. The more the dagger pulled from them, the more the four leaders groaned in pain; Each one draining themselves of every ounce of magic.

"Choose wisely," they said in unison as the last tendrils of shadow formed into the blade. Pulling away one by one, Kyron held the dagger up to them all, the dull gem now filled with a bright purple hue. The torchlight steadied, and the dagger pulsed like it had a heartbeat.

1

The village of SilverDawn was alive with the loud bustle of daily life. Merchants, townsfolk, and travelers gathered at its heart, the town square. A variety of stalls were set up, creating a chaotic yet spacious pattern. Each vendor had a unique combination of vibrant awnings and showcased a different product.

The largest stall, in the middle, hosted the town baker. He stood covered in flour, surrounded by loaves of freshly baked bread. Beside him, a butcher sharpened his cleaver, his table heavy with fresh cuts of venison and pork. Across the way, a weaver sat hunched, unrolling and organizing bolts of dyed fabric. The scent of sage, rosemary, and a variety of spiced ciders wafted from an herbalist's cart, where different herbs were on display.

Blair wove her way through the heart of the bustling market, waving hello to each of the tables. A bundle of lavender from her favorite florist, cradled securely in her arms. Her hazel eyes scanned the countless merchants that surrounded her. She smiled softly and paused, taking in how the sun was beginning to dip low in the sky, casting a soft golden hue over everything it touched.

Following the light as it trailed over the town square, she stepped away from the commotion and rested her back against one of the walls behind her. She observed the glow as it moved fast, consuming everything it touched. It then lingered and continued to the variety of buildings that lined the street on both sides.

Dusk was her favorite time of day. Somehow, the colors of the sunset made her town come to life even more than usual. The golden light poured energy into everything around her. She shifted her bundle and took another moment to take in the beautiful sight of her town.

Blair continued to watch as people wove between the stalls; apprentices carrying bundles of parchment, children darting between carts in a game of chase, and their elders watching from wooden benches, sipping on mulled wine. A bard strummed his lute on a fountain's edge. His song was light and full of longing, drawing a small crowd of listeners. The children, who had been running in circles, began to play in the water as their mothers watched them and exchanged stories. The sound of laughter and conversation echoed off the buildings and reverberated through the street around Blair.

Her eyes flickered between the worn cobblestone streets, the bustling stalls, and the delicate purple flowers that lined the square. A slight evening wind blew, causing her chestnut hair to brush across her face. She smiled at the breeze, sweeping her hair across her shoulders and down her back.

The light from the sunset hit the trees, creating a blended array of colors that shot in multiple directions. They moved as if they had fingers, grabbing onto the walls and consuming everything in their path. The woven colors illuminated the variety of shop signs that hung. Some were simple wood plaques, others were trimmed with metal. Each one swayed gently in the wind, creaking with movement. The biggest placard, The Ravens Nest, was one of metal and stained glass. It reflected the light immediately, sending a flood of colors across the entrance.

The flash caught Blair's attention, a stark contrast to its dark interior. She moved closer, inspecting the sturdy oak doors that were propped open. Peering inside, she observed the interior. The Raven's Nest was where most travelers stayed and recharged with food and ale. She took note of the many people sitting at tables, their laughter and song spilling into the streets.

She continued on and passed the tanner's shop, its pungent aroma wafting through the air. The proprietor was busy stretching hides beneath a wooden awning, but he briefly glanced up to give Blair a curt nod. Coming to the end of the lane, Blair soon reached the apothecary, signaling the last building before the playground that lay nestled beside her Schoolhouse.

She turned back and let her eyes roam the opposite side of the path, where a few other narrow shops resided. The village was small. Stretching just long enough to provide the inhabitants a few options for entertainment, it then gave way to the ring of cottages that lay on the outskirts surrounding the town. Each side of SilverDawn was wrapped tightly in thick forest, creating a screen of protection for the townspeople.

This was her home. She knew everything from the names of the shop owners to the small patches of wildflowers that gave SilverDawn its beauty. Being only one small town in the wide land of Opelysk, it seemed like a hidden gem. It was said all the towns were like that, each one offering a unique personality. Fortunately, she only knew of SilverDawn and its vitality.

Blair continued down the familiar path that led to her house, a cozy little cottage that she had called home for many years. Her home, like many others in town, was simple. A single story filled with the essence of everything she loved.

She lifted the lavender to her nose as she walked, inhaling deeply.

Just as she took another step closer to her cottage, a chilling scream cut through the air. Her heart clenched at the sound, and she froze mid-step, the hair on the back of her neck standing up.

It wasn't a scream of joy or surprise but a scream of pure agony.

Dropping the contents in her arms, she raced back toward the square. As she was getting closer, she could hear the cries more clearly.

"Help! Please help!" The cry was raw, filled with desperation.

Her eyes scoured the crowd first and then moved outward, finally landing on the source of the voice.

A figure appeared, stumbling out of an alleyway, barely able to stand. They were tall, dressed in tattered clothing, and their skin was covered in deep, fresh cuts. As they moved closer, the hood from their robe fell, displaying a man's hardly recognizable face. He was deathly pale, with eyes that were dull and void of life. Parts of his robe had been torn open and blood dripped freely from the gashes that marred his skin. Long, jagged slashes covered his arms, legs, and abdomen.

"Help!" The stranger pleaded again, his voice no more than a hoarse whisper now.

Slowing her momentum, Blair fought the urge to help the stranger as her stomach started to churn. As her feet came to a stop, she just stood there, frozen. Her gaze locked on the bleeding figure.

What had happened to them?

The crowd around her reacted in the same way, gripped by shock and fear. The children, who had been playing moments before, began to cry and ran behind their mothers. Several whispers spread rapidly through the crowd that had gathered.

"Who is that?"

"Where did they come from?"

One individual broke through the murmurs. A woman in an emerald-green cloak waded through the crowd. With eyes set in determination, she approached the stranger, her long gray hair cascading over her shoulders.

Bryn, The Healer.

Blair recognized her immediately, even without the sigil of the Healing Order that was hidden by her hair. The Healer was well known to the townsfolk for her expertise in tending to wounds and illnesses. Most of all, she was commended for the way she remained calm during situations like this one.

With a stoic expression, she quickly closed the space between them. Her hands reached out to steady the bleeding man, "You're safe now." With a calming and reassuring voice, she caught him before he could collapse. "I've got you."

The stranger's breathing was ragged, his body trembling in Bryn's arms. "I can't outrun them," he forced out, fear in every word.

Bryn didn't speak, but her face hardened with understanding. With swift, practiced motions, she helped the man up and turned his body toward another narrow alley that led to her clinic. Blair's breath held still as blood continued to seep into the cobblestones, leaving a trail behind them.

Blair took a step forward, compelled by another overwhelming need to help. But before she could move any further, a man stepped into her path. He was dressed in a simple tunic and a green cloak that mimicked the colors of the Healer. Blair recognized him as Bryn's apprentice, though she couldn't recall his name.

A stern expression met her as she looked up at him. "Stay back," he said. "This is no place for curiosity."

Blair's eyes widened, "But-"

"Stay where you are. It's best not to get involved." The assistant replied, breaking eye contact to glance at the Healer. He seemed to be waiting for a cue or some kind of direction.

Blair went to protest, but hesitated. As much as she wanted to help, she knew the man in front of her was right. She had no idea what was going on, and even if she could help, she was no Healer. She stepped back in submission, imagining what the stranger could have been running from.

As the Healer moved the stranger deeper into the alley, her aide turned and followed them. "Move along," he barked to others who seemed to be battling themselves just as Blair had, "Nothing to see here."

The villagers slowly began to disperse around her. Though Blair found herself rooted to her spot, where a growing unease was settling into her chest.

Who was that person? What had happened? Why had they come here? And most importantly, was there danger following him?

She could feel the weight of each question, but she knew there would be no answers, not yet anyway. Turning her gaze back to the alley, she realized everyone had now disappeared, swallowed by the shadows between the buildings.

The crowd around her had almost completely thinned and the crying had softened, but thick tension remained in the air.

Blair pulled herself away from the scene and slowly began walking the path back to her cottage. The eerie quiet that had settled didn't feel right. SilverDawn's livelihood felt fractured. The warmth that had existed mere moments ago had frozen over, as though something dark and dangerous had entered their peaceful world.

Dragging her feet along the path, Blair imagined possible scenarios that would lead to a blood-covered stranger stumbling into town. As she bent to pick up the items she had dropped, she pulled her jacket tighter. Whether it was the evening wind or the anxiety shooting through her body, she had started to shake.

Trying to remain warm, she hurried the rest of the short walk and approached her gate within a few moments.

Letting the gate swing shut behind her, she heard the soft click of the latch. As she let out a breath and began walking up her walkway, the thought of being home began to melt away her tension.

Following the big flat stones underneath her feet, ones that had been taken from the river, she analyzed her yard. The large pieces of flattened rock broke up the grass and patches of purple flowers that led to her door.

Just before her door, Blair stopped to watch a small bird slip into a birdhouse. The wooden house hung from a low branch near her. It was painted different colors, a gift from one of her students.

Her breathing calmed as she listened to the happy chirping within the house. Within seconds, her shoulders began to lower. She watched for a few more moments before inhaling deeply and reaching for the door handle.

The inside of her home matched the cozy exterior. Her walls were painted a light purple, a color that she had always loved. There were sketches hung everywhere and the top of each wall was decorated with doodles of different flowers. The scribbles covered the perimeter of the room besides a few small areas where they had been erased, almost in frustration.

Blair moved to the kitchen and the paint around her changed to yellow, with new drawings covering the space. This time, they were different fruits and vegetables, all connected by shared vines.

Grabbing a jar, she placed the lavender on her table and looked around her home. One of the many reasons she loved it so much was because of the simplicity. It was open, with different doors leading to a living room, a kitchen, and a single bedroom with an adjoining bathroom. The space was small, but it was *hers*.

A variety of papers hung tacked in different areas, artwork given to her by her students. A fluffy armchair lounged in the corner with an open book lying on top of the middle cushion. A pile of dirty laundry sat in the opposite corner, waiting to be washed.

The bed in her room was a mess of sheets and pillows, but as always, it was where she gravitated to first. She sat on the soft cotton, pulling off her shoes and rubbing out the tension. Rolling her neck from side to side, she thought of the bread she had recently received from the baker and her stomach grumbled in response.

After changing into comfortable clothes, she walked a few steps to the kitchen and grabbed the sourdough. Slicing a few pieces, she took some raspberry jam from the cupboard and spread it on the bread, making a quick snack.

Filling the rest of the evening with small tasks, she found it hard to settle. Picking up her book to try and read a few chapters, she ended up just putting it back down. Next, she tried to organize her books, which failed after just a few minutes.

As darkness fell, she forced herself to settle. She collected a few candles for her bedroom, bolted the door, and headed to bed.

Falling asleep was difficult that night. Every time she closed her eyes, she pictured herself covered in blood. If it wasn't her, it was one of her students or someone from her town. She tossed in bed, wrapping herself in her blanket just to pull it off again.

At one point, she sat up completely and rubbed her temples, huffing at the stress that had returned to her body. The room was quiet around her, except for her heartbeat. The candles had burned through and the only light was the soft glow of the moon shining through the window. Sitting up, her eyes followed the pale light that stretched across her bed and floor.

Taking a deep breath in, she looked up at the ceiling and then turned to find a comfortable position on her side. From this spot, she could see the light again. Tracing the stream of moonlight, she followed it again and again until her eyes started to close.

The hum of the night outside helped her settle, the sound of crickets and a gentle breeze in the trees. Her body had relaxed just enough to drift, and then something moved outside her window. Just a flicker at first that caught her attention, but just when she thought she had imagined it, the moonlight on the floor shifted again like something passed in front of the glass.

She blinked, fully awake now.

Slowly, she turned her head toward the window, her heart picking up pace. Her eyes remained still as the movement happened a third time.

Not the branches.

Not the wind.

Instead, her eyes tracked a figure; a tall form that now stood still, just outside, taunting her as if he knew she was watching. There was no sound in his movement, just his dark shape blocking the moonlight.

Blair's heart thundered so loud now, she could hear it in her ears. She squeezed her eyes shut in an attempt to quiet it, but as she opened them, the shadow was gone.

She jumped up, pulling off the covers to stand in front of the window. The moonlight around her had returned unchanged, soft, and empty. But she knew what she saw, and the fear had kept her up the rest of the night.

2

The anxious energy she had felt from the night before carried into the next morning. When she awoke, her mind was foggy from lack of sleep and the simple task of getting dressed seemed absolutely daunting. Regardless, she rolled out of bed and walked to her closet. Staring at her options, she rubbed her eyes until they focused on a brown dress with a white, lacy trim.

As she went to reach for it, her hand twitched, hovering at her side.

Why couldn't she let it go?

The stranger.

She closed her eyes to reset her mind but instead, she pictured the day before. She had witnessed one little thing and it was like something had settled in her, lodged beneath her skin like splintered glass.

Yanking the dress from its hook with more force than necessary, she pulled it over her head. The fabric clung to her skin where she was damp with sweat. Already frustrated, she tied the string corset that ran down her back and smoothed the fabric.

15

It was one incident. One man. And yet, her mind told her something wasn't quite right.

She knelt to pull on her boots, watching her fingers as they trembled at the laces.

"This is ridiculous," she whispered to the empty room around her. She rose and padded softly across the wooden floor toward the kitchen.

Breakfast, she told herself. *Just eat.*

Food will help.

She sliced an apple with stiff fingers, not really tasting as she chewed. Her mind refused to sit still. Like a candle flame too close to an open window, it flickered, and flickered, and flickered.

"What is wrong with me?" she whispered to herself as she grabbed a pan for her tea.

Watching the water boil, she tried to reason with herself and talk down the anxiety that had festered.

It was common for her to be transfixed on certain things, her whole life had been like that. *She needed to know what was going on, she had to figure it out.* Taking a breath, she listed her options.

"One…" Her voice was dry as she poured the bubbling mixture into a sieve, "find a way to protect myself and my students in case there is *more* to what happened. Something to defend the classroom, maybe?"

This option did the most to calm her mind.

She wasn't a fighter, but she could be.

"Two," she continued, taking the liquid and bottling it into a large jug, "ask someone for a sleeping draught.

Something strong. If I can't fix the fear, maybe I can just... sleep through it."

Her shoulders sagged at that one, it felt like surrender.

"And three..." she grabbed a lemon and squeezed it into the freshly brewed tea, "go to Bryn and see if I'm making myself crazy for nothing."

She paused then, and looked at the brown fluid as it swirled with the citric acid.

The healer's quarters aren't far from the schoolhouse, I can go there after class.

With that final thought, she grabbed her bag and stepped outside into the crisp morning air to begin her walk to school.

Along the way, she made herself stop to observe anything that made her heart lighter, anything that let light in. She did so frequently, finding happiness in the flowers and wild rabbits that ran along the trail.

By the time she had finished the short walk to her schoolroom, she felt better. Propping her door open, she waved to the gathering students. Giving each one a brisk high-five as they entered, she counted them. As the last child stepped in, a little girl with blonde pigtails, Blair realized three students were missing.

Waiting as long as she could for them, she finally closed the door and walked to the front of her classroom. Her eyes surveyed the room and the small children that sat at the scattered circular tables. She had just said good morning, when the door opened and a boy with light brown curls entered. She immediately turned to greet him and noticed his eyes were rimmed red.

Approaching him slowly, she took note of just how puffy his eyes actually were. His body seemed off too, he slouched as if weighed with exhaustion. "Jaycen?" she called softly, crouching next to him. "Is everything okay?"

He stepped into her slowly, a pack slung over one shoulder with his fingers curled around the strap. He didn't look up at her right away.

"No," he answered, voice low.

"What's going on?"

He hesitated, shifting his weight from one foot to the other. "I had a nightmare."

"Nightmare?" she repeated gently. *Him too?*

Jaycen nodded. "About shadows, and not normal ones. These ones moved on their own." A look of fear passed through his expression as he continued, "They looked like people, but... wrong. They're all black, like they're made of dark smoke."

Blair's chest tightened for him as she grabbed his hand and gave him a reassuring squeeze. "That sounds scary," she whispered.

Jaycen looked up at her then, his brown eyes steady, as if he agreed wholeheartedly. "It is. I can't sleep." he whispered, looking down at the floor between them.

A silence settled between them, deep and fragile. Blair inhaled quietly and looked up, glancing toward the back corner of her room where the light didn't quite reach.

"I'll tell you what, why don't you go rest for a while and I'll keep watch," she said with a wink, motioning to the table sitting in the far corner. "You'll be safe, I promise."

Jaycen gave a small nod. "Okay. You'll keep the lights on?"

His words, simple and innocent, hit her harder than she expected. She smiled, even as her hand trembled faintly against his. "I promise," she said, standing and walking with him to the back.

Throughout her lessons, she watched as he finally gave in and fell into a deep sleep. During math, he twitched and while she read out loud, he snored, which caught the attention of a few peers. Blair continued through her teaching, checking in on him when she could. The only time she interfered with his rest was at the end of the day when everyone had already packed up.

Jaycen blinked his eyes open as she rubbed his back. "Hey, it's time to go home," she said lightly, as he continued to work through his drowsiness.

He turned his face to look up at her, his brown eyes brighter than they had been before. "I feel better," he said, stretching.

Blair smiled at him and handed him a small object. "I'm glad, but here's a mini lantern in case it happens again. No matter what, this corner is always available to you when you need it." Blair reassured with a bright smile.

Jaycen stood and nodded, placing the gift into his bag along with his school supplies. After a moment, he paused, "Ms. Griffin. Are they real? The shadows I'm dreaming of?"

Blair watched as he stiffened, waiting for her response. "The only shadows I've seen are the ones on the playground when you play hopscotch and the ones you create with sock puppets."

With that, he nodded and squeezed her tightly in a hug. After a few moments, he let go and quickly hoisted his bag on his shoulder, walking out the door.

Leaning against the door, Blair contemplated the fear she had just witnessed in a mere child.

A nightmare about shadows? Had yesterday spooked him just as bad?

Mentally replaying his words and the worry in his voice, she grabbed her bag and left her classroom, heading down the path to the Healer.

It didn't take long to walk there in her haste, her head filling with a variety of questions. She approached the familiar door and pulled it open, immediately hit by a tidal wave of smells.

Healing oils.

Looking around at the tan walls, she walked up to the counter where Bryn's apprentice sat. "Is the Healer available?" she asked, tapping her fingers along the dark wood.

He looked up from the stone mortar and pestle he had in his hands, "She's preparing a salve, but I'll go ask." He stood quietly and walked down a small hallway that led to a back area.

Blair's fingers continued to tap until she heard footsteps approaching. Turning around, she met the blue-gray eyes of Bryn. She appeared exhausted. Her hair was wrapped into a bun, but some strands hung loose like she had been working endlessly.

"How can I help you?" Bryn implored, a courteous smile forming on her face.

"I-." Blair closed her mouth, forming her circling thoughts into words, "The man that came into town hurt, the stranger- is he going to be okay?"

A strange emotion passed over Bryn's features before she exhaled through her nose. "I can't say much, but I will tell you he is healing. I was able to close most of the wounds."

"I'm glad to hear that." Blair nodded slowly, "Do you know what happened to him? I've never seen injuries like that before."

Bryn didn't respond at first, but Blair thought she saw the smallest dilation of the Healer's eyes. "I don't know for sure, the important thing is that he survived and is now healing."

Blair shifted her weight, crossing her arms in front of her. "I know you said you can't tell me much but I need to know, is there a reason to worry? Should we be concerned about what attacked him?"

Bryn clenched her jaw and stared at Blair for a moment, "I shouldn't give too much information away."

Blair nodded and stepped closer to Bryn. "I understand. I just don't feel right. I feel like something is off."

This time, Blair knew she saw a shift in Bryn, like a subtle tightening of her shoulders. "Thankfully, he didn't remember much about the encounter. The only thing I know for sure is that his wounds felt wrong. Too clean in places, and too ragged in others. Like they didn't come from any natural shape." Bryn paused then, looking at the medical supplies that were on the counter. "I've stitched flesh torn by wolves. I've seen a man burned alive after falling into his own forge. But I have never seen a force that leaves cuts like this."

Now it was Blair's turn to clench her jaw, "It wasn't natural?"

Bryn put her hand on Blair's shoulder, a worried look hidden in her eyes. "Respectfully, I have to get back to my salve. Anything else you need can be handled by Jacobo, my apprentice."

Jacobo, that's what his name was.

Blair nodded quickly to show she understood, "Thank you for your time."

When Jacobo replaced Bryn, Blair decided to test her luck and ask a few more questions.

"I've seen you with Bryn for some time now," Blair implored, meeting Jacobo's eyes, "How long have you worked with her?"

Jacobo nodded, grabbing the pestle and grinding whatever herbs were scattered at the bottom. "A few years."

Nodding, Blair continued, "So have you seen anyone else with cuts like the stranger had yesterday?"

Jacobo didn't answer right away. After a moment, he shook his head as he continued to work.

"I wouldn't think so." Blair replied, her voice low. "I wonder what type of things could even do that." She paused, looking up into a corner of the room. "I can't imagine it was any animals we've seen, especially not around this area of Opelysk." Letting out a sigh, Blair moved her attention to her fingers as she fidgeted with her nails. "What could do this? What else is out there?"

With each word, Jacobo's neck started to turn red as if he was growing uncomfortable.

"Do you have any ideas?" Blair asked, popping her mouth like she was in the middle of thirty different thoughts.

Jacobo looked up then and shook his head for the second time, the redness of his neck moving to his face.

Noticing his flustered state and not wanting to push her welcome, Blair nodded and quietly thanked him for his time.

As the door to Bryn's cottage clicked shut behind her, Blair just stood there for a moment, staring at nothing. The smell of the oils from inside still clung to her, sharp and musky. She wrapped her arms around herself as she began to walk, kicking dry leaves around with her boots.

Bryn had said more than she was supposed to and somehow still said nothing at all.

Cuts like she's never seen.

Blair had come hoping for clarity. Maybe even hope. Instead, she left with more questions, entangled like ropes wrapped around her. Walking blindly, she continued on. Not toward home. Just *away*. Away from the healer's cottage, from the uncertainty, from the image of that distraught stranger covered in his own blood.

Her boots made soft, steady sounds in the dirt. One step, then another. The town around her was quieter than usual. People moved, but quickly with their heads down. Doors shut faster now. Curtains stayed drawn longer. Even the birds seemed to keep their distance. It was as if they all felt what she did.

Option one had failed, she hadn't received confirmation that everything was okay. If anything, she learned her intuition was right.

I need protection.

The thought came loud and clear, like it was no longer a choice. She stopped walking and looked up at the sky. Clouds were gathering in the west, bruised and heavy-looking, a clear indicator that a storm was forming.

Protection, that was it.

For herself and her students.

She began to walk again, eyes drifting to the rooftops of SilverDawn as her thoughts spun.

A knife?

She could keep one hidden in her boot. Not too big. Just enough to buy her time if she had to run.

She shook her head. *No.* She'd never held one with any confidence, and it was more likely to slip from her fingers than strike true. Plus, if the wrong student found it in her satchel…

Charms, then.

Salt lines. Rosemary. Bells at the door.

Some of her neighbors swore by them, even Bryn kept lavender bunches throughout the house. But Blair had a hard time with that one. She had grown up with books and letters, not runes and rites.

Could she ask someone to guard her classroom?

No.

That wasn't safety, that was dependence. And what if something followed them instead? What if it found its way into her classroom, into the quiet corner where the children liked to read? What if it followed one of them home?

She couldn't risk that. *Not them.* Her students were the only steady thing in her life. Their laughter, their smudged hands, their questions about stars, and spelling rules, and why frogs could jump so high. They trusted her and looked at her like she always had the right answers.

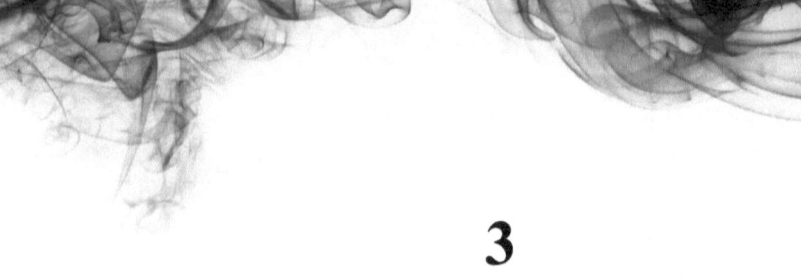

3

As she passed through the market, she noticed just how much paranoia had washed over SilverDawn. People were hunched over whispering, and merchants were engrossed in traded stories of impending doom.

It had only been twenty-four hours since the stranger arrived, and things were already changing. The market she walked through was empty. People spoke faster when trading with each other. Conversations were short and the usual energy had dampened.

A feminine voice pulled her from her thoughts as she reached the middle of the market. "Something is going on, I know it," a dark-haired woman said, as she looked over a variety of loaves in front of her. "Back home, in Keithston, My sister sent a letter that said a darkness was coming. Two people showed up with dark sigils on their bodies. Two! Plus, she swore she saw *shadows* around them."

Orlin, the town baker, looked up at her with an exasperated look as he set down several muffins. "Elise," he said, as if he was used to her over-exaggerating things "That's hard to believe. *Shadows?*"

A man nearby scoffed, sharing disbelief with the town baker. "Don't feed into her nonsense, Orlin." He then pointed at the woman, "Maybe your sister is a loon."

The next day, the healer posted a notice outside her cottage: *If anyone around you is experiencing strange behavior, please file a report to my assistant.*

By the third morning, SilverDawn was not the same town. Not only did people refuse to come outside but they watched each other with suspicion. *Everyone* now claimed the town was in danger. More stories came, spreading whispers of people beyond SilverDawn who were corrupted.

Each variation she heard spoke of the same thing. Each tale consisted of someone with moving darkness that would grow and engulf them, wreaking havoc. People in SilverDawn had even begun taking certain precautions, checking each other for any signs of dark symbols.

Everything seemed to be affected by this growing fear. Blair's classroom, which had once been full of sixteen students, was dwindling down each day that passed.

Throughout everything happening, all Blair could think of was them, her kids. Her classroom was her family, and her students were like her own children. Now, they were in danger from a threat she felt she couldn't see, an invisible fear.

One afternoon, she contemplated whether the stories had any truth to them as she sat at her vanity and studied herself. Her chestnut-brown hair framed her face in waves and fell behind her shoulders to the middle of her back. Strands of auburn sparkled where the sunlight touched it. She lifted her hands and divided her hair into three sections, beginning to braid it.

Hazel eyes stared back at her as her fingers worked, not quite green, not quite gold, shifting in color with every tilt of her head.

Her eyes moved to her freckles that dotted the bridge of her nose and scattered across her cheeks like soft constellations. They stayed there, moving only to observe the skin on her face and shoulders, warm with a sun-earned tan.

She paused her fingers, almost finished with her braid, as her vision shifted to a photo in her reflection. Her eyes lingered on a miniature picture attached to her mirror. The worn snapshot was of her as a child playing in a creek, her parents standing and watching.

She was six in the picture.

Everything had changed shortly after that day.

She closed her eyes and thought of the family she had created for herself, the students who filled her classroom. Most barely taller than her hip, each one a bright light in her darkening world.

At this point, there were only nine students left in her class. She lowered her head into her hands and rubbed her temples with her thumbs. As she did so, images began to flood her mind of her large classroom, empty. A blank, silent room with no little eyes full of wonder or little mouths smiling, asking questions.

As she stood to secure her boots over her pants, she knew she had to figure something out. Her brow set in determination as she closed the door and marched down through the square to the far end of town.

The sun had barely risen, casting a pale light across the village. Briskly walking through the cobbled streets, her hair bobbed behind her like a storm. Her usually composed face was taut, and a scowl lingered in place of her smile. Her brows furrowed deeper as she thought of the stranger whom Bryn had healed. Although she had been told he had recovered, her mind could only recall the scarlet river that followed him when he had first entered. Her pace picked up, and her breath began to come in short, sharp bursts as she hurried toward the edge of SilverDawn.

As Blair walked through the town market, she eyed the selection of vendors out today. These sellers were the only ones left who acted like there was still some sort of normalcy, but Blair knew better. She had seen the anxiety spread. Blair passed the shops, not yet open, and followed the street toward one of the last buildings.

On the outskirts of the village, there was a lodge connected to an old forge with billowing smoke. As she approached, the sound of a hammer on metal rang out with each strike, which meant the Blacksmith was inside.

From the outside, the forge was glowing with an orange light that cast eerie shadows on the stone walls. Blair stood at the entrance and watched the colors shift against the darkness. The scent of molten metal and burning wood filled the air. She paused, not exactly wanting to intrude on him.

Damien was the town's blacksmith, a man of few words, with a craft that required precision and solitude. But if she was going to be capable of protecting herself and her students, he was the one she needed to talk to. He was the only one who was capable of crafting something that could actually help.

Taking a deep breath, she pushed open the door and stepped inside. Adjusting to the flames, her eyes immediately found his towering figure. The blacksmith stood at least six feet tall. His imposing, husky frame was a testament to years of hard labor. Bulging muscles, lined with prominent veins, rippled with every strike of his hammer. The black tank top he wore hugged his broad shoulders and sweat glistened on his brow, but his focus remained unshaken.

Intense glacier-blue eyes watched the metal form. His hair was buzzed short on the sides and left longer on the top. Tousling slightly with each movement, it was streaked with sweat and soot, which gave him a wild, untamed look. His jaw was framed in a refined beard that mimicked the same auburn and light brown tones as his hair..

He paused, sensing her presence, and turned his sharp eyes on her. Even with the look of recognition in his eyes, his face was hard, and his stare was stern.

Blair and Damien had crossed paths a few times in the village, though their words rarely intersected. She was a busy teacher who often ventured out to gather materials and supplies, whereas he only went out when necessary.

He acknowledged her with a shallow nod, wiping his hands on his leather apron. Although not angry, his eyes burned with the intensity of someone who did not want to be interrupted.

Blair raised an eyebrow and relaxed her features enough to show a small smile. "I need your help." she said, stepping toward him. "I need you to make me something to protect me and my students."

Damien set his hammer down, his brows pinching together as he shot her a look that she could only be described as skeptical. "Protect?" he echoed.

"Yes. We both know something is coming." She gave him a leveled look, as if he should know exactly why. "You've heard the stories around town. I need something to keep the children safe." Her voice cracked on the last word, which caught a mere second of attention from the blacksmith as their eyes met.

"Maybe canceling classes would be best then," he said nonchalantly, turning away from her and moving back to pick up the hammer.

Blair stared at him for a long minute, then rested her hands on the table in front of her. Her shoulders straightened as she raised her chin, "Damien. You make swords, chains, anything and everything this village needs."

The blacksmith inspected his hammer, running his finger along a crack in the side. She sighed and nodded to the towering pile of unfinished work in the corner of the room, keeping her eyes on him the whole time.

"Could you use something from there? I'll take anything. A lock. An alarm of some kind. A sword. I don't want to just sit and wait. I need to know I have something."

Damien shot her a sarcastic glare, "A *sword*? Are you a knight or a teacher?"

Blair gave a slight eye roll, pointing to the tool in Damien's hands, "Do you use that hammer to shape your humor?" she replied smugly, raising one of her eyebrows, "You might have flattened it a little too much."

Damien answered with a scowl, though it was hard to tell if he was angry or just perpetually disgruntled. "I'm busy with other orders."

Impatience flared in Blair. "I would argue my request is more important than the others, considering it's about the safety of children, but I'm glad to see where your priorities lie," she seethed, regretting her original plan and already trying to form another in her head.

She went to walk away, but as she did so, her kids slipped into her mind, a look of shock and fear etched on their faces. She paused and sighed, attempting one more time as she reached the door.

Her tone softened as she looked at him again. "*Someone* has to protect these kids. Not everyone has a family they can count on to keep them safe." She turned to leave, but her words had punctured him.

"Fine," Damien muttered, before bringing down his hammer again.

Blair could barely hear it over her shuffling feet, but that one word stopped her movements. He spoke again as her eyes remained focused on the grainy wood in front of her.

"The boys in your class like to sneak here and test their strength using my hammers. Make sure that doesn't happen anymore, and you can have what you need, even if it is a *sword*." He paused there, as if waiting for a reaction before continuing, "Give me two days."

Blair let out a small sigh of relief. She was not about to thank him out loud, not yet anyway. She nodded slightly, in fear he would change his mind or worse, cause her blood pressure to rise again.

With that small gesture, she pushed open the door and walked out, glad to be away from his audacity. "Two days," she agreed, as the door shut behind her.

As she walked back along the road to her schoolroom, she felt lighter. Trailing her eyes over countless rocks in the gravel, her mind soon wandered to a large rock that inhabited a small clearing close to the cottages in SilverDawn. This rock, or more so a boulder, was used as a seat for the town's storyteller.

The large, broken stone that many people gathered around served as a venue for sharing entertaining stories. The area in front of it was open except for a few scattered stumps, and families would come with blankets to sit on as they listened to stories unfold. It provided the perfect space for a makeshift theater.

Although recently, these stories had turned dark and daunting. His words had once held the children's attention, filled with thrilling, well-told adventures. Now, he only fed into their nightmares.

Blair closed her eyes to recall the enthusiasm and excited squeals that used to fill that space before everything changed. Little faces with wide eyes and flushed cheeks had eagerly sat on the lawn, waiting impatiently. Now, the whole space remained empty day after day. She sighed and continued her walk back into town, deciding to clear her mind.

There had been a large influx of wandering people lately, and each one weighed the town down more. Along with the rumors that were already circling about darkness, the new visitors brought more stories that added fuel to the roaming fire. It seemed as if each person spoke of violence and death that consumed other towns. Shadow people, the ones associated with the dark, had become the main topic everywhere.

Blair kicked a small pebble as hard as she could, contemplating the growing restlessness.

Was there any truth to these stories?

Just as images flashed in her mind of shadows ripping apart her classroom, Blair tripped over a broken root in the ground and caught herself on a branch of a tree. Calming her heart, she took a steady breath as a small stinging brought her attention down to her arm. A cut on her wrist now oozed blood. Clenching her fists, her eyes scrutinized the new injury. Her sight shifted then, slowly grazing over the lingering scars she had collected over the years. Faint silver lines and jagged pink scars scattered over her arms, each one a careless signature of years spent tumbling and tripping.

If shadows were coming, what would happen? How could she defend anyone if she couldn't even defend herself against a branch?

She dug her shoe into the ground as she continued on. Her feet trudged on until she was under the Tavern sign. Deciding this could help her mood, she reached for the Tavern handle. The heavy wooden door creaked as Blair stepped inside. The sunlight streamed through the large windows and spilled onto the tables arranged across the room. The comforting smells of stale ale and smoked meat met her as she moved toward the counter at the back. She moved around the large booths and tables.

A warm air filled the room, spilling out of the hot ovens from the kitchen. The heat gave contrast to the cool midmorning air she had felt outside. The clatter of mugs and the low murmur of conversation filled her ears. A fire crackled in the hearth, casting long flickering shadows that seemed to twist and sway in the corners.

Blair's eyes swept over the room as she reached the bar. Her shoulders loosened as she counted the number of people. *At least some were still leaving their houses.*

Finley, the bartender, nodded in her direction as she took a seat. He was a burly man with a warm smile, someone who was meant to work with people. She ordered a drink, her gaze lingering on the patrons around her, their faces worn but full of life and hope.

Soon, a metal clink stole her attention as her drink was placed in front of her. The pink elixir bubbled playfully as she looked up into her friend's face.

"Are the kids giving you a hard time?" Finley asked with a wink.

Blair rolled her eyes and produced a weak smile, to which his eyes brightened. "Try this! I'm sure you're going to love it!" he announced, using his hands to showcase the drink he had just made.

"Thanks, Fin." she responded, using the nickname that always fed into his happy demeanor.

Blair picked up the cup and took a long sip. She immediately recognized a mixture of fruit and tea, but then, toward the end, there was a specific taste. She swished it back and forth.

This game was common. Fin liked to experiment, creating new concoctions to test on his customers. Most of the time, the reactions weren't exactly what he was hoping for. She braced herself as she lifted the cup to her mouth again. The liquid hit her tongue for the second time, and she tasted each individual flavor. This one was a success, and she smiled. "Wine? Maybe honey? Figs?"

His eyes lit up as he laughed loudly. "Wow. You got it! I tried to hide the wine with the honey. Balances out well, huh?" he laughed again, nudging Blair's shoulder with his fist.

Blair shook her head and turned her chair out toward the crowd with her mysterious drink in hand. A few sips later, she felt good, thanks to whatever alcohol was in it.

Glancing around the tavern, she noticed the diverse groups of people. In SilverDawn, each person displayed a different symbol and no two were the same. A burning crown, a jagged mountain, a weeping eye; some were clean and bright, freshly drawn but others were worn and faded, like they'd been there for years. Names were used to identify individuals, but these symbols allowed others to recognize your business and ventures.

Blair's eyes moved to a woman approaching the bar, her sharp voice directed toward Fin. A silver heart showed on her wrist. Blair rolled her eyes and scoffed, recognizing the symbol for an adult companion.

Turning away from whatever proposition Fin was about to receive, Blair noticed an old oak table near the far corner. Two men sat there, hunched over and whispering. Both bore the distinct symbol for merchants, along with a copper insignia she didn't recognize. Turning her head to get a closer look, she wondered if they were from a different town or just passing through. One, was a lanky figure with a ragged cloak. The other, a stout man with a scar running down his cheek. Their voices were low, but Blair's sharp ears caught clips of their conversation.

"They say it's spreading faster now," the ragged man muttered, his eyes darting nervously around the room. "The ones born with shadows, they're not like us."

"They are *nothing* like us," the scarred man replied, his voice thick with dread. "The darkness within them is alive, and they're using it to kill. They're terrorizing towns."

The hair on Blair's arms raised. This kind of conversation had become normal, but she felt like this one hung in the air like an omen. Blair leaned forward, trying to make out more of their words.

"They say they've been born out of the darkest places," the ragged man continued his voice trembling, "places the sun hasn't touched in years, where the air feels wrong. People born with these things on them, they're shadows, but they're not just shadows. They're more. "

"More?" the scarred man repeated, slurring his words.

"The things they do... Some of them are said to have slaughtered their own villages. One town? It was just *gone*. The only thing left behind were pieces of bodies, like shadows had torn them apart."

• Blair's pulse quickened and her fingers clenched around her mug, but she kept her face calm. There were always different types of stories circulating about various things. Stories of dark magic, of curses, that turned people into monsters but this had become something different, it had become a plague.

"I've heard they are born that way," the other man replied. "Born with a curse. A shadow they can't control. They say there's no cure. No salvation, and the worst part? They don't know what they are capable of until it is too late."

Blair's stomach twisted. She couldn't help but glance down at her own shadow, the dim flicker of it stretching out behind her.

What if it were true? What if this were more than just a story?

"You think it's connected?" The scarred man asked, his eyes narrowing.

"I don't know," the ragged man replied, his hand shaking as he reached for his drink. "But something's off. People like that don't just appear out of nowhere. There's a reason so many are showing back up now, but I heard the northern king isn't going to put up with it. He'll take them out, one by one with his Hunters."

The rest of the conversation faded into silence, and Blair felt the weight of a thousand questions settle on her. *What exactly were these shadows? Who were the Hunters?* She took another long drink, although her eyes remained on the two men. She replayed their conversation in her mind.

As her body warmed from the drink that was now almost gone, she ordered another and watched the conversations around her. She stayed there for a couple of hours, just watching the different groups of people and helping Fin when he needed it.

At one point, the tavern turned cold. It was as if her mind had made it seem like shadows in the room had grown darker and heavier. She rose from her seat, slipping out of the door. Even with the drink relaxing her senses, she was antsy. The familiar and persistent need to solve whatever was going on, was clawing at her.

4

Blair was back at the forge faster than she cared to admit. For some reason, after leaving the tavern in a disorienting state, she thought of Damien.

The drinks she finished earlier made her movements slow as she walked toward the forge. After stumbling a few times, she reached the familiar door and suppressed a giggle as she fought to open it. The door creaked in protest so she paused, stopping the noise.

Through the crack in the door, Blair could see the glow from the furnace. The rhythmic clang of metal echoed through the air, the same sound she had heard when she was here before.

Instead of barging in like she had planned, she took a moment to watch him work as she steadied her vision. His face was set in complete concentration over the precise strikes he made and the force behind them. She had never seen a trade like this, where every effort was for a reason.

Damien stood, his muscular frame now bent over the fire. He shifted his body, pulling a long, glowing bar of metal from the furnace with a pair of tongs. She noticed his bare arms, and his hands, which were entirely too close to the flame. Exposure like that would be painful for anyone, probably causing repeated burns or calluses on his hands.

She squinted closely, watching him move with ease as he shaped yet another piece of metal. She blamed her loosened inhibitions as her mind wandered to his rough hands and what they would look like up close, *how they would feel.*

With that thought, heat quickly flooded her cheeks and hiccups emerged, forcing her to cover her mouth. With a hand now covering the bottom half of her face, she internally cursed herself, blaming the rising heat within her on the temperature inside the forge.

Trying to focus on something else, Blair bit her lip and observed the glowing metal that flared as he began to shape it. Shadows danced across his skin as he did so, cast from the light around him. She watched wordlessly as the black wisps moved from the walls to his chest. He continued to mold and shape, stopping every few moments to assess his creation.

Blair inhaled deeply, steadying her breath and the hiccups that had hijacked her body. She then braced against the door to push it fully open, but as she did so, something caught her attention.

The bare skin she had just witnessed, the hands she had just envisioned in her mind, were now covered in what looked like leather. She blinked a few times, second-guessing her memory.

What the ...

At first, she thought she had just missed it. However, the next moment the "leather" on his arms became erratic, twitching and shifting as if it was alive.

Slowly, the gloves dissipated and tendrils of darkness took their place, twisting up from his hands and arms. They looped around his forearms and then his biceps, growing until they met his shoulders.

Blair gawked at the scene in front of her, hoping with everything inside of her that she was hallucinating from the drinks.

It has to be me, she told herself, pulling back from the opening in the door.

But it wasn't.

The proof was right in front of her. The more Damien focused, the harder the darkness around him coiled. He eventually took notice and let out an audible grunt.

As he dropped his hammer and took a step back from the metal, the angry shadows settled. After a few moments, he moved back to his original position, and they glided to his fingers, creating a barrier from the heat.

Blair felt bile rise in her throat as she grabbed the door for support. Paralyzed, she stood, hoping her body and mind would settle. Swallowing down what was threatening to come up, she forced herself to sober up.

Once done, he inhaled deeply through his nose and closed his eyes. With this, the shadows shuddered and slid up his arms, disappearing within the sleeves of his shirt.

Still gripping the door, Blair bit down on her tongue.

The shadows were real.

The stories was real.

The entryway around her seemed to tilt and she swayed. Closing her eyes, she tried to calm her nerves. Peeling one hand away from the mahogany wood, she rubbed her eyes and looked at him again, shaking her head.

This wasn't possible.

She blinked ferociously to try to rationalize what she had just seen.

Damien didn't seem to notice her presence or her crippling panic attack. His focus was on his next task. The moment the darkness had retreated, he had just simply picked up the next piece of metal and began to warm it in the fire, as if nothing was out of the ordinary.

Another wave of nausea hit as the gloves of shadows returned, tightening and shifting as if responding to his movements.

Like a rubberband, her mind snapped back into place, allowing her the ability to move. Slowly, she pulled away from the door. The crack might have been small, but it had changed *everything*.

As she pulled away, the mixture of alcohol and adrenaline caused her feet to slip. She grabbed at the door to catch herself. The tugging force caused the door to slam shut.

Shit.

Had he heard her?

Was he coming toward the door?

The thought sent a wave of panic through her. Her breathing grew shallow as she glanced around the area for a place to hide, but there was nowhere, nothing along this bare road. Her next decision came impulsively; she turned and ran.

As fast as she could, she sprinted away without looking back. The sounds of her footsteps intermingling with the clangs from the forge, a noise she hoped had covered up the slamming door. She couldn't think anymore, but she couldn't stop either. She had to get away from whatever she had just witnessed.

As she turned into the town square, she glanced back at the forge for a brief second, causing her to run straight into the back of a man. Mumbling an apology and avoiding his scowl, she backed away from him and found something to lean on as she bent over, placing her hands on her knees.

Filling her lungs, she shook her head, trying to clear her senses. Looking around, she realized the man was one of many people surrounding the area. It was a rather large crowd, made up of most of the townspeople. She straightened and stood, begging her eyes to focus and her body to calm.

Running may not have been the best decision.

"These are Hunters," a loud, deep voice announced at the front of the crowd. Blair turned her head to the sound, her view partially blocked by the lines of people in front of her. She moved to the back of the crowd, walking until she found a large stone facing the square. She stood on it and looked over the mass of people at three figures who loomed at the front. Two of them stood behind the first, who was holding the reins to black stallion.

The man responsible for the voice was the one in the front. He wore a blue robe adorned with the insignia from the Northern Kingdom. She quickly recognized him as one of the land's Barons. Although rarely seen in town, they handled any business associated with the King.

The announcer repeated himself, and Blair's eyes moved to him, "There will be men like this now stationed in SilverDawn and other surrounding towns. We call them Hunters and they will be patrolling to watch for any danger." With those words, the two men behind him stepped to the front. They were both abnormally tall, their faces hidden by a hood, but both were dressed in black cloaks trimmed with silver. Blair could just make out The King's logo on the back of their cloaks as it rippled in the wind.

"The King sends them with his promise that they will protect you."

She eyed the men, her heartbeat in her ears as her gaze caught the path she had come from.

Damien hadn't followed her.

With that tiny sliver of comfort, she moved her attention back to the people in front of her as the baron continued to speak. "They have been instructed to patrol all areas. They will ask questions that they deem necessary and report any suspicious activity back to me."

With that, the crowd murmured quietly. The reaction was clearly a mix of curiosity and fear. The baron then nodded to the two men before bowing to the crowd and mounting his horse. Without saying anything more, he pulled the reins and veered the horse away from the town square.

Blair watched as the two strange men just stood there, eyeing the crowd in front of them. Their stance was too rigid, almost like statues, and their eyes seemed cold and calculating.

Within a couple of minutes, the crowd had started to disperse, spooked by the men's demeanor.

Once again glancing toward Damien's forge, Blair finally convinced herself he had not come after her. She then turned in the opposite direction, toward the safety of her home.

She walked briskly, pushing through the last bits of sluggishness. Passing the peddlers and pots of flowers, she moved to a slight jog. Once she hit the tavern, she knew she wasn't that far from the serenity of her front door.

By the time she reached her cottage, the air in her lungs burned again but the fog inside her mind had lifted and things were a tad bit clearer. As she stepped over her doorframe, she shut the door with a quick tug and placed her back against the cool, solid wood as she slid to the ground.

Although her brain was already starting to replay everything, she willed it to slow. She just needed to process everything.

First, she needed to figure out whatever that was with Damien. She closed her eyes and envisioned him. The merchant's stories played over the memory of what she saw in the forge. *Was he one of them? One of the things that may have hurt that stranger?*

Next, she thought of the new security detail for SilverDawn. *Why would the Baron announce them? Why would they show up now?* She couldn't help the feeling that everything was tied together.

She stood, steadying herself as she locked the door from the inside. Taking a deep breath in, she forced her feet to move toward her bedroom.

Welcoming the comfort and warmth of her bed, she threw herself down and retreated under the covers. Although now surrounded by her own personal solace, she stared out of her room in the direction of her front door.

Everything in her head yelled that there was a threat but she reminded herself that there was no screaming like that day in the square and there was no blood spilled on the floor. Slowly, she was able to convince herself that she was fine and no danger had followed her. In what seemed like a small eternity, she was finally able to close her eyes and rest.

The next morning, she awoke to a headache and vowed not to drink any more of Fin's experiments. She rolled out of bed and looked in the mirror, taking notice of the dark circles that seemed to form under her eyes. Although she slept reasonably well the night before, she was tense. Rubbing her eyes, she couldn't decide if the visions from the night before were real or if things had been exaggerated by the alcohol in her system. Either way, she had decided to take today and figure it out

Readying herself for the day, her movements seemed slow, heavy from the previous night. She found clothes and tossed her hair up in a messy bun before grabbing a bag and heading out the door.

Tomorrow, she was back in her classroom, which gave her one day to try to find any answers about what was going on.

Squinting her eyes at the glaring sunlight, she battled her headache and silently swore again at Finley. Her eyes had just become adjusted to everything around her as the shops came into view. She passed store after store until she reached her destination; a swinging sign branded with the words 'Inked and Bound'. She repositioned her bag and pushed open the door, hearing the familiar bell that chimed to alert the owner of a customer.

A curly mess of blonde hair sauntered into the lobby, bobbing over the stacks of books. The woman's face was plastered with a giant smile as she greeted Blair. "Hello! Welcome to-Oh!" As recognition hit her, the woman swept Blair into a hug and squeezed tightly. "Hey, honey, you weren't due back until next week! Finish your books?!" she asked, constricting her one more time for good measure before pulling away.

"Hey Penny," Blair said with a wince, jarred from the sudden movement. "Not exactly. I'd like to pick up one more, maybe. If you're okay with it?" she questioned with a sweet smile.

"Ohh, I have just the thing! A new romance was printed! It's about a masked wizard who knows how to *use his wand*," Penny paused, wiggling her eyebrows and winking before continuing, "*if* you know what I mean."

"NO! No,.." Blair answered, clearing her throat and imagining what kind of wonderful filth those pages could be filled with. "I, um,..I was hoping to maybe find some old legends of the town? The kids have been begging for scary stories, and I kind of wanted to surprise them."

Penny sighed, her disappointed face apparent as she motioned to the aisles of books. "Awh man, I was really hoping we could buddy read again, but I get it." A small smile lit up her face as she looked back at Blair. "You've always put those kids first, they are lucky to have you." She shrugged to the back two aisles of books. "Back there is where we keep our history, that includes folklore and stories. It would have anything and everything you're looking for. You know where I'm at, just call me over if you need anything else."

Blair nodded at the hospitality of her friend and walked toward the back.

Penny hadn't been wrong, as Blair skimmed the titles, she came across various ghost stories, old tales of SilverDawn and a few obituaries that had been dramatized. She glanced over each volume before returning them to the shelf. Continuing to brush her fingers along the numerous spines, she stopped on one that caught her eye; one that seemed like it didn't belong. She pulled the small, black leather-bound journal off the shelf. The surface was cracked and weathered with a single brass clasp holding it shut. There was no title, and no markings, just an aged diamond on the front cover.

Blair hesitated, then undid the clasp. Inside, the pages were full of handwritten notes. Turning each page, she found each and every one scrawled with musings and symbols she didn't recognize. Carefully fanning through the journal, she came across a nestled piece of parchment in the dead center of the book. Stopping on that spot, her hand hovered over it then she set the book down and carefully unfolded the paper.

It was a map... and it looked familiar.

There were mountains, streams, and a hot spring that mimicked the ones she heard about from merchants' stories. Along different parts of the region, ridges curved into forests and cities. She knew what this was, it was a map of Opelysk, the land in which they lived.

Except, it wasn't.

Her eyes settled on one of the names on the page. In faded ink, she could barely make out the name Myrth.

Blair blinked and shifted the map in her hands, watching as the ink shimmered faintly. Around Myrth were other towns but none she recognized. Tracing a line over each one with her finger, she read them out loud. "Dunlap, Klamer, Crescentine.." Each name, stranger than the last.

Blair's brain kept retracing the lines, the borders between the towns, along with the rivers, the roads, and the mountain ridges. Everything was so unmistakably familiar. This was definitely Opelysk.

There were markings on the page around the land. Tiny symbols inked in the margins. Some looked like strange lines, others like runes or glyphs. At the edge of the page, someone had drawn a small diamond, like the one that was worn on the cover.

A cold shiver rolled down her spine, like she knew she was on to something. She glanced around at the emptiness around her, the only sound was Penny's distant hum somewhere in the bookstore.

Blair turned back to the journal, her pulse quickening with each second. She had lived in SilverDawn long enough to know the structure of the land. She had studied Opelysk and the sections that made the land what it was.

With fingers shaking, she closed the map and cautiously set it back in between two pages. Slowly moving her hand through the next few pages, she froze when her eyes settled on the word "shadows." Her eyes skimmed the paragraphs until she came across another sentence that spoke of "marked ones."

She snapped the book shut as a fresh wave of adrenaline hit her. *This was it, what she came for.* She slipped the book into her bag and grabbed an orange one next to it titled "SilverDawn stories to tell in the dark." She quickly walked to the desk, ignoring the sweat that had started to cling to her forehead.

"Hey Penny, it was a quick find, I'm gonna take it to school tomorrow, and I'll return it the next day!"

Penny barely looked up, her face buried in the new romance she had told Blair about. She waved her hand, giving Blair a thumbs up, as she continued reading.

Blair basically *ran* back to her house, the book almost burning a hole in her bag. Closing her door, she immediately bolted it and walked to her kitchen. Shutting the curtains, she set the book on the table.

After lighting a candle, she sat down and pulled the book out of her bag. She carefully flipped to the back, where she had found the information from earlier.

Her fingers trembled as she moved over each line, moving closer and closer to the pages she needed. Soon, everything she was looking for was right in front of her. On a half-torn page, with smudged ink, there were answers.

The heading was there, at the top, written in tight, angular script: *The Marked ones of Myrth*. Below it, there was a Diamond, like the one that was on the map and book cover. Beneath that, there was writing.

"ALWAYS FOUR. NOT KINGS. NOT PROPHETS. BUT LEADERS, DRAWN FROM NECESSITY. THEY BORE THE MARKS OF MYRTH, NOT BY CHOICE BUT BY BURDEN. ONE BORE THE MARK OF FATE. ONE BORE THE MARK OF NIGHT. ONE BORE THE MARK OF VEIL AND THE LAST BORE A MARK OF VOID. TOGETHER THEY.."

Blair's eyes strained as she tried to read the rest, but the words faded into nothing. It was apparent that the book was old, but this page in particular was ripped in multiple spots. She flipped forward, realizing it had been the last page that was filled out. The rest of the journal was blank, no words, not even symbols. She read the excerpt one more time before closing the book and placing it on the table.

Movement outside her curtain made her freeze. Glancing in the direction of the flicker, she watched as a shape walked past her window. She followed it, trying to figure out if it was just her brain playing tricks on her. After a couple of minutes, she pulled her eyes away from the window and looked back at the book.

All of these pieces; the stories, the darkness, this map. What could it all mean?

Her head started to pound as she mentally tried to place the pieces together. She brought her elbows up and laid her head in her hands.

Where could she go for more answers?

Breathing deeply, she tried to slow down the onslaught of possibilities. Looking into her living room, she stood and walked over to a small tote.

Maybe if she thought about something else for a little bit, she could figure out the next steps.

Lifting her teaching journal from the bin, she opened it to the next upcoming lesson and reviewed her notes. By the time she had gone over key vocabulary words and verified the objective, her mind was screaming to read the journal again.

After battling herself for fifteen minutes, she grabbed everything and walked to her bedroom. Opening the drawer of her nightstand, she placed the leather journal inside and closed it. Then, she dropped her lessons on her bed, and laid on her stomach to finish planning.

With the book out of sight, she was able to focus for a little while. Falling into a false sense of security, she let her mind drift away from the mystery that was unfolding in front of her. Instead, she focused on her students and her classroom.

Soon, the words in front of her started to blend and her eyes became heavy. She blinked a few times, each one heavier than the last. Finally giving in, she let herself drift to sleep.

The next day seemed to start on a lighter note. She had answers and as soon as she came home, she was going to try and decipher the rest of the things in that journal.

She readied herself, made sure the book was securely hidden, and walked to her Schoolhouse to teach. Although she appeared calm and normal on the outside, her mind had been racing in a thousand different directions.

All day long her thoughts revolved around the shadows and the journal. Thankfully, her school day was cut short due to dwindling numbers of her students. Three more students failed to show up.

After closing down her room, she held onto the doorknob and took a deep breath. It had been forty-eight hours since she had asked Damien for help, and yet in such a short amount of time, she felt like so much had happened.

In a weird way, she felt different. Like her sanity was starting to slip. She was constantly battling herself over turning Damien in and the shadows that seemed to move around her.

At one point, she told herself she was going crazy. At another, she convinced herself it was best to let the Hunters know.

She had only made it three feet toward their station before turning around.

Damien had been in this town for nearly *five years*, and although he kept to himself and wasn't particularly social with those around him, he was never rude or disrespectful. Everything inside of her screamed to leave him be. That was the *one* reason she hadn't turned him in.

That and the fact that she may have imagined the whole thing.

5

Blatant lack of self-preservation.

That's what was wrong with her, or at least the reason she was backed into a corner, hiding.

School had released and she had quickly made her move, situating herself in a hidden corner. Then, she waited there for Damien to leave his forge.

If there was more to him, she was going to figure out exactly what that was.

Her body stilled as the plan came together, and his hammer strikes lessened, then eventually slowed to a stop. It was silent for a minute and then the only sound was a light rummaging. The forge door opened, and Damien walked out of his shop, a heavy cloak wrapped around his broad shoulders, hiding most of his body and face. The only item he carried was a satchel slung across his back.

Blair's eyes followed him as he walked past her hiding place. She cautiously watched, moving out of her spot when he was almost out of her sight. She silently followed him and ducked when needed, even moving behind a flower cart as he passed the town square. Blair watched as a woman standing by the butcher's stall eyed him, her gaze lingering a little too long before she whispered to a friend. A child pointed at him, tugging on his mother's sleeve, but the woman quickly hushed him.

She continued to follow him as he walked past the baker's shop. A man trading coins for roses grinned widely at the sight of Damien, his hands resting on the counter.

"Look who decided to join the living," he called, loud enough for everyone to hear.

Damien's head turned as he nodded in recognition to the man but then he continued walking.

Blair had stuck close to the shadows in the beginning, but now that he was in the market, she could camouflage herself in the chaos around her.

Pretending to examine some fruit, she angled her body so she could watch him as he moved. As he stepped, so did she, moving from stall to stall, she continued to stalk him as he walked through the town center. At one point, she was too wrapped into it and almost ran into an elderly man, but had halted just in time.

She took a steady breath and turned to face Damien again just to find that he had now halted in his tracks. Something had made him stop. Across the cobbled path, a figure stood, framed by a towering archway. The man was dressed in silver and black, a stark contrast to the dull browns and muted greens of the town's inhabitants. The fabric of his attire shimmered in the sun as though it had been woven from moonlight itself.

A Hunter.

The man watched Damien with intense eyes that were too piercing to ignore. His mouth opened and he said something to Damien, but his voice was too low to hear.

Blair crooked her neck to try and catch the words, but she realized she wasn't close enough and quickly recoiled back when a lady selling oils near her took notice of her odd behavior.

For a moment, time seemed to pause. She watched as Damien and the stranger locked eyes, as if sizing each other up. There were no more words but a thick tension filled the space between them.

After a moment, Damien cleared his throat and tightened his cloak around his shoulders as he turned away from the man in front of him. Following Damien's lead, the man quickly turned and walked into the crowd, dissolving among the vendors and townsfolk as though he was never there.

Approaching one of the last booths available, Damien seemed unfazed by the interaction. He talked to the vendor a moment before purchasing a few small things and placing them in his bag. As he opened it, Blair caught sight of a large piece of metal that seemed to have a lock on it.

Why would he be carrying that in his bag?

Damien then returned the bag to his back and situated it as he continued on the path to the last stretch of road before the cottages.

Blair's eyes widened again at the realization of where he was going.

The lock was for her classroom.

Backing out of the market, she sprinted for a common shortcut the kids would take using the building next to her. She hoped it would be enough to make it there before he did.

Thirty seconds was all she had, between sliding into her desk and Damien entering the room. Barely enough time for her to catch her breath and her composure.

He stood at the doorway of Blair's class as he knocked, his back leaning slightly into the doorframe. Blair tried to breathe through her panic as she addressed him.

"What are you doing here?" she asked, trying to calm the winded breathing and frantic nerves in her voice.

He looked at her as if her words had been an insult. "You asked for *help*," he replied, his voice low.

"Oh?" Blair pushed out in a shaky breath. I was under the assumption you might have had other things to do."

Damien made a sound similar to a scoff. "I told you I would do something, and it's done," Damien said, stepping forward. His boots made a soft thud against the wooden floor as he approached her desk. He brought his arm up to the satchel and unbuckled it, dipping his hand in to grab something.

Her nerves exploded as she stood. "Stop!" she said, her voice slightly cracking.

Damien froze in response, slightly cocking his head to the side, assessing her reaction. "What?"

"I don't *need* whatever that is," she said, eyeing Damien and his hand that was still submerged in his bag.

Damien raised one eyebrow as if he was calling her bluff.

Blair's fingers tightened on the edge of her desk in response, as though she were subconsciously preparing for some kind of escape. "I figured something else out. I don't need your help anymore."

Damien's eyes narrowed at her and a twitch of a smirk reached his lips.

Yup, definitely calling my bluff.

"Is that so?" he asked, his words slow and drawn out.

Blair swallowed and moved around her desk, creating all the space she could between her and the man in front of her. "Yes, it is."

Damien's cold glare softened slightly as he clicked his tongue in understanding. "Well, I've already used the materials, so you might as well take it." He said, his eyes looking her up and down.

Blair stiffened as she shook her head. "No need, I just want you to leave."

Damien sighed and rubbed the bridge of his nose. "I'm not interested in whatever type of whiplash this is. I'm just here to give you what you asked for. We had a *deal*, remember? The kids will stop touching my things, and you'll have protection."

Blair's eyes narrowed in irritation. "Like I said, I don't need it anymore. I would just like you to *leave*."

This time, the smirk was apparent, as was the fact he had somehow gotten under her skin.

He inhaled slowly through his nose as he looked at the desks that filled the small space, then he audibly exhaled, as if sighing. "No, you don't Blair. You want to protect these kids." His gaze swept through her classroom and then back to her. "I'll even throw in something *extra* for you, if you can learn to play nice." He shifted his hands to his back, pulling something from his waistband. This caused Blair to take a fighting stance. As she did so, his smirk grew into a smile.

In one fluid movement he tossed a small, glimmering dagger onto the desk in front of her. It landed with a soft thunk and her eyes immediately moved to it. The intricate hilt was wrapped in black leather, and there was a small purple sapphire embedded at the base of the handle. The blade was black and glimmered like it held a million diamonds.

The urge to reach out and grab it was so strong that Blair had to physically ball up her fist. Instead, she looked over it one more time. The beauty of the blade was unmatched and she stared at it for a few seconds before his voice replayed in her head, specifically the last comment. She closed her mouth and shifted her gaze up to him.

Her voice was flat when she spoke. "What the hell is that?"

His eyes sparked as if provoking her was the best form of dopamine. "It's a dagger, Feisty," Damien said, his voice laced with humor. He then stepped closer to her, as if she was just a mere form of entertainment squaring up against him. "An extra piece I had lying around. Let's just say it's rare."

Blair ignored the nickname and slowly leaned toward it, her hand hovering inches above the hilt. "Why would you give this to me?"

Although everything screamed at her to pick it up and take it, she didn't exactly trust him.

Damien shrugged before lifting his arm, pulling another startled reaction from her. "You seem antsy. Figured you could use another reason to feel safe."

Blair glared up at him for a moment, then weighed the options she had. If she walked away, she would be no closer to finding something to help. If she took the dagger, she was accepting help from the one person who she literally wanted to drop-kick.

Damien raised an eyebrow. "Come on, just take it. I'll even look away if it makes you feel better."

Blair's face flushed with irritation and her eyes narrowed instinctively at his remark.

Damien's smile returned along with a small chuckle. He crossed his arms, as he rolled his eyes and acted annoyed. "Look, I'm just here to do my job. You asked me to do something for you. You're the one making this into a thing."

Blair swallowed and moved back, debating whether or not to throw something at him. With every bit of venom she could muster, she spoke directly to him. "I'm not making this into anything. I'm asking you to leave. *You* are the one forcing a gift on me."

"Yup." Damien replied, popping his mouth, just to push another button. "But I mean, it is no *sword*." His mouth then curved into a half smile.

The smirk set her off. "I don't want your dagger," she snapped, picking the small knife up and slamming it down on the desk." I just want you to leave!"

"Okay," Damien answered, lifting his hands in the air in an act of submission, "I'll go, but keep the dagger and the lock." On the last word, he turned again to his satchel and took out a large piece of metal, setting it down on her desk.

She watched the lock land on the table with a thud. Her eyes rose again to meet Damiens before she pointed at the door.

Damien stared at her, another slow smile stretching across his face, "Oh and keep the dagger hidden. It doesn't exactly scream teacher."

"Yeah? I'll remember that when I throw it in the river." she said, challenging him with her gaze.

Damien chuckled. "I wouldn't do that if I were you."

"I'm done with this conversation," she sighed, walking to the door and opening it with a dramatic gesture. "Go. Now."

Damien watched her for a second, finally moving toward the door. "Alright, you win. I'm going to leave and you're going to *keep* the dagger. You're also going to install the lock on your classroom door the first chance you get."

He paused in the doorway, looking down at her. "It's pretty simple, you just need the right size bolts and a hammer."

Blair narrowed her eyes, but after a long moment, she sighed in resignation. "Fine but only because I don't know how else to get you to leave.

"Good girl," Damien said, winking again as he turned to leave. He was almost out of sight before he yelled, "And you're welcome, by the way."

As the door clicked shut behind him, Blair leaned her back against the door and exhaled loudly. She looked at the lock and dagger that lay on her desk, muttering to herself about the man who had just dropped them off.

6

Blair sat in the chair in her kitchen, her eyes glued to the canvas bag that lay on her table. She opened it, slowly unpacking the two items wrapped in cloth. She hadn't dared to carry them out in public after leaving her classroom. Instead, she had laid them at the bottom of her bag and carried them back to her house.

She had wrapped the dagger multiple times in fear of stabbing herself or cutting the fabric of her bag. Cautiously lifting the smaller bundle out first, she unwound the cloth.

Lifting her hand up to a random ray of light that leaked in through a window, she placed the dagger in her palm and eyed the way the sunlight illuminated the details. Size-wise, it was not much bigger than her hand, but the blade extended past her longest finger, about six inches. The detail was what made it exquisite to her. An intricate array of swirls and patterns adorned the handle. The onyx color was darker than any black she had ever seen, but somehow it managed to produce an effect like diamonds, glittering in the light.

She rotated her wrist, watching as light bounced off and reflected. Balancing it on her finger, it felt weightless, not like other weapons. This one was different, unlike anything she had seen before. She swiveled it more to the sides, taking note of how the intricacy was on both sides of the blade. It was the perfect size; very discreet, and easy to hide.

Somehow, in just the small time it had been in her possession, the dagger had dwindled her fear. She *finally* had some form of protection, even if she wasn't sure what exactly she needed it for.

Using a weapon was new to her. She would have to start with the basics to figure out the correct way to hold it. That aside, she was glad she had taken it. Such a small yet powerful thing.

She gazed around the room, her eyes finding small pockets in which she could hide it while inside the house. The instructions were clear from Damien, *keep it out of sight*. There were two options: a hollowed-out book on her shelf and an open canister in her kitchen reserved for flour. Shaking her head, she decided against both. Nothing seemed to fit the majestic nature of the dagger.

She laid it flat in her hand and looked at it again, thinking about ways she could keep it on her.

Could that be an option? Instead of hiding it?

Although it was common for men in town to carry a way to defend themselves, she couldn't have this out in the open around her children. She sighed for what felt like the hundredth time today and wrapped the dagger, placing it back in her satchel.

Next was a crafted lock, if you could call it that. The metal was shaped using a simple method and more so resembled a bolt. As she looked at it, she realized there were two pieces to fit on either side of the door. One was rather large and held a cylinder bolt that would lock into the other side once it was moved into place. Holding it up, it proved to be extremely sturdy and durable. Blair noted the holes on the sides and the weight, figuring it wouldn't require much effort to attach it to the door.

Her thoughts shifted to the person who had given it to her, Damien. She almost dropped the lock completely out of sheer annoyance. Inside her head, she knew he had ultimately helped her. Despite the anger he caused, he did deliver on his word and made something that could help. She set the metal pieces down on the table carefully.

For the rest of the afternoon, Blair made an effort to stay busy. She cleaned her kitchen but found her fingers were strangling the broom. Trying to bake, she dropped a bowl of batter due to the shakiness in her hands. Deciding to settle in and ease her body, she even tried reading but found her foot silently tapping as she reread the same sentence over and over again. Nothing seemed to stop her anxious mind.

As a last-ditch effort, she had taken a bath in hopes of easing the knot of nerves she housed. She ended up leaving the warm water quickly to just stand near the dagger.

It was like every time she was close to the dagger, it seemed to call out to her. She huffed, moving to the bedroom to quickly get dressed.

After dressing, she decided to surrender to the constant pull and grabbed the bundle that was the dagger.

Stepping outside and toward the back of her cottage, she opted for the side that lined up with the trees. Thankfully, she had no neighbors that were close. Instead, a thick layer of tall, exuberant trees fenced her house in from those around her.

She stepped up to a tree and laid her hand on the bark. A pesky, unwelcoming texture met her skin. Slowly building confidence, she unwrapped the dagger once more.

Once it was fully out, she tested it in her grip and moved it around in her palm until it felt right. She raised the dagger to the tree and traced a small spiral into the trunk. The edge of the dagger easily carved into the strong wood, leaving a fine line where Blair pulled and pushed.

A smile was soon plastered on her face. This was not nearly as scary as she had imagined it to be in her head. Soon after her carving was complete, she eyed the other side of the trunk. This time, she wanted to test her boundaries even more. She took a step back and raised her arm, the tip of the dagger touching the bark. She took another step back and another, stopping when there was a distance of ten feet from the tree. Adrenaline began to spike in her bloodstream as she raised the dagger to throw. Bringing back her arm in slow motion, she threw it.

The dagger spun once and thudded, handle-first, against the tree. Then, it dropped to the ground with a clumsy clink. She let out a sharp breath and walked over to pick it up.

"Okay. That was *practice*."

She tried again. This time, it veered left, slicing through a patch of weeds before vanishing into the underbrush around the tree.

"Seriously?"

Her jaw clenched. She yanked the dagger from the ground and walked back, breathing out and trying one more time. It hit the tree, flat side first, and fell. She stood there, hands on hips, staring at the wood like it had personally insulted her.

Her yard was quiet except for the wind in the grass and a bird singing somewhere overhead. It didn't feel like the right soundtrack to failure, but here she was. She rolled her shoulders and picked up the dagger. This time, she didn't grumble under her breath or try to make up a technique. She just inhaled and threw.

Too high.

It was now stuck in a low-hanging branch from the tree. She groaned and flopped to the ground, flat on her back, with arms stretched out. She could just picture Damien's smug reaction to her failing. That mental image made her even more angry.

"What am I doing?" she said to the sky.

She stayed there, letting the evening breeze cool her frustration. She turned her head, watching the last bit of sun slip behind the treetops. Then she sat up. Picking up the dagger for the final time, she stood, eyes narrowing in concentration. Her fingers gripped the hilt, which reflected the faint light of the receding sun.

She threw without thinking. It spun through the air, glinting, then thudded into the tree with a satisfying thunk. Her heart raced, and a grin stretched across her face.

"Perfect," she whispered to herself, stepping forward to retrieve the dagger. She was almost giddy with the rush from the well-executed throw. She stood there for a moment, admiring her work, before hearing something.

A subtle rustle came from behind the nearby oak tree, the sound sharp in the otherwise silent night. Blair's pulse skipped and her smile faltered.

The air around her shifted, and the hairs on her neck stood up. She squinted at the shadow of the tree, but it was too dark to make out anything clearly. A few seconds passed, and then the shape behind the tree shifted again. A movement that was just enough to confirm her suspicion: someone, or something, was there.

The thrill she'd felt moments before evaporated. She turned sharply, her eyes darting in the direction of the house. Realistically, she knew it was only a few yards away, but her fear made it seem much farther.

Without hesitation, she snatched the dagger from the tree, gripped it in her palm, and started to move swiftly toward the door. Her feet barely made a sound on the ground as she moved. She glanced over her shoulder once more, a feeling of dread tightening in her stomach as she reached for the door handle.

7

For most of her life, Blair had been more comfortable with books than blades, but that had changed recently. Her days of teaching turned into nights of training. For the past week after school, she'd been practicing relentlessly, her hands growing steadier with each dagger throw. The first few days had been frustrating; her throws were wild, missing the target entirely or landing with awkward clinks on the ground. But now, the blade danced through the air with a satisfying thud when it struck the target. Even after hours of daily practice, the dagger never faltered or chipped, maintaining its pristine image.

By the end of the week, Blair was almost surprised at how natural it felt. The weight of the dagger was no longer foreign to her, it had become an extension of her arm. She could almost sense the arc of it as it spun in the air, guided by a steady hand and a calm mind. At this point, the dagger always remained close to her.

Knowing that she felt more comfortable carrying it, she'd taken the time to craft something more practical: a sheath for her thigh, made of a few leather scraps and an old belt. It was snug and subtle, designed to be hidden under her skirts.

No one could ever tell she had it, and it filled her with a sense of adventure.

During the day, the dagger remained sheathed and out of sight. Come afternoon, the moment she was alone, it was out and she was practicing. It remained close even at night, when she slept with the blade under her pillow.

She was no longer scared of handling it. She knew it was only a matter of time before she would actually need it. If she was honest with herself, there was also the fact that the dagger gave her a new sense of confidence.

She waited for another stranger to come into town or a scream of agony to signal impending doom, but soon, the exact opposite occurred.. The stories began to dwindle, and SilverDawn's friendly demeanor slowly came back.

Within the next week, all of her students had returned to class. Their rosy-cheeked faces, void of fear.

In almost every aspect, everything was back to normal. Other than the lock (which had never moved from her house) and the dagger that had become a part of her everyday ensemble, everything seemed average. Even Damien had slunk back into the isolation of his forge and had yet to be seen since he presented Blair with the dagger.

Her thoughts rarely visited him and the shadows he potentially wielded. She had almost convinced herself that whatever she had seen wasn't what the traveling merchants discussed, nor what was written in the book. Thoughts about him aside, everything had settled. Besides the stranger who had walked into their town a month ago, no other danger had surfaced.

The Hunters had patrolled the area like they said they would; walking the streets, checking the market, and keeping to themselves. The only interaction she had was once when they walked into her yard while she was practicing. She was just able to pull the dagger from its spot in the tree when a Hunter appeared, eyeing the distressed bark. He watched her for a few more moments, eyeing the marks again before watching her body language, and asking her a couple questions.

"I've been told you visit the town square often. Have you seen anything suspicious or out of the ordinary lately?"

Blair shook her head no, sliding the dagger into the back of her waistband and leaning one arm against the tree beside her. Her mind immediately pictured Damien, and she prayed her face didn't betray her words.

"Nope. Can't say I have unless you count the ridiculous price they're asking for eggs," she responded with a small smile. The Hunter paused, glancing back at the tree and around the yard.

"Do you live here by yourself?" he asked, his eyes squinting slightly in suspicion.

"Sure do," she answered, moving her hand and crossing her arms over her chest. He nodded slightly again.

"Thanks for your time."

She watched him walk away with an uneasy feeling in the pit of her stomach.

She went to bed that night, thinking the worst was over and that whatever storm of unease had blown through, was now behind her. Regardless, she planned on continuing to wield her dagger, even though the need for it may have subdued.

That thought settled her mind, and she went to sleep the fastest she had in weeks.

In what seemed like mere minutes, dawn was awakening, and the colorful lights cascaded into Blair's open window. She awoke with a content smile and slid her hand under her pillow, making contact with the dagger. She pulled it out, stretched her arms, and flipped it easily in her fingers as she sat up. A large grin spread across her face as she registered just how happy she had been recently.

Standing and moving to the clothes she had set out, she pulled on a blue cotton dress and shorts. She sheathed the dagger to her thigh and produced a patterned ribbon to tie her hair into a messy bun. Blair started to hum as she collected her things for the day and threw them into her bag, including the lock Damien had given her. She then descended her walkway, heading out to start her day.

This particular morning seemed bright to her and filled with hope. An optimistic energy flowed through Blair as she decided to use the extra time she had. She walked past her schoolhouse to the bakery nearby. Most mornings, they awoke before the sun to start making breakfast rolls.

The old shop smelled of flour and seasoning, and as she approached, the wind carried the aroma to her. The door was open, allowing the morning air to enter. As she reached the door, she could spot the counter through the window.

Pausing, she noticed a man leaning over the counter, very close to the owner. She set her bag down along the brick that lined the building and moved behind the corner of the door as she watched.

"You've seen something," the Hunter growled, voice hard. "Don't lie to me again, Orlin."

"I told you," the shopkeeper stammered, backing into a shelf of rolls, "I haven't seen anyone who can do that. I don't even know what you're talking about."

With a sudden snap, the Hunter's gloved hand shot out, and he swiped his arm across the counter. Bottles and bags full of flour, sugar, and other contents exploded across the floor, spraying glass everywhere. Orlin cried out, shielding his face as the man in front of him advanced.

"Don't insult me by pretending ignorance," the Hunter said, stepping around the counter.

"I swear, I know nothing!" Orlin's voice cracked, highpitched and pleading.

The Hunter turned again, seizing a wooden chair that occupied a table, and hurled it across the room. It shattered against the far beam with a loud bang. Then came another chair and a jar of spiced salts, each reduced to fragments with cold precision. Orlin flinched at every crash, his back pressed hard to the wall of shelves behind him.

Then, a soft thud filled the quiet. A sound too out of place in the violence to go unnoticed. The Hunter froze and slowly turned his head toward the noise.

At the shop's entrance, half-concealed in the doorway, stood Blair. She had dropped her satchel on the wood floor, clearly announcing her arrival. She hadn't meant to intervene, but she couldn't just sit there and watch the shop be destroyed. It was like her body had moved on its own, walking straight into the heated argument.

The fury in the Hunter's eyes stifled like a candle, caught in a sudden wind. His chest rose once, then again, slower. He turned away from the trembling shopkeeper and stared at the broken remains scattered across the floor as his fists unclenched.

"I'm sorry to hear about the damage that happened," he said, voice flat but no longer venomous. "I'll make sure to report it immediately."

The shopkeeper didn't answer, only watched as the Hunter stepped back and ran a hand through his hair.

"I'll come back later to check on the situation," he muttered, looking up at Orlin. He then turned his body and went to walk out, just brushing past Blair.

His legs stopped moving and his eyes shot to hers, as his expression darkened.

"What is your name?" he asked, his tone flat.

"Blair Griffin," she replied, staring blankly as she picked up her bag and took a step toward the shopkeeper, who was watching with horror in his eyes.

The Hunter grabbed Blair's wrist, stopping her. "I need to ask you some questions."

Her anger rose instantly, and she yanked her arm away from him, "You can ask me *after* I help Orlin, or better yet after I'm done teaching for the day. I'm sure you have others to torment while you wait." Blair walked away, setting her stuff down on the counter to help with the mess.

The Hunter clenched his jaw and pulled his arm back, pulling it under his cloak. "I guess I'll just find you after."

Blair waved him away in response as she found the broom and swept up the glass shards and broken wood.

Once his figure was out of sight, Orlin rushed to her and embraced her in a hug. "Thank you, Blair. I'm not sure what he wanted, but someone sure made him angry."

She hugged him back, dropping the broom. As her arms wrapped around him she sighed deeply. "Yeah, that didn't exactly seem friendly." She pulled away and nodded her head in different directions around the room, "I'm sorry about your shop."

Orlin followed her gaze, stopping to rest on the glass that now covered his floor. "Don't worry too much about it. My assistant will be here soon and he will help. Why don't I grab some breakfast for you, as a thank you."

Blair nodded, gladly accepting the offer. As Orlin moved to the counter and started placing things in bags, she glanced back at the door and thought about the way the Hunter had grabbed her.

Something didn't sit quite right, but her line of thoughts were broken as a bag was shoved into her hand. She thanked Orlin and checked in with him one more time before heading out to school.

The rest of the day was like any other; Blair taught reading in the morning, followed quickly by math and science, and today, there was even art. Each lesson had blended into the next with barely a moment to think. Between tying shoelaces, settling disputes, and reprimanding the boys about the careless play in the forge, Blair barely noticed how quick the time had passed. Before she knew it, the sun was beginning its slow descent over the town of SilverDawn.

Blair dismissed the class and waved goodbye to her students. One student, a loud and energetic redhead, ran back to her and squeezed her tight as she kissed the top of his head. His blue eyes beamed as he said good evening to her and skipped away. She double-checked that all the students had left with their families, and closed the door to her room.

She stood there for a moment, tilting her head back and forth, debating whether or not to go home. Ultimately, she decided to stay and work through the uneasiness of the morning by trying to install the lock.

As much as Blair had connected with the dagger, she didn't want the lock to go to waste. Returning it wasn't an option, seeing how she had no intention of talking to Damien again. With that, she took a deep breath in and decided to install it.

At first, Blair just stood in the middle of her classroom, staring at the heavy iron pieces in her hands with a mixture of determination and stubborn pride on her face. She had just found the tools she needed, and was ready for the next step.

Eyeing it from afar, it definitely appeared to be sturdy enough for a siege. She straightened her shoulders and mentally walked through what Damien had said.

After following the first few self-appointed instructions, she began to struggle holding the lock and hammer up. She paused, muttering to herself and glaring at the lock as if the metal itself was laughing at her.

She kicked off her shoes, rolled up her sleeves, and approached the door with a boost of confidence. The lock was supposed to be simple: just a few screws, a bit of hammering, and maybe some swearing. But the moment she lifted it up to the door, the weight hit her like a ton of bricks.

"Oh, you've got to be kidding me," she grunted, wobbling slightly. It was heavier than she'd anticipated, a lot heavier. Her arms trembled as she tried to steady the lock with one hand and fish around in her toolbox with the other.

She bit her lip as she breathed through the effort it took her to hold it. Lifting the lock higher, she positioned it toward the top of the door. The door creaked, and she tried to level it to the wood. Of course, the weight made it dip on one side. "Come..on..," she said, struggling. "It's like he made this intentionally to piss me off."

After several awkward attempts to hammer in the brackets, hold it up, and not drop anything on her foot, she felt like she had gotten the hang of it. The lock was almost attached, but she was still struggling to get the final screw in. "What is with this thing?" she groaned, rolling her eyes.

Finally, after what felt like an eternity of twisting and muttering, she managed to get the lock almost entirely in place. The final screw was still a little loose, but there was no way she was going to let that stop her.

"Good enough," Blair said with a grin. "No one's getting through that door anytime soon."

She stepped back and admired her work, hands on hips, thoroughly satisfied. With one final break she grabbed the door and closed it. Before the door had even finished rattling, one side of the lock fell hard and hit the floor with a harsh thud. Blair stared for a few moments at the piece on her floor and counted to five.

Nope. Not happening. She was done.

She turned, collected her things, and headed home, almost two hours late and feeling completely defeated.

8

Blair was almost home.

She was walking down the familiar dirt path toward her cottage as the crisp evening air brushed against her face and the sun settled below the horizon. It had been a long day of teaching, planning, and fighting a huge, stupid piece of metal that she was convinced was the wrong size solely to make her mad. She couldn't wait to kick off her shoes and curl up with a book.

But as she turned the corner, she stopped dead in her tracks. The sky was marred by a vast expanse of dark gray.

Smoke.

Thick, dark fumes were rising from the roof of her house.

What was happening.

Her heart slammed against her chest as she squinted, trying to make sense of what she was seeing. It wasn't just a small wisp. It was a full-blown blaze, climbing up the sides of her cottage and swirling in the wind like some kind of malevolent creature.

Her pulse quickened, and before she could even think, her legs were in motion. She dropped her bag and started running, her boots pounding the dirt path. Her stomach churned with dread, and her mind raced with all the things that could've caused the fire.

As she neared the cottage, she saw the truth. Her home, her sanctuary, was burning. The fire was consuming everything she owned. The flames weren't small, they licked all sides of the building. The house was trashed. Windows were shattered, doors splintered were open and the entire interior was engulfed in flames.

Her clothes, the pictures, the artwork.

The journal.

"NO!" Blair screamed.

Before she could take another step, a large hand shot out, grabbing her around the waist and pulling her back.

She twisted in surprise, her heart still pounding, only to find herself face-to-face with Damien.

"Let me go! My house!" Blair cried, trying to pull free.

His grip was firm but gentle, as though he was trying to stop her from making a reckless mistake. His face remained soft, as if concerned rather than angry. Although, when he spoke, his voice was urgent. "Blair, listen to me. Did you talk to any Hunters? Did anyone see the dagger?"

She froze, her mind refusing to cooperate as her heart worked overtime. "W-what?"

Damien muttered to himself as he looked down at her and then raised his eyes to scan her burning house. Blair stopped fighting for just a brief second, as the pieces started to click into place.

This wasn't a misunderstanding or a coincidence.

"I-I didn't talk to anyone," Blair stammered, her breath coming out in short bursts as she stared at her house spitting flames. "No one knew about the dagger and I-I really haven't spoken to anyone."

Damien's expression darkened, his grip tightening for a moment as if restraining himself. "They've been watching you, Blair. They know your schedule. They most likely thought you were home." His voice lowered, "We need to move fast."

A sick realization hit Blair like a punch to the stomach. *Her home wasn't just destroyed; it was a message. A warning.* Whoever was after her didn't care about her things or her house. They had been looking for *her*.

She recalled the past few weeks; every incident, every interaction. Her mind caught on two specifically; The Hunter who had approached when she was practicing and the Hunter from the bakery.

Could one of them be responsible? Had she embarrassed the one from this morning? Had she been too cross with him?

"I don't understand. Why would they do this?!" Blair screamed, trying to move toward her house again but Damien's arm only tightened as he pulled her into his chest.

She struck his chest over and over. "Why?" she screamed again, her voice filled with anger. "Why?!"

Damien's face was stern as he looked down at her, "We leave. Now."

Without waiting for her reply, he pulled her toward the edge of the path, away from the flaming ruins of her house.

Her mind was spinning; her life, her safety, her very sense of security had just been ripped away, and she felt broken as her feet mindlessly followed him. After a few moments, her mind finally caught up and her legs froze, defiantly pushing into the ground beneath her..

"I'm not going anywhere with you!" Blair said, ripping her arm away from him. "I know nothing about you. You could be part of this!"

Her words had no effect on Damien as he leaned down and picked up her bag, along with the things she had dropped. "There's no way you can fight this alone, Blair. Remember they're not after your *house*, they're after *you*."

She opened her mouth to argue, but his words were like cold water to her nervous system. In a way, she knew he was right. They'd come for her. And no matter how hard she tried to deny it, she couldn't fight whatever was happening without help. Still, every instinct in her body told her to flee from him.

"I said that I'm *not* going anywhere with you." Blair repeated, enunciating her words.

Damien looked her up and down before clicking his tongue. "Just know, if you scream, they *will* find you."

With those words, he bent down and threw her over his shoulder. In reflex, her mouth opened to protest but she knew what he said was no threat, it was a guarantee.

Instead, she kicked her feet and thrashed against his shoulder. Fighting the whole way, she watched upside down as he took her through the winding streets, away from SilverDawn and into the woods beyond.

The shadows of night were quickly descending and that made her fight harder. Kicking her knee to the side, she managed to make contact with his jaw.

Dropping her quickly, Damien groaned in pain and rubbed the tender spot as she found her footing. She braced, expecting a fight but as his eyes met hers, an avalanche of feelings bombarded her. She was vulnerable. She had been foolish. And now, for the first time in a long while, she was scared.

This fear materialized when something in the air around them changed. Damien broke eye contact, moving his gaze from her, to the space around them, and then back again. The shift in the environment made her stomach drop. At first, it was subtle, an unnatural stillness, like the world itself was holding a breath. Then, a low rumble echoed from the forest to the east, followed by a dark shadow that seemed to crawl across the ground itself. Damien grabbed her wrist and pulled her next to him into the closest shadow given by a tree.

They stood together, Blair's heart pounding. The town square was out of view, but the bustling sounds carried from the path they had followed.

SilverDawn's livelihood, the one that had carried on the wind, suddenly stopped. Another cold wave of dread rolled over her as she heard a scream in the distance.

A noise that was sharp and desperate.

Another one followed.

Oh god.

Around them, the air crackled with an invisible presence. A wave of shadow moved, and creatures leaped from the darkness. Twisting and writhing like living smoke, their eyes glowed with malice as they headed straight for the town.

Her eyes bulged in disbelief at the creatures that rushed past her. Moving in waves, they ran toward the town like a plague. People continued to scream, and she could only imagine them fleeing in every direction to escape. Blair's feet moved on instinct, her hand grasping for the dagger she'd concealed on her thigh. The safest bet would be to run, but the town was descending into chaos. Her students' faces flashed in her mind, and there was no time to think, only to act.

The ground beneath her feet shook as more of the dark creatures surged past, their claws tearing through the stone. Damien's arm reached out and encased her against the tree behind him, sensing her urgency to move.

"I need you to stay still and be quiet." he hissed through gritted teeth, shielding her body. His face was grim, his dark eyes scanning the chaos around them. His breath was shallow, almost like he was tempted to hold it until everything had passed.

Pushing up against her body, she began to fight in protest which resulted in him pressing a hand over her mouth. "We need to get out of here. Now." His grip was firm as he pulled her into the forest, away from the shadow beasts but she still refused to cooperate with him.

"Come on," he commanded again, urging her to follow him. For a moment, her mind went blank, and her feet shuffled with his as the adrenaline pounded in her ears. They passed through the trails like ghosts, slipping between the large trees and avoiding the sounds of panic. Damien never spoke, only pulled Blair by her hand. She watched, as the world around her became a blur of darkness and fear.

Finally, they reached a clearing, a space far enough away from town that the smoke was as distant as the screams. Damien paused, glancing over his shoulder to ensure they hadn't been followed. He took this second to take out a small pouch of water and offered it to Blair.

Blair's eyes roamed over the pouch and darted back to the path they had just walked. She blinked a few times, willing herself to reassess what she had just seen. If she returned, it would lead her to her schoolroom and the children she needed to ensure were safe. Her mind screamed at her as they took a second to breathe, keeping out of sight. Another minute passed and she could again hear the echo of screams. She knew the creatures were probably everywhere, easily tearing through the town. That was enough to clear the panic-induced fog that had rendered her helpless.

"I have to go back Damien!" Blair turned to leave, but he wrapped a steel-like hand around her arm.

"You are no match for them," he stated blankly as he tugged her back to him.

She immediately whipped around and dug her heels into the ground. "You don't know a goddamn thing about me." She grabbed for the dagger and fought to move back in the direction of her students.

Damien snarled loudly and blocked her path yet again, pushing his chest up against hers. The whites in his eyes seemed to darken as he pushed into her space. "We don't have *time* for this. They are after you, not the town."

Snarling back, she pushed her shoulder into his torso and glared up at him, "I'm not asking. Let me through Damien!"

He took a deep breath in and out, "Sorry, but you leave me no choice." Then, for the second time he bent to hoist her over his shoulder.

She tried to fight him off but as he grabbed her, the world around them was swallowed by shadows.

As she succumbed to black, she feared the monsters invading their town had found them.

9

Blair's eyes opened to an unfamiliar canopy of leaves. The shapes faded in and out as her eyes adjusted to the darkness. The air around her smelled of damp earth and pine. There was a dull ache in her head as she tried to recall where she was. Groaning, she brought her hands up to rub her temples and tried to refocus her eyes on the sky above her.

Attempting to sit up, the world tilted beneath her. Instead, Blair held onto the soft, moss-covered ground for stability. A sharp breath escaped her lips as she finally registered her surroundings as well as a figure who sat a few feet away.

The moonlight was almost a spotlight on Damien and the long sleeves he now wore. The silver light created shadows on his face, which only brought out his stone-like features. Small areas of soot still covered his skin, now mixed with lines where sweat had fallen. He was sitting on the ground, a couple of feet from her, with his back to a large tree.

Giving her mind a minute to register the darkness, Blair realized how late it had to be. The sky around her was drastically different, which meant it had been hours since she had fallen asleep.

Was that what had happened? Had she fallen asleep?

The last thing she remembered was arguing with Damien. Her body tensed at the thought.

Damien was looking at her with a quiet, intense expression. His posture was relaxed, yet alert. His eyes watched her with a mix of curiosity and caution. "You're awake," He said softly, crossing his feet and leaning back into the tree behind him.

Blair's mind flashed back to the moment before she lost consciousness, the urgency she felt, the screams that echoed to her, the absolute wall that stood in front of her as she tried to return to the village. Like a defense mechanism, her hand slid to her thigh for her dagger. Finding the empty sheath with her fingertips, her eyes widened, and her mouth went dry.

Blair's eyes ignited in anger as she slowly stood and narrowed her eyes at Damien. Holding onto a nearby rock for support, her voice rose with each word. "Where is my dagger?"

"You've grown awfully attached, huh?" His eyes flickered in response to her growing rage as he stood alongside her and replied with an indifferent tone, "Your dagger is in your bag, along with a spare set of clothes and a canteen of water."

Blair's fury escalated as she focused on him. "Damien. What is going on? What happened back there?

Why are we in the middle of nowhere?" She stepped closer to him and pointed at him. "Why were you asking me about the dagger?!" On the last question, she shoved into him, using force to send him a message. As her hands made contact, his body didn't budge but something else did, a small flicker of movement.

He said nothing as his nostrils flared, and a flash of black grew across his neck. He closed his eyes, breathing deeply, and after about three seconds, he opened them. His blue eyes darkened with restraint as he just stared at her for a few moments. Then, with a deep sigh, he folded his arms and pushed into *her* space. "The Hunters noticed you. You were in danger. As for me being here with you? It turns out we are *both* now wandering around because our home is no longer safe."

Those were not answers. At least not the answers she deemed acceptable.

Blair's eyes caught the movement on his neck and she could have sworn she saw something recede back into the collar of his shirt as he continued to speak, "The other questions you have, I cannot answer simply. In order to explain it, there are other things that you have to know first."

Blair backed up, crossing her arms and nodding, clearly waiting for the explanation.

So, he continued, "First off, what do you know about Hunters?"

The question threw Blair off. *That's where he was starting?* She scoffed and straightened her stance, making sure to keep a reasonable distance between them. "We were told their job is to protect us, to report anything suspicious. They showed up and started patrolling," she paused, thinking of the bakery, "Maybe investigating. I'm guessing they might be looking for specific people."

Damien nodded, wiping a piece of dirt from his leg as she continued.

"Would you happen to know *anything* about that, Damien?" she asked, raising her eyebrows.

He gave a simple nod. "I know that Hunters have one job, and it is not to protect, it's to *hunt*. The King sent them to collect those who have shadows."

Blair looked up at the moon, registering his words. After another second, she froze, remembering what she had witnessed in the forge. "It's you. They want you."

The brief nod that Blair received was all the confirmation she needed. Her face flamed at the thought of her house, her things, and the distance between her and the town she loved. "*You* are the reason for this. *You* are the reason my house is gone. The reason we had to run." Her voice lowered on the last word as her eyes grew in rage.

This time, it was Damien's turn to peer into the sky for an escape. "Yes it's because of me, but you had to leave too. Someone sensed my shadows and I think they assumed they belonged to you. If we hadn't left together, they would have found you eventually." His glacial blue eyes met Blair's as once again, the moonlight highlighted his features.

He sat again, shifting his elbows to his knees. She still stood a few feet away, with her jaw clenched and her eyes fixed on the surrounding woods.

Damien gave a small sigh as his tone lightened. "As much as it's my fault, I didn't mean for this to happen. I swear."

Her silence was louder than a shout.

He gave her a second to think and then continued, "I gave you the dagger to help and I think that's what they sensed." He ran a hand through his hair, frustrated.

"All of this over a stupid dagger," she repeated flatly. Looking away from the dark woods, she turned her head to him, her expression sharp with disbelief. "Why would they sense the dagger? What is so special about it?"

He met her eyes but didn't respond.

"I need you to tell me everything," she said, her voice still laced with anger. "I need you to tell me about the dagger. I need you to explain what is going on. You at least owe me that."

"You asked for help," Damien replied, his voice clipped but sincere.

"To protect the students that you took me *away* from!" she yelled.

He flinched. Her voice cracked on the last word, raw with fury that was held too long. "I asked you for help because I had no one else," she whispered.

He opened his mouth, then closed it. The defeat in his eyes was apparent despite the darkness around them. "I'm sorry," he said, quieter now. "I really am."

She turned, crossing her arms and staring at the sky with her back to him. "Keep your apology," she said. "I'd much rather have an explanation."

After a few moments of silence, Damien sighed and stood up as well, walking next to her and directing his attention to the stars above them. "I've had the dagger since I was young, it always gave me a sense of security. For some reason, everything in me was screaming to give it to you."

With a small inhale, Damien pulled his gaze away from the dark sky and looked down at her, "I'm guessing the fire was set by someone who sensed the shadows in the dagger. A cloaked Hunter was at your house waiting for you after work, but you never showed up. I'm assuming he was going to ambush you."

Blair shook her head slightly, focused on the stars. "And how would you know that?"

Damien didn't answer.

Blair quietly shifted toward her bag and took out her dagger. Turning toward Damien, she stepped closer and attempted to swipe at him with heated emotion.

His reflexes pulled his body back, which was expected, but the blunt force that hit her wrist was not.

The dagger hit the grass beneath her with a soft thud, and Blair stared at the reason why.

Shadows had stopped her.

Large tendrils of smoky, black lines appeared out of nowhere. They hung close to his body, as if protecting him.

As fast as they had shot out and defended his body from harm, they had curled back in, leaving no trace of what had happened.

She gestured to the area around him, "What the fuck was that?!"

Damien bent, picked up the dagger, and blew off a loose blade of grass. "Blair, meet my shadows. Shadows, meet Blair."

"How do you have any humor about this?" Blair yelled, her eyes wide with disbelief.

He then turned to his own bag and took out a sheath made of black fabric. "Because I don't know how else to handle it." He offered the fabric to Blair, keeping his eyes on his outstretched hand. "I made you a new sheath." Blair stared at the cloth, not moving. "Also, wanting to hurt me is valid. You *can't*, but I'll give you a point for effort." Damien said with a smirk, lifting his eyes to hers.

Blair glared at him, "A sheath?! Absolutely not! I don't even know who or *what* you are. Besides, the last time I took anything from you, it ruined everything."

Damien's stare was blank as he lifted the sheath to her, gesturing for her to take it."You couldn't even install the lock on your door. Besides, I'm just trying to help, maybe make a crappy situation into something a little better," he replied, one of his eyebrows. "I was intending to give this to you anyway."

Blair continued to stare at him, flabbergasted, and backed up. Fighting back tears, she sat down on a log near her. She hung her head in her hands and sighed, looking at the ground. The anger she felt moments ago seemed to suffocate as the situation sucked the air out of her lungs. Dizzy, she closed her eyes and inhaled deeply.

She looked up after a few moments. "Damien, I need you to answer me. How did you know he was waiting for me and how did you know about the lock?" She looked up after a few moments, thinking back to the shadows outside of her windows. "Have you been watching me?"

"Yes." Damien replied, moving to sit next to her. He placed the dagger and sheath on the log beside her leg.

"Why?" she asked, still seething with emotion but picking up the items and holding them. Goosebumps pebbled her skin as a cold gust of wind blew by. She wrapped her arms around herself in an attempt to ward off the chill that gripped her body.

Damien noticed and threw her bag at her. "I think you should be more focused on the fact that I was able to save you."

Blair rolled her eyes in response, "You didn't *save* me. You dragged me out unconscious and without the ability to fight back. Kidnapping would be a better term actually, because now I'm stuck with you in the middle of nowhere, with no answers, about anything."

"*Ashwood.* We're near Ashwood." Damien responded, as he once again turned and walked away from her down a dark trail.

Within his absence, Blair could finally breathe a little, even if that meant she was alone in the darkness. The growing fear from that was shattered when she repeated his words in her head.

Ashwood?! That was a whole town over from SilverDawn. How long had she slept?!

Once again, anger tore through her and she hung her head in her hands, elbows balancing on her knees.

After several long moments, a click in front of her made her raise her head. She could just make out the outline of Damien and the fact he was holding something. She focused as much as she could through the darkness and then held her breath as Damien moved. The next moment, there was a small flicker of light. A couple seconds later, another spark, and she realized it was from stone hitting stone.

This happened two, then three more times before a flame ignited, lighting up the face responsible. Damien blew into the small fire that now sat on top of a pile of kindle. The flames easily grew, eating the small bits of grass around it. Damien sat back on his knees and placed several small twigs at the base, causing the flames to grow.

His eyes rose to Blair's as he pushed back from his knees into a sitting stance. One knee was up, bent with his arm dangling over it, and the other lay crossed in front of him. Even in the dark, he demanded too much space. "I thought you might like a fire," he said casually, staring at the moving light.

Blair pursed her lips. "I would *like* more answers." As the words left her mouth, the heat warmed her skin, and she pulled her arms away from her face at the tiny bit of comfort.

"Mhmm. I guess someone is going to have to learn to communicate better," he said into the flames as his gaze flickered to her shoulders that lowered as she relaxed.

Blair gaped at him and then snarled, standing up in front of him with her chin raised in defiance. "I can communicate just fine. For example, I would rather find all the answers I need on my own, than have to deal with you."

Damien's eyes dropped to Blair's foot, his eyebrows raising in amusement. "Yeah, I'm sure you could *totally* do that on your own," he said, voice dripping with sarcasm, as he pointed to where she had kicked dirt on the fire, putting out half the light.

Her face flared in embarrassment, and she pulled her foot back. Turning herself away from him, she walked a few paces away. "You're infuriating."

"Also valid," he called after her, "but you'll get used to it."

She shot him a look over her shoulder, "Don't count on it."

He laughed this time, his shoulders rising and falling with the sound. Despite the anger, despite her desire to throat-punch him, a part of her knew she wasn't getting out of this alone.

Blair's thoughts were interrupted as Damien grunted, pulling his bag over to him. Placing it on his lap, he used his hands to turn it towards him and motioned with his head for Blair to sit next to him. "Come back over here before you hurt yourself."

Blair scowled at him in response.

He smiled, "And stop making that face, you know I like it."

This time, Blair rolled her eyes and looked away.

"That's no different, feisty." he replied, chuckling at himself, "Come on, I'll give you more answers."

That caught Blair's attention and she moved slightly closer to him but refused to close any more space between them.

As Damien looked back at his bag, he unlocked the small clasp that held the material closed.

Blair noticed a small diamond symbol etched on the metal. She squinted, trying to remember where she had seen it before.

"I have small things to keep our strength up, but we will need to find a food source soon." He produced some dried meat and a few pieces of bread, offering half to Blair. She stared at his hand, wondering how many other items were in his bag and how they all fit. Ultimately caving and knowing she needed nourishment, she accepted the bread and ate it quietly.

"Honestly, the rest of what I have to say isn't what you want to hear. But the truth is, I don't have all the answers. All I know for sure is that the Hunters were after you. If they find you, they'll kill you, just because you had the dagger. If they find me, there's a good chance they'll try to take me out too. So, right now? We have to stay together, at least until we figure everything out." Damien looked up, taking a bite out of his bread.

Blair continued to chew slowly, her attention resting on Damien.

He had finished his portion and had methodically gotten to work. His hands were steady despite only having the light from the fire. With only a thin, weathered sheet and a single metal rod, she watched as he made a tent to sleep in. He drove the rod deep into the earth, angling it just right to support the makeshift roof, then stretched the sheet over it, securing the corners with rocks and carefully knotted twine. The fabric billowed slightly in the breeze, but Damien reinforced it with additional stakes fashioned from broken branches, tightening every edge until the structure held firm. The sheet draped low enough to offer privacy, its edges tucked carefully to keep out the creeping chill of night.

Satisfied, he stepped back, surveying his work.

He then turned and laid another sheet down within five feet of the tent. "I can take the first shift. Why don't you go to sleep in the tent, and I'll sit out here by the fire."

Blair contemplated that and shook her head slightly, "I'd rather watch first. I'm not tired anyway."

He nodded, then grabbed his satchel and took out two pieces of clothing, bundling them up and placing them on top of the sheet that lay on the ground. He lowered his body onto the forest floor, laying on his side and turning toward Blair.

"Give me four hours. I'll be right here if you need me." With that, he closed his eyes and rolled over. "Don't get us killed."

The first hour passed quickly, most of which Blair found herself watching the fire consume itself over and over again. She spent the second and third hours reciting the names of her students. Recalling their little faces and the personalities that she had come to love. Memories of lessons that left the students in bewilderment and surprise. The determined look in their eyes as they faced a new challenge and the heartbreak when they felt defeated. This collection of thoughts brought tears to her eyes, and she took a deep breath. A silent tear fell as she realized what she left behind. The life she built, the children she loved.

Wiping the tears and returning her focus back to the dancing flames, she sorted her thoughts and weighed her options. Damien had claimed they were safer together, but it didn't feel right. Not when she wasn't sure what had happened to her town or if she could trust him.

She needed to get away from him.

She needed to go back.

She would just have to wait for the right opportunity.

Around the four-hour mark, Damien began to stir, and his eyes opened in a sharp movement. He registered her, the fire she kept alive, and the darkness around them. He said nothing as he sat up and looked toward the tent, motioning her to go inside. Once she gave him a few moments to fully wake up, she stood and entered the tent.

Like outside, there was a small bed made of cloth on the floor, and she was suddenly thankful for a moment of solitude. She lay down, letting the tears fall silently. She cried until her body was weak and begged for sleep.

It wasn't long until she gave in, offering herself one of the only things she could control right now.

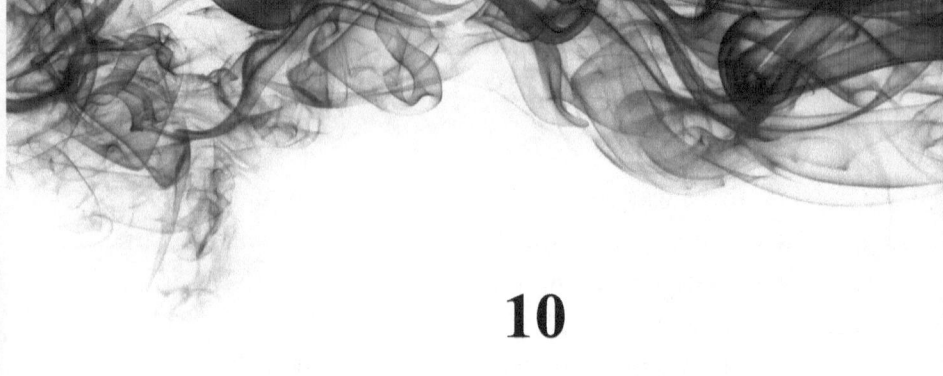

10

Blair's eyes fluttered open to the sound of a soft scrape against steel. The dim light of dawn filtered through the thin fabric of the tent, casting long shadows on the ground. Her eyes began to close again, but the sound of metal-on-metal made them spring back open. Rolling to her side, she adjusted the way she was lying to peer out of the crack in the tent's fabric.

Sitting cross-legged just outside the entrance was Damien. Carefully running a stone along a blade, he looked like he hadn't slept much.

Damien didn't acknowledge her right away as she emerged from the tent. He kept sharpening his blade, his sharp features shadowed by the low overcast light.

Blair took a small moment to look at him. Besides the apparent lack of sleep, he seemed relaxed, his dark auburn hair glinting faintly in the dimness.

"Morning, princess," he said, stopping the movement of the stone to look over his blade.

"Don't call me that," Blair replied, her tone sharp as she stood in front of the tent and stretched her back. She pulled her eyes from him and looked around, pretending to blink the overcast light from her eyes.

It seemed dark, like rain.

Damien took one last look at the small hunting knife he had been sharpening and placed it through a loop in his belt. "I would suggest changing into the other clothes you have, they have a better chance of withstanding the weather. We have to head out soon."

She nodded and stepped back into the tent. The smell of smoke clung to her hair as she moved her head around, pulling her shirt over her head. She found the other outfit in her bag and quickly pulled the long-sleeve shirt on, as well as matching pants. The clean clothes felt warm but did nothing for the dirt that coated her skin. Pushing the thought of a hot bath aside, she pulled her hair together and threw it up in a bun using a small piece of twine from the bottom of the bag.

For the next few hours, Blair blindly followed Damien as they hiked a path through Ashwood. They both remained silent, only stopping to use the bathroom or take a small drink of water.

Each moment that passed gave Blair more time to think. She thought of her warm bed, the tavern, and the million reasons she couldn't trust Damien.

By the time her legs weakened, they had been walking through the dense forest for close to half the day. The afternoon air was cool and fresh against their bodies, but their stomachs growled in unison as they turned down a new pathway marked with purple flowers, similar to the ones she loved.

Blair pushed past the hunger pangs and sharp cramps in her stomach but a few minutes later, her stomach complaining again, rather loudly.

"We need to find food soon," Damien muttered, wiping sweat from his brow. His eyes searched the trees for anything that they could cook.

He paused, taking off the bag that was bound to his back. It was larger than Blair's satchel, and she had guessed it contained more than just clothes and water. He opened the top by unlatching the brown leather and pulled out a small bow and quiver.

"So, not just blacksmith skills, huh?" Blair suggested, nodding her head at the bow.

Damien shrugged, "Something like that. I guess you can say I like hobbies." He looked around again, positioning the bow against his shoulder.

Blair's mind flashed with the animals that filled the forest. The wild rabbits and deer that brought her such happiness on her walks.

Reluctantly, she stepped toward him.

He eyed her suspiciously, lowering the weapon. When she made no effort to move again, he prepared the bow. The tension in his body was taut as he aimed toward a flickering movement in the woods ahead of them.

Another vision of a baby deer popped into her head, and she stepped in front of the bow as he lined up the shot. "I-uh, I can't let you."

"What did you just say?" Damien retorted, keeping the bow in place as his eyes glued to the trees ahead of them.

Blair rolled her eyes and stood straight, "I'm not here to debate my morals with you."

Damien ignored her, pulling back the string and readying the arrow. As a result, Blair found a large twig close by to stomp on. The snap was sharp and loud in the stillness of the forest. The animal that Damien had found, a deer, bolted past a nearby tree, its tail disappearing into shadows.

Damien sighed in frustration."Out of all the people in the world to be traveling with," he whispered, turning toward her, "I get stuck with you?"

Blair smiled widely, feigning innocence.

His eyes narrowed in annoyance. He shouldered his bow and aggressively shoved the arrow back in his quiver with another sigh. They continued to walk for a few minutes until Damien came to a halt. A white rabbit, small in form, caught his attention. Eyeing Blair from the corner of his vision, he unslung his bow and wrapped his fingers around it. "I suggest you look away," he muttered, his voice barely audible.

Another sound bounced off the trees around them, a rock that clattered loudly on the ground. Before he could even knock his arrow, the rabbit bolted away, vanishing into a thicket of green nearby.

Damien ground his teeth, "Stop. You're doing this on purpose."

For the first time since leaving SilverDawn, Blair released a genuine smile.

I see why he likes to make me upset.

"Wow. You do have emotions, look at that." She looked down at her hand, still full of pebbles and tossed another one in the opposite direction of where they stood. That caught Damien's attention just long enough for another deer in the near distance to run away.

Damien stepped toward her, his lips in a sneer.

She looked up at him and smiled again, lightly pushing him. The movement wasn't out of fear or anger, it was purely to agitate him. In a mocking tone, she whispered "Oh come on, who's the *feisty* one now. Or is that just when you get hungry?"

Damien let out a long breath. "I'm not doing this with you. If we don't eat, we won't have any strength."

Blair looked around, her expression shifting as she became aware of the situation at hand. "Alright, alright, I'll be quiet, but only under the circumstances that we find some type of nuts or berries instead of cute little woodland creatures."

Damien looked at Blair with an irritated stare, "You've got to be kidding me."

He looked like he was about to say more, but then a strange expression crossed over his face and he smiled smugly. "Fine." He agreed, a certain gleam in his eyes, "but when your stomach starts to eat itself, you have to *beg* me for food."

"Deal." Blair cocked her head to the side, her smile returning. "But you will wait a very long time for that."

Damien smirked, "Good, it gives me time to teach you how to play nice."

He shifted his bow to his other hand and opened his bag, carefully placing it inside. He then put an arm through one strap, shifted the bag to his back, and stood, staring at Blair.

Blair watched him, trying to anticipate his next move. He waited a few moments before glancing at the trees around them and then landing back on her hazel eyes. "Alright, you're up. Find us something."

Her face blanched, but she turned before he could register it. Recalling anything and everything she knew about plants in the wild, she followed the path in front of them.

After searching for a few minutes and turning over different leaves, she came across blue and purple berries sprinkled across knee-high bushes. Her eyes lit up at them, a fruit that she knew, Crescent berries. A rare treat that only bloomed during a certain type of year. She smiled at the large patch and recalled just how much her class had enjoyed them as a snack a few weeks prior.

She pulled the bottom of her shirt away from her stomach and gathered them, holding the fabric up high. She started to pluck them off the bush, tossing the berries one-by-one into her makeshift pouch.

Damien stood behind her and just watched, as her face filled with satisfaction. After she had filled her shift to the brim, and some were starting to fall to the ground around her, they moved to a nearby patch of grass. Damien took a small blanket out and laid it down underneath them.

"So," Blair said as she knelt, dumping the berries before popping two in her mouth. "Where are we headed?"

Damien picked one up, cautiously examined it, and bit into it slowly, pulling away the fleshy skin and assessing the soft purple filling. "We'll keep moving until we are in a safe area. We need to stay out of sight for a while, especially with the Hunters around and multiplying. We can either go northwest toward the Gorge for refuge or northeast toward Lynnwick." Damien bit down on the fruit he had obviously never tried.

The look of relief that washed over his face confirmed Blair's assumption that he would like it. "Okay, so let's say I'm going to stay with you and *not* because I want to but because realistically, I have no other choice. What does that mean for me?" Blair said, shoveling another handful of berries into her mouth, the juice beginning to dribble down her chin.

"You *will* be staying with me and that means you won't die immediately," Damien said, smiling at her as he carefully placed a few more in his mouth.

Blair rolled her eyes at his remark. "Cool, but that's not exactly what I meant," she pulled her hand away from her mouth and leveled her stare at him, "I have to be able to trust you."

Damien paused and looked at her, his eyebrows raising slightly, as if in disbelief. "I'll give you five questions," He replied, tossing another berry into his mouth, as a playful smile replaced his previous reaction.

"*Five*?!" she coughed out, almost excited.

He nodded, clearly content with her reaction. "On one condition, you find more of these berries." He lifted the last handful and popped them into his mouth.

She scoffed at him with a dramatic tone, "Some of those were mine!"

He shrugged, shooing her away with his hand.

"Fine." She stomped away, grabbing her bag, "I'll use this, so I don't have to ruin my shirt more than I already have." She then stuck her tongue out at him and headed in the direction of the bushes.

Damien watched her closely as she walked away, crossing his feet and leaning back on his elbows. "Stay close."

Yeah, right.

As soon as he was out of her sight, she ducked behind a tree and looked around. This is what she had been counting on. Steadying her nerves, she took off in a dash back toward the way they came. Ten feet, twenty feet, she kept going until her lungs burned from exertion, only slowing when her head pounded with adrenaline. Gasping for breath, she hunched over with both hands on her knees, sucking in the air around her.

A branch snapping to her left stole her attention.

"Huh, you didn't make it as far as I thought you would." Damien chuckled, walking out from the shadows of the trees that lined her path. "Good effort, though." he reassured, with a wink.

Blair's face flooded with heat and anger so strong it escaped in the form of a scream.

Damien watched, appearing unfazed. As her voice cracked and dwindled out, he leaned against a tree behind him. "You done?"

All the adrenaline left Blair in a rush, and she collapsed onto the ground. Slowly, tears began to streak down her face and when she spoke. "I just want to make sure my students are safe. Don't you care about your friends?" She sniffled, the tears coming harder as she looked up at him. "All of the people in town? I just need to know they're okay."

Damien watched as her body sagged and her walls crumbled. Sensing this, his demeanor instantly changed and his face softened.

He knelt beside her and sighed. "I wouldn't consider anyone there my friends, but I understand what you're saying."

As Blair looked up at him, soft droplets of water fell on her face from the sky.

They sat in silence for a few moments as the rain began to fall harder, the droplets soaking into their skin and clothes. As Blair gained control of her breathing and stopped the tears from falling, Damien placed a rough hand on her knee and spoke over the incoming thunder.

"Listen, I understand that I didn't have connections in the town that you did. I guess I wasn't thinking about anything else except getting us out of there, but Blair, if the Hunters get hold of you, they are going to do anything they can to extract information. They know about the dagger, and it wouldn't be as easy as handing it over or telling them about me. They would torture you, and you would never escape. I've seen it." His soft tone continued as he squeezed her thigh and let go. "This isn't about me kidnapping you or not letting you return. It's about staying away from them. If one of us gets found, it dooms the other." He pulled her up from the ground, raising his hand to shield her from the rain as it picked up in intensity. "If we go north to Lynnwick, it's only a half-day's journey. Once we get there, I can hire a runner and send them to check on your students and see what damage was done to the town."

With his words, Blair physically relaxed and even stepped toward him, closing the space between them. "You would do that?"

He looked down at her and for a brief second, his eyes traced her lips. "I would do whatever to get out of this rain, Feisty."

11

The half-day journey went faster than expected, even with the rainfall. By the time they reached Lynnwick, the rain had stopped, but they were now covered in mud. Blair exhaled with relief as they approached the town, her skin covered in cracked, dried dirt that was becoming extremely uncomfortable.

Stepping into the entrance of the town, she could immediately tell the village was bigger than SilverDawn. Even from here, it seemed like twice the size. Like their town, it was nestled between towering trees and hills from the outside but this one opened up into a much larger space.

As they crossed under a large archway, the hum of activity instantly filled their ears. The streets were not cobbled but smooth, the dirt flat and soft. The paths were crowded with townsfolk weaving through each other, carrying boxes, laughing, and speaking in lively voices. Her eyes scanned the surrounding area and immediately settled on the colors that were so prominently displayed. The town was full of pastel hues, different forms covering multiple areas. Ribbons decorated the trees in light blues, pinks and yellows. Woven banners of those colors stretched across booths.

Blair squinted against the sun which was now peeking out from around the clouds and took in the town in front of her, which was bustling with movement.

Damien eyed a table nearby and walked up to the vendor, asking about the towels displayed. He soon returned with two small ones that had been dampened. He offered Blair one, before using the other to wipe his brow and arms. The mud attached to them was in thick patches and cracked as they wiped at it. The larger chunks fell easily, but a thin, dusty film clung to the fabric they wore, staining it a dull brown.

"I guess we'll have to figure out a way to wash these," Blair said, tugging at a particularly stubborn clump on her thigh.

Damien made a sound in agreement as he turned toward her and knelt on one knee. Taking the towel from her hand, he ignored his own legs to help with hers.

Blair stood frozen with her hand in the air, as his hand wrapped around the back of her thigh.

Fighting whatever warmth his hands were causing, she clenched her jaw and forced her eyes to move, looking everywhere besides at him. He ran his hand up he thigh and then down her calf before moving to the next leg and repeating the motions. Each time he pulled or tightened his grip, she found herself fighting off certain thoughts.

Once done, he pulled back, content with his work and shifted over, moving to clean his own pants. Blair watched him and *those damn hands* as they moved with an intensity that was no longer slow or careful, but rough, as he tugged through the clumps that clung to him.

He felt her stare and looked up, holding eye contact with her until the intensity caused her cheeks to flush. He chuckled then, and threw the towel at her as he stood.

"Look at that," Damien said, pointing to a curious shop that was across from them. It had a large wooden sign swinging above its entrance that depicted a quill and a book.

The window next to the door displayed several bound books wrapped in different pastels that towered in different heights.

Blair leaned closer to the shop, her eyebrows raised. "It's twice as big as the one in SilverDawn," she muttered, intrigued. He nudged her toward the door with his shoulder, encouraging her to check it out.

As they walked closer to the shop, his voice was soft. "Go inside and check it out. I'm just going across the street." He pointed to another building, a few doors down. 'Runner's Guild' was painted on a birchwood sign nailed to the wall.

She nodded absentmindedly, her eyes glued to the intricately carved door in front of her, which was covered in swirls and small illustrations. Damien only shook his head at her as he watched her enter, before turning toward his destination.

Walking in, her eyes immediately took in the expansive shelves. Each one towered over her with rows and stacks of books. Every inch of space was filled, from floor to ceiling, with books; Some novels were perfectly lined up, others stacked haphazardly. She began to stroll, lifting her hand and running her fingers over the countless spines. Blair barely noticed she was now alone, her mind consumed by the magic around her. She picked one up at random, turning it over in her hands. The writing inside was foreign and intriguing to Blair. She sat and turned the pages, finding pictures that depicted different parts of the story. She read through what she could before choosing another and another.

Finally tearing her eyes away from the words, she pulled herself back to reality, finding Damien leaning against an exposed beam with his feet and arms crossed.

She smiled up at him, "That was fast."

His eyebrows shot up in surprise. "It's been two hours, Blair."

Her jaw popped open, "I'm sorry!" she said as she stood, causing the books on her lap to fall to the ground. She quickly bent to pick the books up and stacked them on the chair she had been sitting on.

Damien cocked his head to the side as she approached him, looking at the ground in embarrassment. He only shook his head and opened the door leading back out to the village. Nudging her with his shoulder as she passed, Blair responded with a sheepish smile.

They turned down a new street, taking in a different view of the village. "I sent the fastest runner. He will return within four days. The job was to check on the town and deliver a message to Finley. We will have to stay until he returns but I found some lodging for us while we wait."

Blair nodded, stopped, and turned to him, "Thank you, Damien. I really mean that." Taking a moment to meet his gaze, she placed her hand on his chest briefly. He went rigid in response, and she pulled away quickly, returning her attention to the city before them.

They wandered farther down the street, taking in the different vendors that were scattered around. It almost mimicked the one they knew from their home, except here, stalls lined the roads in a line. The booths were in different shapes and held mostly perishable items. A large U-shaped table was bursting with fresh fruits; orange melons, purple berries, and ripe apples. Another booth was lined with chests that were filled with different varieties of flowers peeking out of them. As Blair scoped out the tables, a group of children ran past. Her eyes caught on a toy that most of them held, a strange wooden rectangle that made musical sounds as they spun it through the air.

They continued, passing a blacksmith's forge. Damien paused to watch the smith hammering some kind of sword into shape. The air was thick with the smell of burning coal and hot metal.

"Do you miss your forge?" Blair asked, sensing a change in his demeanor at the sight.

Taking a moment to think, he sighed as he responded. "I miss not having to worry about anything around me. It was the only place I didn't have to hide."

Pulling his eyes away, Damien motioned in the direction of the outskirts of town. "That's where we're headed."

Following his gaze, Blair caught something in the distance through the gaps between the buildings, something unusual. Steam rose from the top of a small hill just outside the town, and as they approached, the scent of warm minerals and earth grew stronger.

"A hot spring," Damien expressed, watching her face for her reaction.

Blair eyed the distant mist, where pools of steaming water shimmered under the last rays of the sun. It was a beautiful sight, pale green water steaming gently from the earth, surrounded by rocks that seemed to glisten in the light. The area was secluded, bordered by tall trees, and even from this distance, the warm, inviting steam seemed to call out to them.

"I've never been to one before," she said softly, curiosity lining her voice. *After days of walking, the idea of soaking in those warm waters was tempting.*

"Good, it's our home for the next few days," he responded, as if happy with her thoughts, "At least until we get word back."

Blair's mood shifted, as if she was now uncomfortable. "Damien, I don't have any money for this. I barely have clothes left to wear." She then gestured down to herself. "Everything I owned," she paused, defeat filling her eyes as she continued, "It all burned."

Damien shook his head at her "Technically, it's my fault we are in this mess. Let me attempt to make some of it up to you."

Blair started to protest, but she realized it wouldn't matter, he was the only one with money, and if he wanted to spend it on the hot springs, who was she to deny him? She looked up, shrugging in agreement.

A small smile of victory spread across his face.

They walked together through the lobby, greeting the receptionist with a wave. Arriving at the double doors, they opened them to the courtyard. A massive area of grass was fenced in, leading to the springs. Several small buildings encircled the water on both sides. Each brick structure showcased a different number, but were relatively the same size and shape.

As they approached the room labeled 23, Damien took out a single key. Blair looked at him, raising one eyebrow.

Damien noticed her apprehension and raised his hands innocently. "I'm going to be in the water most of the time anyway." She lowered her eyebrow as he placed the key in the lock and turned the handle. With no further sign of reluctance from her, he pushed the door open.

The room was small, offering one large bed, two nightstands, and a table in the far corner. The walls were bare but shined with a simplistic beauty, showcasing different grains of wood. Walking to the only other door inside the room, Blair discovered a small bathroom attached. Jumping up and down excitedly, she grabbed her bag and closed the door, calling out to Damien. "I call the shower first." His response was muffled as she tore her clothes off, and turned the faucet on.

There was no ecstasy quite like this. Her body almost melted in pleasure from the warmth that now surrounded her. She scrubbed everywhere once, and then again before moving to her hair.

Not wanting to use all the water, she hurried through the last bits of skin that had stubborn dirt attached. After another minute, she walked out in a towel.

Damien, who had been putting his clothes away, looked up just in time for his eyes to catch rogue drops of water that fell down the exposed skin on her chest. He cleared his throat and looked down just as his eyes darkened around the crystal blue.

Blair caught it and took a step toward him, angling her head to try and see better. "What's going on with your eyes? Is it your shadow?"

As the word left her mouth, dark tendrils moved down his arms, moving toward her. She jumped back just as he grabbed his things and took her spot in the bathroom, avoiding eye contact and the question.

With a slight shrug and feigned ignorance, she placed her dirty clothes outside the door and stepped back in, finding her last outfit at the bottom of her bag. Tugging it on, she nodded in approval at the bed. Grazing her fingers over it, she felt the soft texture of the cotton blankets that lay on top. With a content sigh, she laid down, flopping on her stomach and groaning in approval. She quickly tugged the blankets and wrapped them around her, savoring the way she was instantly hugged from all sides.

"Okay," she murmured to Damien, who she *knew* couldn't hear her, "I don't hate you right now. Right now, I'm completely content."Closing her eyes, she listened to the water run as her body relaxed into the bed.

Soon after, the smile that was plastered on her face loosened, and a soft snore replaced it.

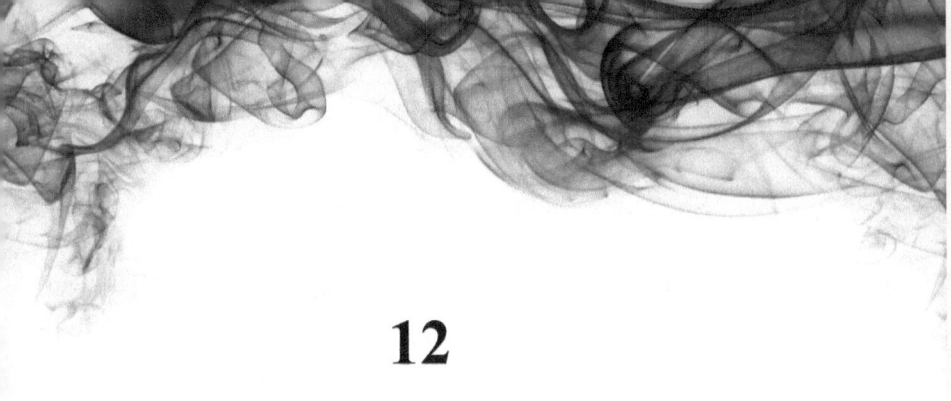

12

When a strand of moonlight leaked in and crossed over her, Blair stretched and unwound from the blankets that were wrapped around her. She sat up, remembering where she was, and looked around. The room was empty, there was no sign of Damien.

Knowing him, he hadn't strayed too far. Pausing mid-stretch, she imagined him sleeping in the tent outside.

He wouldn't do that, would he?

Scoffing to herself, she turned toward the edge of the bed and swung her lung down. Inhaling deeply, the scent of the hot springs outside flooded her senses.

Looking up at the moon through her window, she guessed she hadn't slept for more than a few hours. The darkness indicated it wasn't close to dawn, so maybe a perfect time to test out the water. She moved out of bed, checking the bathroom for any signs of Damien and shrugged when she found nothing.

She was definitely the only one in their room.

Walking from the bathroom, she looked down at her clothes and decided to undress. If she was going to try the hot spring, she was going to do it the right way.

She shimmied out of the light fabric and grabbed a robe that hung next to the sink. Wrapping it around herself, she opened the door leading outside and took a step into the darkness. There was just enough light to see, courtesy of the moon and stars from above.

Closing the door behind her, the night air felt crisp against her skin. She looked around on the ground for her dirtied clothes, the ones she had set out earlier but the patio was clear, which she found annoying. *Who would steal mud-riddled clothing?* She shook the thought out of her head, huffing in irritation as she walked the stone path that led to the water.

The closer she got, the louder a faint bubbling filled her ears. As she reached the edge of the pool, the welcoming steam filled her lungs. The vapors hovered just above the water, lingering over the large rocks that enclosed it. In some places, thick wisps covered the dark water as they curled lazily against the surface.

There was no one in the water.

Relief flooded her.

Becoming more comfortable, Blair dipped a toe in and gasped at the unexpected heat before laughing softly to herself. She had never experienced this before, and although she heard stories of the hot springs, she couldn't help feeling vulnerable. Opening her robe, the feeling deepened as she looked down at her body. Running a hand across her chest and then abdomen, she watched as goosebumps followed.

Slipping the robe off her shoulders, she waded in slowly. The warmth instantly wrapped around her, making her sigh in relief.

"Look who's up."

Blair jumped, causing the water to splash around her. Her eyes darted toward the far side of the spring and focused in on an outline of another person occupying the water. Someone she definitely hadn't noticed before.

Half immersed, the figure lounged against the rocks along the ledge. From the dim moonlight that flickered over his sharp features, Blair could tell it was Damien.

Words refused to form as she realized she had just openly flashed him. Pushing past it, she gathered the courage needed to answer him. "Yeah. I woke up and wanted to try the water out," she admitted, sinking deeper to hide her flustered expression.

He smirked and tilted his head slightly. "How's your first time?"

Blair blew bubbles underneath the water before popping up to answer him, "Five seconds ago? *Great.* Now? Uncomfortable."

"Just pretend I'm not here, then." he chuckled. "It obviously didn't bother you when you first showed up."

With that, Blair turned away from him and tried to focus on the warmth that seeped into her bones. After a few seconds, the tension in her shoulders and neck started to melt away. Maybe she didn't care how naked she was. Maybe he was farther away than she realized, and he couldn't see anything anyway. Within a few moments, her worries seemed to lift as she focused solely on the water that enveloped her.

Another few minutes passed before she glanced over at Damien. His eyes were half-lidded with ease and he seemed just as relaxed as she was.

Like always, he knew she was staring. "Unless you want to use your five questions now." Damien casually murmured in her direction, not opening his eyes.

She peeked at him, shaking her head at the absurdity of the situation. *Casual conversation in the nude, why not?*

Swallowing a chunk of discomfort, she sighed back at him in submission. "And you won't lie?"

"I have no reason to," he answered, before lifting his head and holding her gaze in a direct stare.

She nodded slowly before clicking her tongue as the first question formed in her mind "Are your shadows dangerous? I mean, they are shadows, right?"

He responded quickly, a smile leaking through his words. "I think technically you just asked two questions, in a matter of two seconds."

She cursed under her breath."Will your shadows hurt me?"

Damien opened his eyes and exhaled sharply, running a wet hand through the top of his hair. He stared at his arm as he brought it back down in front of his face. "Controlling them isn't that simple of a task," he admitted, his voice low, almost hesitant. "They're part of me, but they don't always need direction. It's like they feed off my emotions, slipping through the cracks when I get too angry, too scared, too anything." His gaze flickered to the sky. "I've had them for as long as I can remember. I try to keep them in, but the more I fight back for control, the worse it gets. They lash out when I don't mean them to, and sometimes it's hard to stop them." He clenched his fists under the water. "So no, I don't think they will hurt you. I just have to keep myself together and hope they don't decide to tear everything apart."

At the brazen truth and sheer unease of his voice, Blair believed every single word but still, it wasn't an exact answer. "That's not really reassuring," she stated, eyes opening to the sky above.

"You have two questions left," He stated as he moved away from the rocks, splashing water now louder than the gurgles that surrounded them.

Another question nagged at her, one that she hadn't quite figured out for herself. "Are you the bad guy?"

His answer came out like he had rehearsed it. "No. I am what some people call Shadowborn or Duskborn, depending on what legend you grew up with. I'd like to think I'm *not* the bad guy but the truth is, some of us lose control and that's when things can get messy."

Blair bit her lower lip as she processed the information he was giving her. She then focused on her last question, another thing that had been swirling in her head since meeting him. "Okay, here's my last one: Why are you always such an ass?" She asked, a giggle cracking on the last few words.

He picked his head up and looked over at her. "You really decided to use *that* as your last question?" His warm laugh echoed off the water around them. "Call it a personality trait."

Another shift of water signaled that he was close to the entrance of the pool now. As she glanced over, he stood, water running down his chest. Each step caused the water to run more, and soon, Blair found that he too was wearing nothing

Blair quickly averted her eyes, her cheeks staining with color. *Did he have no shame?* She listened as he moved to another rock outside of the water. Grabbing a towel, he wrapped it around his waist and sat to dry off.

Trying to get her mind off what she had just seen, she cleared her throat. "Well, I guess it's my turn but I'm only giving you two because you tricked me." Blair said, turning the attention away from all the exposed flesh in the vicinity.

Without missing a beat, Damien responded. "I want to know why you're alone all the time."

Taken back by the quick response, Blair swallowed and thought about the question. *He was truthful, so she could be too.* "It was always just me and my parents," she said, her fingers curling in and out of the water as she tried to comfort herself. "My father wasn't the best man. He favored alcohol." She paused, fighting the lump trying to rise in her throat. "Most days he'd come home angry."

Blair's voice wavered, and she took a moment to steady herself, "When I was fourteen, he died," she went on, her hands trembling slightly as the memories flooded back. "They told me it was a heart attack, though I think his body just gave out from drinking. And my mother, she was sick. She'd cough for days, and I'd try to help her, but there was only so much I could do."

Blair's eyes turned down to her hands, the scars on her palms a reminder of the years she had spent trying to shield herself from the chaos, the pain. "A few years later, she died. It was a slow kind of death. Some random sickness that the healers couldn't help with. I was sixteen when she passed. After they were both gone, I didn't really want to get close to anyone else." She paused then, the weight of her words hanging in the air.

After a long breath she blinked away the stray tears threatening to spill.

Damien remained quiet, focused on her story, but his second question followed soon after the first. It came out slow and methodical. "How did you end up in Silverdawn?"

This wasn't just a logical follow up to his first question, he genuinely wanted to know her story.

"I didn't know where to go after my mother died," she continued, her voice gaining strength. "I wandered for a while, not sure what to do with myself. Where I lived before, you couldn't even call it a town, it was just a few houses grouped together. When I found SilverDawn, I found kindness there in Finley, in the traders, and in the children that littered the streets. It gave me life, and I quickly became obsessed with it. I knew I didn't want to be the same kind of person my parents were. So, I became the mother I never had, in the teacher I am... or *was*." Blair took a deep breath, unaware she had been holding it as she talked.

Suddenly, everything was too much. Whether it was the water, the conversation, or the walls that had seemed to come down so naturally for him, she wanted to be back in bed, surrounded by comfort.

Standing, she moved toward the shallow water. "I think I'm going to head in for the night."

As the air hit her wet skin, she remembered just how vulnerable she really was. A hard lump formed in her throat, but she swallowed it. *He wasn't going to win, not tonight.* She turned her body, exposing herself to him.

All color drained from his face before lines of black moved up from his jaw. His body tensed as he watched the water drip down every inch of her skin.

Walking up to him, she reached for her robe, but before she could get any closer, shadows wove around her, concealing her.

She gasped at the contact, and watched as the writhing smoke moved with ease, twisting and turning like it was alive. The shadows were not forceful, but they caressed her skin, shielding her gently from the outside world. Her most intimate body parts had been concealed, leaving some strips of her skin open to the night air.

She looked up and into Damien's eyes which widened for a second, before the blue was overcome with black. His jaw tightened as he managed to ground out a few words "You could have warned me."

Her eyebrows furrowed. "Warned you?"

He tensed again as he gave an abrupt nod and looked away.

With that, her confused expression morphed into one of annoyance. "Get over yourself." She dropped the robe she was holding and turned, walking several feet back to the room. The shadows stayed in place until she was inside, disappearing only when the door slammed shut behind her.

13

Bright morning light invaded Blair's eyes, and she blinked against the sun filtering through the window. Shielding her eyes with her hand, she pulled the blanket over her head and rolled. Everything hurt and her mind was heavy with exhaustion. She wasn't even sure what time she had gone to sleep. Once she had stormed inside, she had regretted her attitude and waited up for Damien, who never showed. Ultimately, she had given in to her drowsiness, and fell asleep.

Trying to fully wake up, she pulled the blanket off and took a deep breath. She pulled herself into a sitting position and turned, noticing a large frame across the room on the floor.

So, he had returned.

Catching sight of the way he huddled on the floor, she almost felt bad. His large frame was awkwardly placed, clearly uncomfortable despite the blankets he had used to try and create cushions. He had one arm under his head for added support, and his legs were extended out as far as they could go before running into the wall.

She slipped her legs out from under the covers and moved them to the cold floor. Standing, she carefully balanced herself and stepped over him. The world outside was still asleep as she peeked through the blinds at the other rooms of the inn. She considered returning to the hot water outside but quickly dismissed that idea, remembering how distasteful last night had been.

Opting to be outside and in the fresh air, she decided on dagger practice instead. Carefully, she went to grab her bag for her sheath. She froze as her hand touched the clothing on top; A folded pair of pants and a shirt, the outfit she had worn yesterday. She picked up the pants, unrolling them to look at the legs. There was no trace of mud, as if they had been scrubbed. She glanced back at Damien, who hadn't moved.

Did he do this?

No, there was no way.

As quietly as she could, she stepped into the bathroom and put on her clothes, strapping her sheath to her thigh. She then moved lightly toward the door, pausing only for a brief moment to listen for any sounds from the sleeping man on the floor.

Putting her ear up to the door, she heard nothing. Other than the breathing next to her, the inn was quiet. No one else seemed to be awake, which meant there was no one to disturb her. She eased the door open just enough to slip through, closing it gently behind her.

As she stepped out, she winced at the chill, but it didn't matter. She had a moment of freedom and needed to feel the weight of her dagger in her hand again. Not being able to practice her skills the last few days had made her antsy.

The dagger she had come to love hung on her thigh, nestled in its new sheath. She reached for it now, fingers brushing the cool hilt as if it were a lifeline. She took in the sight around and looked up, admiring the colors that had painted the sky. Blair moved swiftly, finding a place she could practice that provided some type of privacy. Her footsteps were soft as she moved, the only sounds coming from the small rocks that crunched under her boots. She made her way behind the huts, finding a corner that backed up against a hill of the hot springs. This area was enclosed and would be a perfect spot for her.

The space was quiet, almost eerily so. The only sounds were the bubbling water and birds waking up in the distance. Blair looked around, noticing a stack of old crates against the wall. Knowing they would make an improvised target for her practice, she grabbed them and restacked them.

She positioned herself at a distance, her body moving instinctively as she reached for the dagger. The weight was familiar in her hand, smooth, cold, and solid. She ran her fingers along the blade for a moment, a brief ritual she had adopted to calm her nerves before she threw.

Blair raised her arm, her focus narrowing. Her breath slowed as she fixed her gaze on the center beam of wood on the crate, the distance almost non-existent in her mind. The world seemed to disappear as she inhaled and released it, the movement fluid and precise as she hurled the dagger.

The sound of metal slicing through the air was like music to her ears. The dagger hit the crate with a satisfying thud and buried deep into the wood. Blair let out a quiet breath of relief, the tension in her shoulders easing. She approached the target, inspecting the strike. It was good, close to the center, but not quite perfect.

She retrieved the dagger, wiped it clean, and took a few steps back. This time, she adjusted her stance, shifting her weight slightly. The second throw was faster and more confident. The dagger flew through the air, spinning once before it embedded itself firmly in the wood. Blair couldn't help but smile a little. It was a perfect hit this time.

For a moment, she stood there, letting the quiet victory settle in her chest. She had trained diligently to reach this point. These skills would be the ones that kept her alive, the skills she wasn't willing to let slip away.

As she retrieved the dagger again, a voice broke the silence behind her.

"At least you didn't run away this time."

Blair froze, her heart skipping a beat. Slowly, she turned around, and there, standing casually with his hands in his pockets, was Damien. His eyes were drowsy with sleep, but there was an amusement in them. His arms were crossed, and his disheveled hair only made him look more mischievous than usual.

Blair's lips parted in surprise, but then she looked away. "I guess you aren't lucky enough for that," she said, her voice rigid.

He shrugged, pushing off from the wall and strolling toward her. "Lucky?" He eyed the dagger in her hand. "I would have found you."

She let the silence hang for a moment, her gaze shifting from Damien to the dagger, then back to him.

Damien raised an eyebrow. "You've gotten better."

Her response was intentionally clipped,"I know."

He tilted his head, looking at her with an unreadable expression. "Blair-"

She interrupted him before he could continue, "Did you wash my clothes?"

His gaze lingered on her for a second before he shrugged in her direction.

Blair rolled her eyes before turning away from him, lining herself up to throw the dagger.

Before she could throw, Damien reached out, gently taking her wrist in his hand. His skin was warm, and Blair couldn't help but notice the way his touch lingered, just a moment too long, as though to steady her.

"I'm glad the stains came out," he murmured, grabbing her wrist again and guiding her arm into a better throwing position. His other hand moved, pressing lightly against her back.

Why did that feel so good?

His fingers brushed against the fabric of her blouse, sending a ripple of warmth down her spine. Blair held her breath as the contact sent a shock through her. He adjusted her stance, his hands firm but not forceful, his body close enough that she could feel his presence, his warmth.

Damien's breath skimmed the shell of her ear, "I'm not sure what thoughts you put in your head about last night, but I can tell you, they are *wrong*." He moved his hand to her elbow, guiding it slightly higher. "Relax your grip a little," he instructed, his breath warm against her ear. "I already forced you to leave with me, I'm not going to force you to be uncomfortable around me or take anymore of your free will." He shifted slightly and his hand trailed the skin on her wrist. "My shadows respect you. They wanted to comfort you, to give you a sense of privacy." He pulled his mouth away from her ear and moved his hand to her shoulder, tapping lightly. "You're too tense. You need to flow with it, not fight it."

Blair nodded, swallowing against the unexpected flutter in her chest. Her fingers loosened slightly around the hilt of the dagger, and she adjusted her posture as he guided her, his hands now resting gently against her lower back, steadying her. The touch was intimate in a way that caught her off guard. For a second, she felt a little lost, as though she had no idea how to separate the comfort of his touch from the focus she needed.

Damien stepped back, his hands slipping away, but the heat from where they had touched lingered on her skin. "Now try."

Blair nodded, forcing her thoughts aside. She raised her arm once more, her body already feeling different. It was something about him, and the way he raised her confidence without even trying.

With him next to her, she was more balanced, more controlled, and her mind was clearer. She threw the dagger with ease, watching as it flew through the air and buried itself deep into the crate. The strike was perfect.

Damien grinned, stepping closer to her again.

"There you go," he said, his voice warm with approval. He stepped to the side and watched as she positioned herself to throw again. Damien's hand rose up and for a split second, Blair hoped he would touch her again, but they moved to his neck instead, as he leaned backward and stretched.

Hiding her disappointment, she bit her bottom lip. "About last night," she stated, her shoulders sagging, "I'm sorry."

"Sorry for what?" Damien asked, his tone flat.

"Making you think you had to sleep on the floor."

Damien showed no reaction as if she didn't own him anything. Smiling, she flipped the dagger once over in her hand and eyed him up and down. "I think I'm going to visit that bookstore again today, if you want to come along."

Damien didn't respond, so Blair shrugged, "Suit yourself." She began to walk back in the direction of their room, only pausing when she came to the door. Damien tilted his head in the direction of the town and Blair smiled, stepping forward to lead the way.

As they walked, she felt his eyes on her, watching. She turned to address him but her attention was caught by something else. A small group of girls, no older than seven, sat in a circle on a patch of grass. Their laughter was light and carefree while their hands were busy at work. Blair took a few steps closer, intrigued by the ribbons they held.

The girls, with their untamed hair and bright eyes, were focused on weaving colorful ribbons into intricate braids. Some had already formed delicate patterns, their little fingers nimble as they worked. Others sat next to them, watching and practicing with each other still trying to master the motions. The sight was charming, like something out of a storybook.

Blair stood for a moment, watching them, a soft smile curving her lips. This is why she loved being a teacher, small moments of innocence where children displayed true kindness and curiosity.

One of the smallest girls, a blonde with a crown of daisies in her hair, noticed Blair. Her eyes brightened as she stood up, her hands still clutching a bright blue ribbon. "Would you like us to braid your hair?" she asked, her voice full of eagerness.

Blair hesitated, her fingers absently brushing through her long hair. With only one shower during this journey, it was still pretty tangled. Although, the idea was intriguing. She had always worn her brown waves loose, often too tired to bother with much more than tying it back at the end of the day. The thought of it being braided with flowers made her heart flutter a little.

"I would love that," Blair said, her voice soft and inviting. "You'll have to brush it though."

The girls erupted into excited giggles and chatter, their eyes wide with glee. It was as if Blair had granted them all some great privilege. They scrambled around her, hands outstretched to untangle her hair, their laughter like the tinkling of tiny bells.

The little girl who had spoken first guided Blair to sit down on the soft grass. "You have such pretty hair!" she exclaimed, reaching up to gather a section. "We'll make it beautiful, just wait!"

Blair sat still, her chest swelling with a kind of warmth she hadn't felt in a long time. She closed her eyes for a moment, just taking in the good feelings.

The girls worked in unison, their small hands gentle and sure. As they braided, they wove tiny wildflowers into the strands. Daisies, buttercups, and lavender, each flower adding a touch of color and sweetness to Blair's hair.

Blair could feel the energy of their joy in every tug of the braid, and in every flower they carefully placed. The simplicity of it, of sitting here, letting them create something beautiful for her, was more soothing than she could have imagined. It was like she had stepped into a small, perfect moment to remind her that everything was going to be okay.

It didn't take long before the girls had convinced Damien to join. He did so willingly, sitting on the ground with his legs crossed beneath him. Two girls moved over to him and stood on their tip toes behind him. He knelt back, sensing their struggle, and allowed them to put a crown on his head. The gift was made from broken twigs, vines, and random flowers. When it was securely placed, he stood and the girls moved away, giving him a unified curtsy. He smiled and bowed back.

As the others finished Blair's hair, the little girl with the daisies stepped back to admire their work. "There!" she said proudly, her eyes shining. "You look like a flower queen now!"

Blair chuckled softly, her fingers touching the delicate braids. "You've done such a beautiful job," Blair said, her voice filled with warmth and gratitude.

The girls beamed up at her, their faces flushed with pride. "Thank you for letting us do it!" the little one with the daisies said.

Blair's heart ached a little at the sincerity in their eyes.

How many times had she seen this in the eyes of the children she used to teach?

"No, thank *you*," she replied softly, her fingers tracing one of the flowers in her hair. "You've made my day brighter."

The girls giggled again as if pleased by her words. Then they ran off toward the town square, their laughter trailing behind them.

Blair watched them go, trailing joy with each step. She stood up slowly, running her fingers through the braids once more. Marveling at how something so simple could feel like such a gift.

She took a deep breath, looking at Damien, who was now standing next to a tree. "I think my students would have liked you." She stepped closer to him and flicked the crown on top of his head.

Damien smiled in response and held out his hand, asking for permission to escort her. "I probably wouldn't have minded them."

Blair laid her hand on top of his and gave a small curtsy, They both laughed as they walked toward the stalls and shops.

14

The bookstore was easy to find this time, the carved door like a beacon. Damien had said nothing to her as they entered, only held the door open and walked behind her to the back. She made a straight line to one particular book, recognizing it on a small shelf. Damien smiled at her as she grazed the spine and stepped back to the chair behind her. She plopped down and crossed her legs, wiggling into a comfortable position and kicking her shoes off. Damien stayed next to her for about an hour before muttering something to her and disappearing into town.

By the time Blair looked up from all the stories she had read, the sun was shining brightly through the upper windows signaling the afternoon.

At this point, she now had three different novels in front of her, each spread open to different pages, displaying various symbols of the language she was trying to decipher. She had been able to decode some of the words, guessing at the stories that filled each one. A grumble reminded her that she had yet to eat today. She closed the books and stood, reshelving them in the area where they belonged.

Stretching her arms over her head, she stretched her back.

A short woman with a brunette bob poked her head around the corner, startling Blair. "I just knew you'd get lost in my books!" The owner, Blair assumed, beamed with pride as she continued, "I had come in here to see if you had any questions, but you were so enthralled that I decided to come back later, and here I am!" The corner of her brown eyes crinkled with enthusiasm as she raised her hand to wave. "I'm Mar! I own the bookstore."

Blair took a second to take in the woman before her. At a whopping five feet, the woman in front of her carried a large sense of confidence and enthusiasm. Her smile was kind and contagious, somehow making Blair feel warm and at ease.

"Hi. Thank you for checking on me." Blair looked back at the books she had just returned, "I'm sorry I hadn't noticed you before. I was trying to decipher some of the words, and I guess I got a little carried away."

"Ah, you must have found my journals in Veldusk." Mar nodded, gesturing to the small books Blair was looking at. "I work on those when I have time too. A rare mystery they are! This is a lost language to most, but they say it originated here."

Blair nodded, conversing for a few minutes and then dismissing herself. Mar let her go, but only after she promised to come back to discuss the other "wonderful mysteries" that lived within the pages of her books.

She chuckled as she walked out, closing the door and turning her attention to the figure that lingered outside.

Damien lay under a nearby tree, a large brown bag at his side and a book in his hands. Blair halted, eyes grazing over the sight. She tilted her head in disbelief and approached him with a look of bewilderment.

Damien looked up at her. "About time you came out. I was about to come check if you were alive."

"Are you *reading*?" Blair asked incredulously.

Damien pointed the book at her as he stood. "That's insulting."

Blair smiled at him and swung at him as he stood, hitting him with a soft punch.

The walk back to the Inn was quiet. Blair was lost in her head, focusing on the details around her and the journals she had been looking at. It had seemed like only minutes before the ground under them soon turned into the familiar mud of the hot springs.

The Inn was busy today, alive with hordes of people. She nodded to each one as she passed them, acknowledging them as they waved. The whole time, Damien watched her, often gazing at her hair and the flowers that adorned it.

As they finally entered their room, Blair threw herself on the bed. Bouncing once and then settling, a loud grumble came from her stomach.

Damien looked over at her, "Have you eaten yet?"

She shook her head at him before staring up at the ceiling.

Damien walked to the side of the bed and placed a brown bag down, one that he had brought back from town.

He reached into it and grabbed something, pulling it out to show her. At the sight, Blair's mouth started to water.

The insignia on the side of the bag showed a slice of bread with a heart in the corner. She immediately recognized it from the bakery that had been next to the bookstore. Many times during the day, the smell had wafted in, causing her to pause for a moment before jumping back in.

Opening his hand, Damien held out a pastry filled with blueberries and topped with a crumble. He lifted it to her nose, offering to let her smell it.

"Is that for me?" She looked at the pastry and licked her lips.

"You're hungry, huh?" he teased, his mood lifting slightly. He moved the treat closer to her before quickly pulling it away. "I do believe you owe me a certain something to get this."

Blair's mouth snapped shut and her eyes narrowed in irritation. "What?"

Suddenly, she recalled the conversation from the last time they ate. She looked up at Damien who seemed to be smirking. "Damien, please don't be childish. " she murmured, her voice almost a whisper.

He paused and put his hand up to his ear as if he couldn't hear her, the grin on his face spreading. "You know what you have to do," he reminded, his tone playful. He looked down at the treat before taking a bite, rolling his eyes in satisfaction. "I mean, I think this is definitely worth *begging* for."

Blair looked again at the warm pastry in his hands, the smell invading her senses and making her stomach growl louder. "Damien," she began again, more desperate now. "Can I please eat that?"

He raised an eyebrow, as if it wasn't good enough. "More."

Blair bit her lip, feeling her resolve slip. Glancing at the food in front of her, she took a breath. "Damien," she said softly, the words finally escaping her lips, "You big idiot, I'm begging you. I'm hungry. Can I please eat that?"

Damien's grin widened, clearly satisfied by the admission. "You know," he said, lifting the pastry and handing it over, "the green comes out in your eyes when you listen." He handed her the food, and Blair eagerly grabbed it. With a grunt of annoyance, she bit into it, and a small moan escaped her. The hunger that had racked her body receded instantly.

Damien sat down beside her, watching as she ate in silence. He didn't need to say anything more. The game was over, he had won.

After she had finished and licked her fingers clean, he had reached into another bag, and pulled out different outfits. He placed them on the bed next to Blair and took a step back. "Before you bite my head off about them, consider this me still trying to make things up to you."

Expecting an aggressive response or to be *punched*, Damien tensed up and waited for Blair to attack. Instead, a heavy silence hung between them for a few moments, and then Blair stood. She took them off the bed and folded them, placing the outfits in her bag. A soft "thank you" barely made it to Damien as she closed her bag. When she walked back to the bed, Damien saw it, the tear that had fallen down her cheek.

The rest of the evening was filled with a unique tension between them. Damien had ventured out for dinner, returning with a small bowl of noodles for them to share. They then took turns in the springs outside while the other stayed in the room. When the moon was high in the night sky, both of them had settled for the night.

As Damien rummaged through his bag, taking inventory of their supplies, Blair glanced to the floor. She fiddled her fingers as she eyed the spot on the bed next to her. Fighting internally with herself, she weighed the pros and cons of what she was about to do. Eventually, she huffed at her decision.

The final pillow was yanked into place as she looked up at Damien who had just closed his bag. She cleared her throat and motioned to the barrier on the bed. The contraption stood two pillows tall, an uneven wall of cotton and defiance.

"This is your side," she said, pointing to the other side of the bed. "Touch that line and lose a finger."

Damien smiled and crossed the room, lying down next to her and propping himself up on one elbow. Eyeing the pillows in amusement, he looked over them at her. "You built a border," he said, trying and failing, to hide the grin tugging at the corners of his mouth.

"I didn't build a *border*," Blair corrected. "I *enforced* a boundary. Don't test it."

He chuckled and twisted on his back, folding his hands behind his head. "Has anyone ever told you that you can be a lot sometimes?"

She glared at him through the flickering light of the bedside lamp. "Call it what you want, just stay on your side."

"I like it." He turned his head toward her. "Besides, I think you're only doing it because I'm growing on you, and you know it."

She grabbed one of the spare pillows and smacked it against her side of the wall, fluffing it aggressively. "If you cross this line, snore, or wake me up, I'm pushing you off the bed."

He smiled lazily, moving his eyes back to the ceiling. "Noted. No touching, no breathing too loud, and the pillow wall is sacred."

"Good," she muttered, sliding beneath the covers and pulling them up to her chin. "We understand each other."

A few moments passed in silence. The room settled around them, dim and warm, filled only with the soft rustle of fabric and the light from the lamp.

Then Damien whispered, "But what if the pillows happen to *fall* over?" he asked, a smile in his voice. "Or we happen to get really cold and need body heat?" There was a pause, then a heartbeat later, Blair's eyes caught the slight movement of a thin tendril of shadow peeking over the top pillow, rocking it back and forth.

Blair's voice struck out in a stern tone. "Try it and die, Damien."

In response to her savagery, he smiled into the dark and said nothing more.

15

On the third day in town, Blair awoke with the soft rustling of the wind outside her window, mingling with the faint chirp of birds. She moved to her back, taking a moment to feel the stillness of the early morning seep into her bones.

"Damien," she murmured, turning and glancing over the untouched fort where he lay. The blankets were tangled around his body, highlighting the muscles that seemed to stay strained even when he slept.

She called his name again and he grumbled in his sleep, before rolling over. His tousled auburn hair was almost cute, pushing out in every direction.

Blair sat up slowly, the sheets falling from her shoulders as she glanced out the window. The town was still wrapped in the early hours of the morning. She gave Damien another glance, watching the slow rise and fall of his chest before moving the pillows and gently nudging him.

"Damien," she said softly, her hand brushing his shoulder. "Today is the third day. Do you think the runners' guild might have news?"

He groaned but slowly sat up, his face crinkling in sleepy confusion. "Runner's Guild?"

Blair smiled, amused by his groggy state. "Finley! He could have sent word back!"

Damien rubbed his eyes and yawned, stretching his long limbs. "Okay, so you're a morning person. Got it."

Blair pulled a pillow over, hitting him on the chest with it.

"Alright, alright. You don't have to smother me. I'll -" he yawned the next word,"check, but I can't promise anything."

Blair nodded. "Okay! I'll keep myself busy."

She watched him slowly stand and walk to the bathroom. There was a brief sound of water running and then he came back in the room with a new set of clothes and his hair down flat. His movements were still sluggish as he made his way to the door. "I'll be back soon. Make good decisions."

As the door clicked shut behind him, Blair sighed. She hoped there was some type of word, but she let her body settle as the quiet of the room wrapped around her. She moved to her side, her gaze finding the small bundle of wildflowers she had taken out of her braids the previous night.

An arrangement lay on the table of daisies, lavender, and buttercups, all mixed in a loose bouquet. She knew the little girls in the town had grown fond of making braids with them, and she thought maybe it would be a good chance to collect more to surprise them.

She imagined their excited faces as she played out a scene in her mind. Showing up with a big bucket of vibrant, new wildflowers to say thank you.

Yup, that's how she was going to stay busy.

Blair stood up, finding a simple top and matching pants set. She brushed her hair with her fingers before pulling it into a ponytail. Moving to her boots, she pulled them up, tying the laces loosely as she grabbed her sheathed dagger and a small basket. The town outside her window was still waking up as the light of morning fog was growing, revealing the beauty around her.

As she watched the awakening light through the glass, it moved to the stone houses surrounding it, and the patches of green that lay between. It reminded her of SilverDawn and she smiled softly. She thought about where she'd find the best flowers as the colors in front of her continued to build.

Remembering a clearing that they passed when they entered town, she turned to grab her things and stepped out of the room. Making her way through the courtyard and out into the empty street, she wandered toward the edge of town.

It wasn't long before Blair found the clearing and rows of fresh flowers. Crouching down, her fingers brushed against possible options and she took her time, choosing the best ones. With each bouquet she gathered, her mind drifted to the girls and their eager faces. It made her smile, the thought of something so simple bringing so much joy.

As she worked, the sound of footsteps approached, and Blair turned, expecting Damien.

But it wasn't him.

Standing within ten feet were three men in dark cloaks trimmed with silver.

Their figures seemed simple at first, but within moments, two were engulfed in shifting shadows. Black tendrils curled around their arms and shoulders like a living darkness, one that seemed rough and sporadic.

She blinked as she looked over the men. There was a noticeable difference in energy between them. Although all three were menacing, the two who bore shadows seemed to pulse with a distinct life force. They wore longer cloaks than the other, not just silver and black but inscribed with an unknown symbol.

The taller one, with brown hair tied on the top of his head, wore a large pendant around his neck and had a scar above his right eyebrow. The shorter one had thick black hair that was carved into a mohawk. His face was more mature, with lines of aging. He too had gaudy jewelry, but his was in the form of a thick bracelet shaped into black chain links. Their eyes were dim; A cold, unnatural murkiness that showed no light, devoid of humanity. The longer she stared at them, the more their shadows snarled in impatience.

The one with a scar took a step forward, his voice low and laced with annoyance. "We've been looking for you," he sneered.

Although scared, Blair refused to show it. She set down her basket, sliding out her dagger as she straightened. The shadowless Hunter took notice and lunged toward her. She twisted quickly, narrowly avoiding his grasp, and swung at his side. She missed, his reflexes being too sharp.

In that opening, he turned his fist, making contact with her jaw. The sound of her teeth snapping together rang in her head, and she swiveled at the last second, twisting her wrist and throwing her dagger.

The moment the steel pierced his flesh, a hiss-like sound escaped him. His amber eyes flickered with anger as he pulled away to protect the now-injured shoulder that was sliced by the dagger's tip.

Remembering how Damien had positioned her during practice, she eyed the man who was backing away slowly. Without thinking, she moved and grabbed the dagger, throwing it again toward his neck.

The black blade glinted for a split second before making contact, his eyes growing wide in surprise. Blood gushed from the wound where her dagger protruded, and for a brief second, she held a victorious smile. It faltered quickly when she realized the shadows of the other two men had grown furious.

Moving quickly to pick up her dagger, she faced them, her knuckles white. For a brief second, she held confidence, but as the men moved in, she could feel the dark weight of the shadows pressing in on her, constricting her movements. She wasn't just fighting them, it was like she was fighting the very air itself, thick with gray smoke-like tendrils.

The second man who was shorter and stockier, chuckled. "You think you can win?" He asked, transforming the smirk into a cold smile devoid of emotion. Blair tried not to focus on his twisted demeanor but instead sought the best method of attack.

Her muscles screamed as she moved, the invisible weight pushing down around her. All she had practiced was aim and throwing, there was no way she could go up against these people. Taking a steadying breath, she lunged forward, her dagger aimed at the gaunt man's chest.

Just as they had with Damien, shadows appeared defensively, grabbing her arms and blocking the attack.

As Blair's mind raced, she couldn't help but notice the differences between *these* shadows and Damien's. They were lacking depth and appeared gray, almost a watered-down version of Damien's. Even the sense of power was small in comparison. Still, it was way more than anything she had to offer. With a flick of his wrist, more shadows materialized and surged toward her, faster than she could react.

The first tendril struck with the speed of a viper, wrapping around her wrist and yanking her arm downward. A loud, popping sound filled the air.

The pressure was immediate and agonizing, like a vice gripping her bones. She screamed as she tried to pull away from the tendril, but another one shot from the ground, lashing across her ribs with a brutal crack.

Pain flared across her side, but she didn't have time to focus on it. She had to keep fighting. She swung her dagger again, but the shadows danced around her. A third tendril snapped out, aiming for her other arm but missing and striking across her cheek. The darkness burned like acid, tearing through her skin, and a blood-curdling scream escaped her as it swung at her again and the cuts deepened. The world blurred as the wound pulsed with pain, blood seeping down her face.

Blair's body soon became a battlefield, each slash of shadow carving new wounds into her flesh. The dark tendrils whipped around her faster than she could react, leaving deep, jagged wounds along her arms, legs, and torso. She could feel the cold sting of each one as the shadows scraped across her skin, the pressure building with every movement, like the darkness itself was trying to slowly suffocate her.

Her dagger was heavy in her hand but useless against the twisting, slashing shadows that seemed to come from every direction. Each time she tried to step forward or defend herself, another cut would appear across her cheek, her side, and her back, blood trickling out, mixing with the darkness that clung to her like a second skin. The pain was unbearable, and her body was growing weaker with every passing moment.

"You're already losing," the gaunt man said, his voice gleaming with dark amusement. "Can you feel it, sweetheart? Our darkness, cutting you apart."

Blair tried to stay on her feet, but the shadows were closing in faster now. She could feel them moving like cold, wet fingers around her, coiling around her limbs, dragging her to the ground. Her heart raced, each beat echoing in her ears as she tried to push herself up to regain her balance. Her eyes grew heavy as the pain overloaded the adrenaline coursing through her veins.

She fell to her knees as another shadow struck out. A shadow that felt like ice, cold and merciless. It struck across her eyes, searing into her vision. She cried out, falling backward as the sharp tendrils blinded her. The world twisted and the darkness blurred. Her vision faltered as the sharp burn of the shadows lit like fire in her skull.

Despite her injuries, the unrelenting shadows didn't stop. They continued to cut through her skin, attacking her. A black blanket laid across her vision, sealing her off from the world around her.

"I know you have power. Why are you not using it?" he snarled. "I can sense it on you. So fight back, make this fun for me."

"NO!" she screamed, but the word was a strangled sound in her throat. The world had gone dark, and every movement she made felt sluggish, as if her limbs were no longer her own. Her dagger slipped from her fingers, falling to the grass below her, as the shadows continued to slice through her skin, each strike worse than the last.

The men's laughter rang in her ears, cruel and triumphant, until it stopped a moment later. She sensed the second man stepping forward, closing in on the space between them. "Was all that power coming from this?" he sneered, bending over to pick up the dagger. With her last bit of strength, she tried to reach out, grabbing for the blade.

Another shadow struck, this time across her chest, cutting through the thin fabric of her clothes and into her flesh. The pain was everywhere, it was everything.

"So, it wasn't *you* at all. You were just a distraction, hiding what we were searching for all along." Bending down closer to her face, his tone flooded with rage. "Where did you get this?!" he snarled, kicking her side.

Blair rolled, pulling her knees up to her chest as the darkness crushed in around her like a suffocating, cold shroud. Her breath hitched, and she tried to focus on anything besides the agony that tore through her body.

Then, the world shook.

A surge of power split the air, thick as thunder, humming with something ancient and deadly. The shadows that swarmed around her paused and started to recoil back to their owners.

A familiar voice rang through the clearing, filled with a cold rage and sharp as a blade.

"Let. Her. Go."

16

The presence of something far darker than her attackers filled the space around them. Even without her sight, Blair could feel it thrumming in the air. This power pushed up against her skin.

Damien's eyes immediately assessed her as he approached, skimming over the blood coating her body. As his eyes met the Hunters, his lips rose in a snarl and his chest became rigid. His eyes, always the blue of a summer sky morning, immediately cascaded into blackness.

Webs of black grew from his temples and moved down his face, eventually overtaking his whole body. They writhed as if angry, as if they were alive and eager to obey him. The ground beneath his feet darkened as he walked, leaving a trail of shadow behind him. He stepped forward, his eyes glancing to Blair's bleeding form again, causing his shadows to surge in anger around his body.

"Would you look at that, sweetheart," the taller Hunter taunted, cocking his head and lifting his eyebrows in recognition as his voice dripped with malice. "We found our answer."

Damien didn't respond, he only continued toward them. When he was a few feet away, he stopped again as the shorter, older Hunter stepped in front of him. "Look at that, we were hunting little Ian the whole time."

Damien tore his gaze from the woman lying helpless and bleeding on the ground to find the face responsible. The shadows reacted viciously in response, swarming around his body, ready to attack.

At that moment, the other man lunged at him. A sharp whip of darkness shot forward, trying to ensnare Damien, but his shadows blocked the attack easily. Another tendril of darker gray shot out, intending to pull him to the ground. Damien sidestepped and twisted his wrist. A stampede of black shadow bombarded the short older man, attacking from all angles. In response, the Hunters' lighter gray shadows reacted, moving swiftly to block and counterattack.

Focusing back on Blair, Damien progressed toward her while the Hunter was occupied.

"Don't worry about her. We already had our fun," the larger Hunter taunted again as he watched Damien move closer.

Damien's response was a feral growl, a low, guttural sound that came from deep within his chest. The shadows stopped moving and instead, began to pulse around him, the air itself turning dark.

A blade of pure shadow struck out, slicing through the air where the Hunter had been standing. Moving in just the nick of time to save his life, he looked at Damien and smiled. The sound of a wet thump followed a second later and he looked toward it, watching as his arm dropped to the ground.

A wail filled the air, and a wall of gray shadow shot up around him as he tried to create distance. Damien didn't react but instead focused his attention solely on the Hunter in front of him, who barely avoided his previous attack.

Damien moved fast, breaking through the wall of gray. Different tones of darkness began swirling around each other as they attacked. The typical sound of clashing steel was absent, this was a fight of silence and shifting forms.

The shadows halted for a split second as the Hunter reassessed and charged at him again in a different way. A knife glinted, catching Damien's attention but he didn't move. His shadows twisted again, forming a dark shield that the knife slid harmlessly off. The man stumbled back, disoriented from the blood loss of his arm. As he caught himself, Damien's shadows wrapped around his leg, pulling him up. Damien raised his hand, and the shadows responded, slamming the man against the ground with brutal force, crushing his skull in the process. He landed with such force that multiple other bones snapped, and his thick black bracelet shattered, expelling shards all over the ground. As pieces broke apart, an eerie black mist dissipated from them.

"One down," Damien muttered, his voice barely recognizable. His black eyes were as dark as the onyx dagger that was poised in the older Hunter's hand.

He turned slightly, clearly adjusting his stance to challenge the last one. This one showed no sign of fear but smiled somewhat in response to the fight. He dodged the first lash of shadow, rolling away to create distance. His gray shadows shot forward toward Damien, aiming to take him out at the knees. Damien retaliated, sending a magnified whip of blackness at the Hunter's back. He turned at the last second.

"Nice try, Ian, but do you remember who trained you? I know all your moves." he taunted with a smirk.

They mirrored each other like a reflection, anticipating and countering each other's attacks and movements. One leaped onto a large oak tree for an advantage; their shadow stretching unnaturally upward to grasp the large branches and pull them higher. His opponent followed, launching themselves upward on tendrils of living darkness. They met midair, a brief collision of shadow and forged weapons before parting, landing opposite each other in the clearing.

The Hunter chuckled when he landed, "Just like old times, huh?" Damien's eyes remained motionless and inked in black. The few words spoken sparked a reaction within Damien, and he retaliated with twice the fury. There was no hesitation now, only the desperate, instinctual drive to destroy.

Damien's shadows bent and stretched in unnatural ways, forming spears, claws, and tendrils that clawed for flesh. The trees around them shuddered under the force of the blows, branches cracking as darkness itself rippled through the air.

As they broke apart, the Hunter eyed Blair, her breath becoming extremely shallow. He smiled at her, returning his gaze to his opponent. With that, Damien's shadow grew into a pretentious wall of black, sending a tsunami of black clouds surging across the ground. The shadows beneath the Hunter's feet darkened, stretching into long, snaking forms. Before he could react, the ground cracked open, and from the darkness, long shadowy hands shot up, grabbing at his ankles and pulling him down. The Hunter cursed and fought, but the shadows tightened like a vice, pulling him deeper into the earth's cold embrace.

"You might have trained me," Damien spat, "But you have no idea what I can do."

With a twist of his hand, the shadows came crashing down. A resounding boom echoed from the final movement as the gaping hole sealed, causing the crack in the earth to vanish and remove any proof of the man's existence. Damien gasped for air. His power was too much, his anger too overwhelming.

Blair coughed, groaning when her body moved. The sound caught Damien's attention and gave him a chance to regain control of himself. His shadows moved to her, each one stretching across the earth like they were crawling to her. Damien watched them as he wal;ked over and knelt beside her, reaching to pick up the dagger that was stolen from her.

Blair grunted as the shadows brushed her face. She tried to open her eyes, but was unable to make out the figure above her.

Damien's face was carved in fury, as his hands grazed her mangled body. Though his shadows moved to cover her wounds, she was still losing blood. As his eyes examined her and his shadows worked to staunch what they could, the rage within him softened, replaced by something else.

He blinked a few times, and the shadows finally lifted from his eyes, revealing the familiar blue. As if sensing his need to protect and care for her, the shadows around her tightened, cocooning her in darkness.

Blair let out a shaky breath, groaning again at the contact. Damien's eyes lingered over body. His finger twitched, fighting the urge to console her.

His voice was rigid with worry as he spoke to her. "I'm going to get you help, but we need to get back to the village."

Blair tried to nod, but her body disobeyed her.

He stood, and as he did so, the shadows softly lifted Blair off the ground and into his arms. Not once did he take his eyes off of her, as he counted the number of times her chest rose and fell. The only times he paused was when she shuddered from pain.

It wasn't long before they were close to the Inn. Damien's shadows morphed and took the form of a thick, folded blanket. His eyes then darted around the shops, landing on the rough, brown door he was looking for. The window next to it was adorned with different bottles of elixirs and medicines.

He looked down again at the woman in his arms, pulling his shadows back and exposing Blair's face. As slow as he could, he used his shoulder to open the door and willed the shadows, along with his markings, to recede into his body.

Within a mere second, they were gone.

The young man who stood at the counter turned to greet them but his smile soon fell away when his eyes moved down, taking in the bleeding woman.

Damien carefully stepped into the apothecary, placing Blair on the counter. "We need any Healers in the area immediately, along with anything you can give her for the pain," Damien said grimly, eyes still focused on Blair's breathing.

The man didn't move at first, overwhelmed by the sight of the broken and battered woman.

"Now!" Damien barked, his attention still focused on the woman in front of him. The boy blinked, breaking the trance that had robbed him of thought, and turned, running out of the room.

Damien placed his hand on Blair's forehead, rubbing his thumb across the skin that wasn't broken. "Just stay with me."

Blair tried to respond, but every ounce of her energy had been spent, and her body felt light and weightless.

Damien's thumb stopped moving, releasing her forehead. "Come on, Feisty. Don't you dare leave me."

It was the warm skin of his lips that she felt next, as her consciousness started to falter. They rested on her forehead as he pleaded with her to just breathe. Soon, his words and her thoughts became muffled, and a haze settled over her mind as everything went dark.

17

Damien's face.
Black eyes turning blue.

There were moments of excruciating pain and other times where memories faded in and out as she fought to stay conscious. In between these scattered images, she would hear different voices talking above her. Then, there would be a sharp sting that jolted her arm.

Her eyes refused to open, even as she screamed at them to do so. The world constantly wavered as she felt more of the small, sharp pokes that seemed to riddle her body in patterns. This time, it was only a few moments before her mind went hazy.

The next time she was aware enough to think, something cold was on her skin. The soft material felt nice, and the coolness brought a sense of relief to her body. She willed herself to be more coherent this time. Fighting through the fog in her mind, she tried and *failed* to identify the voices around her.

Blair then moved her attention to the areas of her body that were in pain. Pinpointing them proved useless, because as she did so, each place was poked with something that helped ease the suffering. Another wave of darkness came and she wordlessly thanked whoever these people were as her body relaxed, and she fell back into slumber.

Blair continued to drift in and out of consciousness. Every time she became alert, her mind struggled to catch up, tangled in a haze of pain and confusion. When she tried to open her eyes, her body would not cooperate. The overwhelming ache was a constant battle that pulled her away from her surroundings.

"Is she healing? We need to-" A voice said quietly, just out of her reach. Blair couldn't make out the last words clearly, but the tone was one of concern and something heavier.

Guilt, maybe?

She tried to focus, but her eyelids felt too heavy, and a strange sense of dizziness overtook her.

Another voice spoke, "You need to get some rest, Damien."

The name pricked something inside of her, and a figure formed in her mind. *Damien.*

She hadn't been able to piece together who was taking care of her, but hearing his name meant he was the one. He was there, with her. A cool touch on her forehead followed the short conversation and Blair felt her body flinch in response to the tenderness of it.

It was quiet for a few moments before there were footsteps and a third voice. "Here are some of the books you requested, the owner had a few suggestions as well."

"Thank you." Damien replied, his words clipped with exhaustion.

Despite the fog in her mind, Blair felt a strange tug in her chest. The pain in his voice made her want to reach out, to tell him that she was okay. Although she tried, her limbs were still too heavy, and her body *still* would not cooperate.

The more Blair came around, the more she could piece together what was happening around her. Other times, words were missing, and she couldn't figure out who Damien was talking to. It became *his* voice that pulled her out of the depths most. At first it was just a few words here and there but then he would speak directly to her.

"I'm here, Blair." There was a long pause before more words came, softer, filled with more emotion than Blair had ever heard from him before. "I'm not going anywhere, I promise." He then began reading from a familiar book. A faint memory of a bookstore lingered in her mind, with him in the doorway staring at her. The image stayed for a mere second and then fizzled out.

A deep humming awakened her the next time. Blair felt a cool, damp cloth press against her skin again. It moved over her chest, her arms, and the back of her neck. The sensation was calming despite the ache in her body and the throbbing of her wounds. The touch was gentle and the movement slow and soothing. It was the kind of care that made her feel like she wasn't lost in a sea of confusion.

Her eyes fluttered open, just for a moment, and she saw the outline of someone leaning over her. The humming stopped, and words filled the air instead. "Just a little longer," his voice murmured. "Your body is still healing."

As the fabric moved down her leg, the motions then stopped, and she sensed Damien taking a seat at the foot of her bed. The sound of pages being turned held her straying focus before a story began; it featured a woman sailing across the sea on an exciting adventure. The reader paused at the start of the next chapter, his voice drifting, and Blair couldn't help it as she fell back to sleep.

The shuffle of footsteps cleared the haze this time, a slow exhale of a breath following. "It should be any day now. You should use this time to rest."

"No," he snapped, and for a moment, it seemed like the world held its breath. "I'm going to be here when she wakes up."

Blair's heart ached with his words and the rawness in his voice, the desperation. But still, no words came from her as the arguing quieted around her. Blair felt the tension begin to ease as a rough and steady hand found hers, gentle but firm.

The touch was everything, and she knew it belonged to *him*. It held her in place, kept her tethered to something real, something tangible.

"You can wake up any day now, feisty." Damien's voice was close, but strained, as if he hadn't entirely given in to his fatigue.

Her fingers twitched as if responding to his touch, and Blair felt the warmth of his hand tighten. With that, Blair let herself drift one more time, sinking into the embrace of darkness, a place where she was free from the pain. As she went, she clung to the sound of Damien's voice and the memory of his face.

The next time she became aware, the fog not only lifted, but also thinned. Although still there, it became less of a wall and more like a layer that separated reality from her dreams. She couldn't remember how long she'd been here, nor could she place the aching in her body. As she focused, the pain seemed more subtle than what she remembered.

As the last bit of haziness broke, Blair felt a new level of recognition. The more her mind cleared, the more she focused on her senses. She could feel the softness of the bed, smell the scent of disinfectant, and hear the faintest rustling. Blair tried to blink, her eyelids heavy as if she'd been holding them shut for days. Then, she felt the pull of something inside her urging her to finally wake up.

The dim light from above stung her eyes as she managed to open them fully. For a moment, everything was blurred but then, as if by instinct, she focused on one spot, and it became clear.

Damien.

He was sitting beside her, hunched forward, elbows resting on his knees, his face pale and worn. His dark auburn hair was disheveled, and his eyes were bloodshot. Books surrounded him. Most were closed, but one laid opened halfway, showcasing one of the stories she vaguely remembered from her small moments of awareness. She blinked faster, focusing on him. Damien lifted his head, his gaze meeting hers, and something in him shifted.

His posture, which had been tense and coiled, immediately relaxed. He stared blankly at her, blinking rapidly as if he might be hallucinating. When a look of realization came over his face, his breath came out in a shudder, and a visible weight seemed to lift from his shoulders. He leaned back in his seat, the corners of his mouth twitching into a faint, almost imperceptible smile.

"Hey." His voice was a hoarse whisper, breaking through the stillness of the room.

Blair's chest tightened at the look in his eyes. The intensity almost rattled her as she tried to put herself in his shoes. She couldn't remember much of the recent time frame, just fragments. She quickly played through the most recent memories she had gathered between waking and sleeping. Her days had been blurry and inconsistent, but his days had probably been full of anxiety and panic.

Her throat had a raw dryness as she tried to speak. "Hey." she rasped, her voice just above a whisper, "I'm okay."

His eyes widened at the sound, and for a heartbeat, neither of them moved. Damien stood suddenly, the book on his lap falling to the floor. He immediately moved to her side, but hesitated as he approached.

"You're awake," he whispered back, almost as if the words were too fragile to say out loud, like saying them would make her go back to sleep.

"And you're here," she managed again, forcing the words through the dry ache in her throat. She lifted her hand and grabbed his, giving a simple but firm squeeze. Damien looked down at their hands, his fingers trembling slightly as if testing the waters to see if this was real.

He smiled again, "Of course I am feisty." His voice lingered on the last word, a raw sound of affection spilling out that made her chest tighten again.

She didn't know how she had gotten here or how long she had been unconscious, but what she did know was that Damien was looking at her *differently*. A new emotion filled his eyes, brighter than the one they shared previously.

"What happened?" she croaked, her eyes scanning his face for his reaction.

He exhaled deeply like he knew that question would come sooner or later. His hands tightened but then relaxed as though afraid to hurt her.

"The Hunters found you, like I said they would. You had to deal with their shadows for a while before I could get there. You did so well, Blair. Most people wouldn't have survived this." His brow furrowed as he studied her. It was like he was searching for any sign of anger or resentment toward him, for not being there during the attack.

Damien swallowed hard, his voice low as he continued. "I brought you back as fast as I could. The Apothecary helped me find a few Healers. You were unconscious for days." He let out a soft, bitter laugh, a trace of relief mixed with something darker. "I told them you would wake up soon. There was no way you could go that much longer without yelling at me." Blair's eyes softened as she looked at him, feeling a strange sense of comfort in his presence.

Her gaze lingered on him and then shifted to the walls behind him. They were not what she remembered. The yellow paint and wood trimming signified that she was not in the Inn at the hot springs anymore. Shifting her sight, she moved her head around the room she was in.

"Where-" she started to ask, trying to sit up, but her body protested. A sharp ache in her back made her gasp. Damien was immediately there, his arm sliding behind her to support her, his other hand resting gently on her shoulder.

"Easy," he murmured, his voice soft, protective. "I had you moved once you were stable. I didn't want to chance them finding you again." He motioned to the bed with his hand. "I opted for more room. Even the bed is bigger, so there is no need for any more pillow forts." He said with a wink.

Blair leaned back into bed with a small smile, but her eyes never left him. As hazy as some parts of her life were right now, the one clear aspect was Damien; his witty expressions, his way of caring, and his dumb nickname. Despite the situation, despite the pain, she wasn't alone.

She took a second to continue to look around the room. The only other pieces of furniture were a small leather chair and a tray table next to her bed. The wooden rectangle held dirty wrappings that were covered in dried blood.

Wincing, her eyes moved down her own body. Her arms, mostly wrapped with new bandages, were covered from her wrist to her shoulders. She lifted her right arm, bending it at the elbow. Her muscles protested from the lack of movement, and she grimaced, lowering her arm to move the blanket from her lower body.

More wrappings adorned her torso and legs.

"It's been over a week," Damien explained, following her gaze and looking down at the bandages as well. "Our goal was to stop the bleeding. Your cuts were deep, some even getting close to the bone." He looked up, finding her eyes.

She sighed and grinned as she pulled the blanket back and motioned for him to join her. "I'm willing to bet the Hunters looked worse."

He looked at her and shook his head no, trying to lay the blanket back on top of her.

She scowled and lifted it once more. "Stop being stupid and come lay next to me."

He opened his mouth to protest but stopped, eyeing her injured body. Moving slowly, he sat next to her and then swung his legs on the bed. As he did so, she thought that this might not have been the best idea but in her battered, and pain-filled state, she couldn't bring herself to care.

She closed her eyes and turned into him, laying her head on his chest. She had expected him to tense or turn but he just laid there, running his fingers over the skin on her arms.

His voice was deep as it filtered through his chest and into her ear. "I'm sorry, Blair." He then inhaled deeply and placed his hand on the back of her head. "This whole thing has been my fault but I need you to know that I'd rather be torn limb from limb, by the darkest parts of my soul, than ever have to see you like that again."

Her eyebrows rose at the statement, but she didn't reply. *He couldn't mean that, could he?*

She pushed past the way her heart fluttered and thought about an answer that could reassure him. A way to accept his apology, and reassure him that it wouldn't happen. Filing through the smart-ass remarks she had in her arsenal, she opened her mouth to reply, but as she did so, she heard slight snoring coming from him.

She smiled, tightening her grip as she voluntarily welcomed the haze this time.

It won't happen again, because I'm staying by your side.

18

Blair gritted her teeth as she tried to sit up, her body protesting with every movement.

Today, it was an overall, intense pain that moved as she used different body parts. That didn't matter though, she had woken up determined to challenge herself. She wanted to see just how much she had healed and in order to do that, she had to push her body and the many muscles that were still recovering from her injuries.

She glanced over at the clothes laid out on the chair by her bed, just a simple shirt and shorts. It seemed like such an easy and insignificant thing, a task she had taken for granted previously. Now, she would have to endure multiple layers of discomfort just to get dressed for the day.

Since waking up, she had spent time rehabilitating herself by doing small things just like this. Her muscles had been torn and she basically had to spend the majority of the time retraining them. Damien helped when he could, *more like hovered*, not letting her do anything on her own. He had even taken time to explain it all, walking her through how two different Healers had come and attempted to repair what they could. Because both had a strong set of skills, they had been able to work quickly to start the healing process.

Although thankful, she had reached a point where she needed to prove to herself that she was regaining her strength and could conquer things on her own. Despite the fact there were no permanent injuries, the whole ordeal left Blair with numerous scars and bruises. Not to mention the soreness that plagued her.

"You can do this," she muttered to herself, wincing as she tried to lift her arm and pull her shirt over her head. Her body screamed in protest, and she let out a groan of frustration.

"Need a hand?" came a familiar voice from the doorway.

Damien, of course.

She turned to him with a raised eyebrow, "Well, if it isn't my babysitter." She tried to sound sarcastic, but the pain in her voice came across as a plea for help.

Damien leaned casually against the doorframe, his arms crossed, looking impossibly appealing in contrast to her awkward flailing. "Out of all the things you could call me, you settle on that?" his eyebrows raising as well.

Blair shot back an offended glare, even though her arm was stuck halfway through the sleeve, and her face was red from the effort. "What else am I supposed to call you?" she grunted, trying to shimmy her arm farther into the hole.

Damien's smirk deepened as he watched her with a mix of affection and amusement. His eyes rolled playfully as he stepped toward her, "Let me help."

Blair responded with a dirty look even as her shoulders sagged. "Fine, but I'm not letting you dress me like I'm some sort of helpless-"

"Relax," Damien interrupted with a chuckle. "I'm still going to make you work for it."

Blair looked up at him with her hazel eyes. "What's that supposed to mean?"

Instead of answering her, Damien stepped flush with her, his shadow flickering at his feet as though they felt playful. His blue eyes glinted with mischief and he stretched out his hand. "Here's the deal, feisty. Get the shirt on as far as you can, and I'll pull it over your head for you."

"What if I don't need your help?" she said, raising an eyebrow. "What if I can handle this?"

He chuckled, the sound smooth and warm. "Just shut up."

Before she could respond, he lifted his arm and traced the scars on her skin. Lowering his fingers, his eyes fell to where the shirt hung on her body. "You went up against some crazy strong people, almost died because of it, and now you're going to let a piece of fabric win?" he asked with an antagonizing grin.

She shook her head, scoffing, "No," she said, trying to pull her shirt down, her frown deepening as her muscles continued to protest the motion.

Damien tilted his chin in encouragement as the darkness of his shadow swirled around her. "Alright, I'll help you now." His voice was soft, but the teasing undertone was unmistakable.

Blair raised an eyebrow at him as he stood just out of arm's reach. "You're ridiculous. Maybe I'll just hire help instead. I'm sure there's someone capable of getting me dressed."

Damien's grin widened. "Oh, trust me, you wouldn't want that." His finger skimmed her back as he grabbed the seam of her shirt. "No one is allowed to take care of you, besides me."

Blair chuckled, even as her body fought back. "That sounds a little unhinged."

Damien smiled and winked at her, "You haven't seen anything yet."

Tugging the rest of the shirt over her head and shoulders, the fabric finally fell into place.

She sat back against the bed, breathing a little easier. "Thank you for everything you've done for me."

"Thank you?" Damien's voice was light with amusement as he folded his arms again. "I don't think you owe me that. It's my fault you're in this situation anyway." He looked her up and down as he continued, "You healed from the Hunters with just sore muscles and a few scars. Maybe I'm just trying to impress you a fraction of how much you impress me."

Blair smirked, leaning back, wrestling the soreness that was still very much present in her body. "Maybe if you could make breakfast, I'd be impressed."

Damien laughed, the sound was genuine and warm. "I'll see what I can do but I draw the line at omelettes."

Blair audibly gasped like she was wounded, "Well, now you're just *disappointing* me."

Damien smiled subtly, and then a look of concern crossed his face like he was deep in thought. He took a step closer, his eyes meeting hers with a quieter, more sincere look now. "You okay?"

Blair's heart gave a small thump in her chest, though she wasn't sure if it was from the pain or something else.

"Yeah," she said softly, glancing up at him with a small, genuine smile. "I think I'll survive."

Because of you.

Damien's gaze lingered on her for a moment, his expression softening. "Good."

Blair snorted, and Damien tilted his head slightly, "I guess you're the one growing on me."

Blair rolled her eyes but couldn't suppress the smile tugging at her lips. "Well, I did learn how to *play nicely*."

He winked, clearly pleased with himself. Blair laughed, and for a brief moment, the pain seemed distant, swallowed up by the comfort of his presence and their banter.

"Help me to the kitchen, please?" she asked, blinking as if she had large eyelashes.

The warm feeling from her chest continued to spread as she hobbled in the hallway and toward the kitchen. She sat at the counter, eyeing the items already out for breakfast. Damien had set her down, making sure she was comfortable before grabbing her some water and listing the ingredients he had.

They had chosen pancakes and Damien had not dissapointed. He had used berries from the surrounding area and mixed them in, winking when he handed her the plate.

"Berries, because *obviously*, that's a tradition now. Actually, we'll let it be a reminder of what happens when you run from me." He looked up at her over his plate, "You won't ever get far."

She licked her fingers and smiled, "I bet I could right now. I mean, I would be *so* fast." A sarcastic thumbs-up accompanied her words.

They ate in silence for a few minutes, savoring every bite. As she finished her plate, traces of blue and purple juice stained her mouth and fingers.

Putting down the empty dish, she looked around the room and noticed how different it was from the Inn they stayed at when they first arrived. That one was bare, offering only a bed, some nightstands, and a small bathroom. This was an actual cottage that had two rooms, a shared bathroom, and a kitchen. It had been two days since she had first ventured out of the bed and investigated the home they were in.

Her mind shifted to life recently, contemplating the first memories she had since waking up. The very first thing she remembered was that the guild's runner had returned. As soon as she was coherent enough, Damien relayed his message.

She replayed the conversation many times since then. Knowing she couldn't ask her own questions, Damien had asked them for her. Without prompting her, Damien had found all the information she had been worried about. He had reports about the people she loved and the students from her class. It turns out that SilverDawn was safe. Although it was torn apart pretty badly and shops had been wiped out, the attack had been brief. The shadows that had invaded, left shortly after they presented themselves.

It was explained that they had been looking for something or someone, and when they figured out it wasn't there, they left. A few adults had been hurt from the chaos of the incident, and only two had been killed from trying to stop the shadows. This information had helped her through the healing process.

Blair took a deep breath and stood, setting her fork down next to her plate. Damien immediately stepped close to her, hands out, ready to help with whatever she needed. Blair looked at his hands and then shifted her gaze up to his face.

"Damien, I am not broken. I just want a bath. That's all." He nodded and stepped away toward the bathroom.

Blair stood and looked down at her body. Cloth shorts hung tight on her thighs, and she counted the marks on her legs. Four on one and six on the other, where the shadows had sliced her. The scars were thin white lines that adorned her skin. The small marks were all that was left from the attack, thanks to the Healers.

One of them had taken the time to ensure the bleeding had stopped while the other followed behind and focused on each cut. The healing time had then been expedited using elixirs and lotions.

Although her exterior injuries had healed at an impressive rate, the inside of her body was still stiff. At this point, she was relying on massages and baths to help soothe the constant ache.

Blair took another small breath and ran her hand over the scars, feeling the raised skin and remembering how she had felt small pokes in the hazy memories between clouds of black. She lowered her hands and stood tall, peering into the bathroom. Damien had the bath running and was putting some kind of oil into the water.

There had been a major shift in him since the attack. He was no longer full of silence and distance. He watched her with his full attention, tending to whatever she needed and never making any comments, no matter how small the accommodations were.

It had been like that since the first night she remembered seeing him. That night, he slept on the floor next to her bed, often waking to check on her.

It was every night after that, that he had been next to her in bed. This room had become *theirs*, even though there was another one down the hall. She had grown accustomed to this, having him next to her at all times.

Her legs moved slowly as she walked to the bathroom, just in time for the water to stop. He set the bottle down and pulled her to him. Keeping his eyes on hers the whole time, he pulled her shirt off and then her bottoms before he sat with his back against the tub, just as he had every other time.

Blair sighed in acceptance and stepped into the warm water as the scent of eucalyptus hit her. Blair smiled slightly, wondering when he had refilled it since the last bath.

Blair bent, using her knees, as the water hit her waist and then chest. Her hands guided her as she slowly lowered herself until she was covered in water. The water sloshed in the tub, making ripples that mimicked the lines in her skin. She rested her head back on the rim of the metal tub and took a deep breath.

"Need anything?" Damien asked quietly.

Blair answered with a sigh, "No."

The bathroom was quiet except for the soft lapping of water and the occasional drip from the faucet. Blair stayed leaning against the edge of the tub, her body finally relaxing.

Next to her, Damien's head rested on the rim as well. His legs were extended straight out, and his hands rested on his lap, with his fingers intertwined.

She studied the back of his head, contemplating asking the question that had been heavy on her mind.

"So, what is this? *Us*?"

Damien exhaled, his body stiffening slightly. He didn't look at her right away but then slowly turned his head, meeting her eyes over the edge of the tub. "I don't know."

Her pulse quickened.

Damien was always cautious, but now, he was antsy, as if searching for an answer he didn't have. "I don't know how to explain things." His voice was low and steady, but something in it felt fragile. "I just know that I can't leave you alone, I don't *want* to leave you alone."

The bathwater rippled as Blair shifted, the weight of his words pressing against her in a way that made her breath catch. She should have said something, should have asked what that meant, what he wanted, but she didn't. Instead, she sat up and watched him over the edge of the tub. The way his fingers tapped anxiously, the way his throat bobbed when he swallowed.

Damien finally met her gaze again, his turquoise eyes unwavering. "I tried to ignore it, but it's like every part of me is drawn to you. Even my shadows."

Her fingers drifted lazily through the water at his words. The air suddenly charged with electricity.

"Well, maybe I don't want you to ignore it," she replied in a small voice.

Damien stilled, "Good."

Neither of them moved until Blair had said the water had gone cold, and then he stood, leaving only to return with a towel. She dressed with him outside the door, calling him in when she was done.

Over the next few days, this became their routine: cooking food together, reading, and talking.

Blair focused on healing, while Damien focused on her.

19

"Please?" Blair asked.

"Nope. Not happening." Damien answered, displeased.

Blair stood with her hands on her hips, looking at Damien. "Come on, I'm hungry, and I want to go out."

Sitting on the edge of the bed, he paid no mind to her theatrics.

"Let's go to dinner! I'm almost completely healed, and I've been stuck here for over a week." Blair begged, adding a dramatic flair by doing small arm circles with her arms and then gradually increasing the size of them.

"I'm not risking it," Damien responded, not looking up from the book he read.

"Listen, we'll hide ourselves in the back and I'll eat quickly. I can't stay here any longer, I'm literally going crazy. Plus, you're going to be with me, so everything will be fine!"

Blair placed her hands together in front of her chest, kneeling on her knees, pleading with him.

Damien raised one eyebrow at her and sighed. Shaking his head in defeat and closing his book, he looked down at her. "I like you better when you're feisty."

Blair's eyes widened, and she stood, jumping up and down but stopping quickly. She had put in a lot of work to earn the forgiveness of her muscles, and she was starting to understand her boundaries.

She moved to the door, grabbed their cloaks and handed his to him with a large smile on her face. He stared at her for a moment and then took it, shaking his head again.

The cottage they were temporarily staying in was closer to the shops. They didn't have to walk long before the smell of food hit them. The old tavern they chose was a miniature mock-up version of The Raven's Nest. The wooden beams were dark with age, the scent of roasted meat and spiced ale thick in the air.

Blair and Damien stepped inside, the low murmur of conversation wrapping around. There was no fire in this one, but the roof opened in multiple areas, showing glimpses of the night sky and the stars that littered the canvas of black.

They found a table near the back, where the light from the lanterns was softer, and settled into their seats. Blair stretched her legs beneath the table, running her fingers over the rim of her glass as she glanced around.

"I like this place," she said, her voice light, thoughtful. "It's got character."

Damien nodded his head in agreement, "Definitely. If by character, you mean a unique smell of horse stall and stale beer." he said sarcastically, rolling his eyes.

Blair chuckled in response and kicked his leg playfully under the table.

They ordered and ate slowly, with different plates of meat and vegetables now in front of them. Blair took some bites while admiring the food and atmosphere. A musician in the corner plucked at his strings, the melody weaving its way through the room like smoke. The rhythm was smooth and inviting. Before Damien could react, Blair was rising from her chair.

"I love this song," she murmured, her body swaying as she stood. She stepped into the open space near the musician, her movements fluid as she swayed to the music. The candlelight around the musician highlighted the soft brown tones in her hair, her smile gleaming bright and effortless.

Damien leaned back in his chair, watching her, his lips curving upward as she twirled lightly on her feet.

It wasn't long before someone *else* noticed her too. A tall man sauntered over to her after watching her for a moment. Filled with the confidence of someone who had spent his life charming women, he moved into her space and Damien sat up.

Leaning in, he watched as the stranger murmured something to Blair that he couldn't hear. Blair laughed and the stranger's hand found hers as he pulled her into a dance.

Anger bled into his veins as his shoulders tightened with restraint.

Blair laughed loudly as she was spun around. She moved in step with the stranger as the song picked up, his hands moving to her waist.

Damien watched the man's grip tighten around her waist and move to her lower back.

The song seemed to stretch on far longer than it should have. By the end, Damien wasn't just angry, he was visibly seething.

As the song came to an end, the man took Blair's hand and pressed a slow, deliberate kiss to her knuckles.

Damien's shadows shot out, ready to grab Blair and pull her close. They made it halfway before they reluctantly stopped and started to recoil.

Damien met them as he charged toward Blair, grabbing her wrist and turning her toward him.

Blair looked at him, breathless, flushed from the dance. "You okay?" she asked, noticing his demeanor and tilting her head slightly.

"It's time to go," Damien said, his voice tight, controlled.

Her smile faltered as she caught the look in his eyes. She noted the tension in his shoulders and the way his jaw was locked as if he was holding something back. She didn't argue. She simply nodded as he grabbed her hand and went to follow him toward the door.

Within that exact second, a foreign touch tugged her other hand, and her body was pulled to a halt. Blair turned, meeting the eyes of the stranger she had shared a dance with. Her mouth gaped open, and she tried to pull her hand away but he yanked at her first, breaking the hold Damien had on her.

"I want another dance." the man whispered into her ear as her chest collided with his from the force.

A sharp snarl from behind made goosebumps erupt on Blair's skin and Damien's warmth was immediately there, at her back.

She turned, ready to tell him everything was okay, but his eyes were glued to the man's hands on her.

"You will *not* touch her again." Damien commanded as he pulled Blair behind him and pushed the man up against the wall, his hand instantly around his throat.

In reaction to the hostility, the man swung. Damien turned his head, avoiding the sluggish punch. When he looked back at the man, Blair noticed black wisps had begun to peek out of his collar. Damien raised the arm that held the man's throat, and his feet dangled off of the floor. As his foundation gave way, his eyes filled with fear. Blair watched in horror as the other patrons' attention shifted to the brawl.

Blair looked around and then back to Damien, his shadows so very clearly teetering on releasing. She moved to him then, aligning herself to his back. Molding her chest to his shoulders, she put her arms around his waist and squeezed gently."Damien, we need to go."

His breathing had escalated, and his body was now rigid.

"Damien, please!" she whispered loudly.

With that, he relaxed his hand and the man fell to the ground in a pile of exasperated inhales. Blair stepped in front of Damien, placing her hand on his cheek, and stole the attention of his darkening eyes.

Taking his hand, she pulled him towards the door and away from voices that were starting to shout. "Let's go."

As the door swung open and they stepped outside, the night air cooled her flamed face. Once a few steps away, she turned to him and pushed into his chest. "What is *wrong* with you?"

"Nothing," he muttered, averting his eyes as his hands curled into fists at his side.

Blair studied him, her anger shifting and her brows lifting in concern, "Don't lie to me. What happened back there?"

Damien didn't answer. He just exhaled sharply before addressing her. "You," he snapped, "*You* happened Blair." With that, he turned and walked away from her, back toward their cottage.

She followed him, keeping her distance as they walked, a silent tension thickening with every step.

Damien entered the cottage first, with Blair close behind him. As soon as they stepped in, the door slammed shut, courtesy of the force from Damien's shadows.

Blair froze and turned to look at Damien, who had gone straight into the kitchen to sit at the table. His whole body was tense as he held his head in his hands, his eyes directed at the floor. She walked up slowly, approaching him with caution.

His neck was the first thing she noticed, a pattern of angry black swirls cascading down under his shirt. As she stood there, more shadows materialized around his hand, weaving between his fingers as he tapped the side of his head.

Without thinking, Blair reached out and traced one of the black lines on his forearm. Damien inhaled sharply at the contact and his shadows raced to Blair. They traveled up her arm, hugging close to her skin. She flinched and closed her eyes, remembering the pain she had once experienced.

Slowly, she opened her eyes and realized this was different. Damien's shadows were not only soft, but they caressed her, gently.

Damien watched for a split second before he abruptly stood and walked around Blair. "I need a minute."

Blair moved fast to block his exit. She stood in front of him and placed both hands on the doorframe. "Not until you talk to me."

Damien stilled, closing his eyes and breathing through his nose as his nostrils flared. "Blair. Move."

"Just tell me what's going on." Blair urged as she watched his shadows coil around his shoulders, surging with power.

Taking a step toward him, Blair bumped her chest to his. Within that split second, Damien's eyes popped open, completely devoured by black.

Blair gasped and stepped back.

His demeanor was the same, but *he* was not. He no longer held a silent authority, but a dominating aura that surrounded him.

Was this what it meant to be Shadowborn?

Whatever it was, Blair felt oddly calm. Even with all the power radiating off him, she wasn't scared.

Tilting her head up at him, she straightened her shoulders and yet again, closed the space between them. Her chest brushed up against his as she brought her hands up to his arms, rubbing the back of them slowly.

"Talk to me." Blair pleaded, staring into the black galaxy of Damien's eyes. Her hands stopped moving as her fingers gripped the back of his biceps. "Are you okay?"

As if answering, the shadows lashed out around her. Like living tendrils, they coiled around her wrists before moving down her arms and settling at her waist. They pulled her in until she was completely flush with him. Blair gasped in surprise, her hands now pressed against his chest. His muscles quivered there, beneath her fingers, as if trembling with restraint.

"No, I'm not." he muttered, his voice rough and uneven as he brought his forehead down to hers. "Give it back."

His shadows began to move around her, ghosting over her bare shoulders and curling around the nape of her neck. They moved again, tracing the dip of her spine like unseen fingers.

Blair shivered, her skin warming beneath his touch. Her lips parted, her breath shaky. "Give what back?"

Damien exhaled sharply, his mouth moving to her forehead. "My control." His hands, real and shadowed, moved to her waist, his thumbs grazing the soft curve of her hips.

She said nothing, just tilted her chin up at him as he towered over her.

His mouth formed a tight line, and he slowly looked down at her. "Tell me to stop, Blair."

She swallowed silently and met his intensity, slowly shaking her head no.

It was a mere second before his mouth crashed against hers.

The kiss was deep, searing into every part of her soul. His shadows moved with him, gliding over her like invisible hands. They touched and teased along her arms, her sides, the curve of her throat. Settling for a brief moment, they wrapped around her thighs and lifted her. She responded instantly by folding her legs around Damien.

Blair gasped into his mouth as his arms locked around her. Her fingers dug into his shirt as the dark tendrils continued to caress her skin. Warm and cool at the same time, they traced patterns along her back and hovered around the most sensitive parts of her body.

A small moan escaped her, and that sound shattered what little control Damien had left.

His shadows riled in response, ripping the back of her shirt in one smooth motion. There, they stayed, licking every inch of exposed skin.

She pulled away from his kiss to shimmy out of it, letting it fall to the floor,

His grip loosened as he looked down at her exposed chest. With a low growl, his shadows gripped her hair and pulled her lips back to his.

Blair trembled against him as her body completely surrendered to every touch. Her hands moved on their own, removing his shirt and then tracing his shoulders, running over every line of carved muscle. He was still so tense, even as she wrapped her fingers in his hair. With each movement, she matched his possessive need, demanding more.

Everything from the past few weeks; the attack, the scars littering her body, the tavern, it all just disappeared as Damien's hands claimed her, the same hands she had fantasized about all along.

Nothing else mattered besides his grip, and the feeling it left on her skin. There was only the heat between them now. That, and the way he was slowly worshiping her body.

Damien stiffened, and Blair watched as he struggled to regain his composure. With a small smile, she whispered his name and he exhaled in resignation.

Blair's back hit the wall first, a soft moan leaving her lips as Damien pressed into her. His thumbs dug into her skin, hard enough to leave bruises as he held her in place.

When his mouth wasn't on hers, it was trailing down her neck, nipping at the soft skin there. His black eyes burned into her as she pulled back, almost panting.

She watched his lips as they parted slightly. "You took it from me," he murmured, his voice rough, almost desperate.

Blair barely had time to respond before his lips crashed back into hers. This kiss was all-consuming. She melted against him, her fingers yet again threading through his hair, pulling him closer, *needing* him closer.

Another shred and she felt it, her bottoms, ripped to pieces with just one quick movement from his shadows. Every single inch of her was now completely vulnerable and exposed to him.

The shadows around her eventually slowed, and Damien set her down to take a step back. Her gaze locked onto him as his eyes trailed over her body. It wasn't long before his shadows reached out for her again, and she instantly relaxed into their touch.

As she did so, more tendrils curled up from the floor, silken and merciless, as they wrapped around her ankles.

"What-?" she breathed, but the word barely left her lips before her legs were yanked apart, forced wide by the living dark that pulsed around her. A few more moved to her arms, pulling them high above her head and securing her wrists together against the wall. They then lifted her, until her feet were completely off the ground.

A few shadows moved on their own, attaching to the wall and creating a small ledge for her to sit on. As she did so, they wrapped around her thighs. Slowly, they lifted her legs up and opened them, pushing her knees to the wall behind her. She looked down at her body, which seemed to not only be exposed, but *displayed.*

Blair watched as Damien smirked with approval, his eyes glancing at her wrists and legs, which were now held into place.

She strained, her chest rising and falling with a rush of adrenaline. The shadows didn't hurt her, but they held her deliberately, as if waiting for permission to do more.

The final wisps of black that had lingered around Damien moved toward her, tracing over her body. She shivered, her breath catching as they trailed along her shoulders, brushing against her skin like ghostly fingertips.

Damien never moved, he just watched as his shadowed extensions bound and teased her. They traced the curve of her back, then slid down to her hips, circling around her thighs.

The sensation was intoxicating.

"Do you trust me?" he asked, as a shadow grazed her cheekbone.

She let out another shaky breath as his gaze wandered down the length of her body.

"Yes." she panted.

A low growl formed in Damien's throat as his eyes landed between her legs. As soon as the noise hit the air, the shadows lifted her hips up to him, revealing every inch to him. Two shadows moved over the inside of her thighs and rested between them, pulling her completely open for him.

His breath became erratic as he noticed how she glistened for him. After looking over her body one more time, he stepped up to her and returned his lips to hers, consuming every sound she made. After a few moments, his lips moved to her jaw, then lower, pressing heat against the sensitive skin of her neck. The shadows followed, caressing every inch of her as though they wanted to memorize her.

"Damien," she whispered, fighting the shadows to touch him.

His hands gripped the outside of her thighs. His touch was almost bruising, counteracting the soft grazes from the shadows.His breathing grew more ragged as he continued to kiss her deeply.

She gasped into his mouth when she felt pressure between her legs.

His shadows.

They circled her, sliding back and forth until she arched her back. With that, they formed together and pushed inside of her in one swift motion. A moan tore from her throat as he tightened his hold on her and leaned forward, biting down on her neck.

This only fed into the shadows, moving as if they had a will of their own now. Her body shook as they continued their assault, allowing her no time to adjust to their size. Her eyes rolled back just as Damien stepped back to watch again. The shadows continued to thicken until she made a pained noise and then they pulled back out. The motion was repeated over and over again as Damien watched.

The speed was tantalizingly slow at first but started to pick up as she rocked her hips, meeting their movement.

Damien dipped his hand inside his waistband, gripping himself as he stroked slowly. "Do you know how long I've wanted this? How long I have sat next to you, thinking of this moment?" His nostrils flared as his hand moved faster. "You are so goddamn beautiful Blair. From here on out, you are *mine*. I'm the only one who gets to touch you."

Blair tried to agree, but one of the shadows binding her wrists loosened and moved to her neck, cutting off her ability to answer. A muffled sound of pleasure escaped her again as the shadows continued their relentless exploration.

The one inside of her moved faster as another one fondled the curves of her body.

Starting at her collarbone and moving down to the curve of her waist, it only fed into the sensations that were building.

Damien stepped toward her and knelt, his lips moving to meet the shadows. He took his time, gliding his tongue across her and savoring every inch. She squirmed against him, needing more.

Damien noticed her movements, and released her wrists from the binds. Her hands immediately moved to grip the back of his head.

"Make more sounds for me baby." Damien instructed, his voice no longer his own but a rough imitation.

Blair moaned and rocked her hips against his face as the shadows around her throat allowed her to speak, "Give me a reason to."

Damien lowered into her again, his eyes glossing over with an even darker onyx. The shadows inside her shifted, creating a unique pressure as Damien's mouth found her center. He lowered his lips to the sensitive area and rolled his tongue over her swelling bud. A shock of warmth traveled up her body with every flick.

Blair sucked in a sharp breath.

Damien snarled in response, closing his mouth completely over her and moving his tongue in fast motions. Blair thrashed in response, but the shadows around her held firm. Damien continued to work in tandem with his dark extensions, creating a response that made her muscles quiver.

"Damien!" she half-screamed, subdued as yet another shadow bound her mouth. Her muffled screams faded in and out as his tongue slowed, just to pick up pace again. As she began to build, the shadow inside of her continued to move, creating layers of pleasure.

Being completely held down by his shadows meant she couldn't fight back, she couldn't escape what was coming. Within seconds, release tore through her and the shadows tightened, magnifying the feeling.

Damien's tongue slowed to almost a complete stop as he lengthened his licks, forcing her to work through her body tremors. Eventually they slowed and the shadow that had been inside retreated, as well as the other shadows.

Damien looked up with a sly smile, his eyes slowly turning back to blue. He held her up for a moment as she adjusted to having her own weight back.

Breathing through the aftershocks, she felt Damien rub the faint lines his shadows had left. Next it was his lips, kissing her skin everywhere the shadows had secured her. Crouching, he repeated the same movements on her thighs and ankles.

Finally, he picked her up, cradled her in his arms and walked her to the bathroom. Lowering her down into the tub, he started the water.

The absolute bliss that consumed Blair was unexplainable, especially as the hot water hit her skin. Moments later, she felt a shift in the water as he stepped in, sitting across from her.

His hand found her leg and pulled it above the water. She opened her eyes just enough to see him staring at her. His expression was soft and his eyes were now completely crystal blue, void of the feral darkness she had just experienced.

He smiled as he motioned for her to come closer. She listened, scooting her butt down as his focus moved to a soaped cloth. His eyes roamed her skin as he moved the cloth in circular motions.

Once he hit the indent of her hip, he lowered that leg and picked up the other, repeating the process. When he was finished, he pulled her to his chest and turned her around, so her back was to him.

Sudsing the cloth again, he slowly washed her arms, chest, and face, leaving her hair for last. When it was time to wash that, he doused his hands in soap and massaged her scalp.

She had never been taken care of like this.

After the final rinse of her hair, he wrapped his arms around her and held her, moving his mouth to her ear. "I'm tired of fighting this. I'm tired of fighting whatever you're doing to me," he whispered, his voice barely loud enough to hear. "You've ruined me without even trying. I'm yours, Feisty."

Blair smiled at that. "I ruined *you*? I don't think I'll recover from what you just did to me." Blair replied, her body clearly exhausted from her release.

Once the water turned cold, Damien produced a towel and helped her out of the bathtub, wrapping the cloth around her. He then walked her to the bed, unwound the towel, and pulled one of his large shirts over her head.

She moved the blanket and laid on the bed, inviting him next to her. He accepted without a second thought, ultimately pulling her onto his chest.

His fingers traced her cheekbone, her ear, and her neck, a repeated cycle that soon made the drowsiness hard to fight.

"I need you to know that everything has changed for me." he whispered out loud. "The first time I saw you, you had this light in your eyes I had never seen before. It dimmed the day the Hunter's found you." It was quiet for a few seconds as Blair's blinks became longer, and her body begged for sleep. "I want to be the reason it stays lit." It was in that last word that Damien's grip tightened around Blair. She turned to him, placing a soft kiss on his lips.

"I want that too." she confessed, drawing small circles on his chest with her finger, "If I'm being honest, I think I've wanted that for a while now."

He kissed her again, pulling her flush against his side. Blair relaxed into him, feeling the safest she'd ever felt.

Her eyes closed, and her mind drifted.

20

Blair stirred, groggily pulling herself from the depths of sleep. For a moment, she just lay there, blinking up at the ceiling. The weight of exhaustion tried to pull her back, but then the images of last night flashed through her mind.

His shadows.

His hands.

She sat up, eyes immediately darting around the room for Damien. He wasn't next to her, but a soft sound from the kitchen told her he wasn't far.

She stretched slightly, her cheeks flaring at the dull soreness that settled between her legs as she moved around. Rubbing her face with her hands, she let out a small breath.

Memories of the night before, and what he had done to her, played through her mind. It was exactly as she had imagined it would be, except replaying the events, she realized everything last night had been for *her*.

Damien hadn't even taken off his pants.

She pulled the covers off just as the hickory smell of bacon wafted into the room. Her stomach growled at the caramelized sweetness that filled the air, and she quickly moved off the bed toward the kitchen.

The morning light leaked through the blinds in soft gold slats, painting the kitchen in pale warmth. Damien stood at the stove, barefoot and quiet, whisking eggs in a bowl with practiced ease.

As she approached, his shadows awakened and moved across the floor to caress her legs and face. She smiled at them as moved up her skin, and then watched as they retreated back to the floor, swirling around her feet.

She looked up at Damien as he poured eggs into the pan. They hissed faintly, curling at the edges as they encountered the heat. A shadow drifted toward the counter, leading Blair to a chair. She followed, taking a seat at the island to face Damien.

For the next few minutes, the kitchen was quiet. Just the soft sounds of cooking, the occasional creak of the old floorboards, and the subtle stirrings of darkness that moved as if they belonged there.

Damien opened the oven, and a light billow of smoke erupted as he pulled the pan of bacon out. Setting it on the counter, his shadows returned to him, lingered around him lightly, as if perfectly content. They soon melted back into his arms as he set Blair's plate down in front of her and walked around the island to the seat next to her.

They ate in a comfortable silence as the sun rose higher outside the cottage, warming the room. Blair would occasionally look at Damien from the corner of her eye and shyly smile before returning her attention to her food. "Top three?" she asked, softly.

Damien's gaze found hers with a slight bit of confusion. "What?" he asked, his mouth full of eggs,

"I can never figure out what you're thinking. So, right now, at this moment, what are the top three things on your mind?" Blair asked, shoveling a forkful of eggs into her mouth.

Damien lowered his hand and rolled his tongue over the bottom of his teeth. "Okay, top three: One, I liked taking care of you last night. Two: I want to taste you again. Three? There's something I want to tell you."

Blair didn't flinch. "Okay." She said with a blushed smile, pointing her fork at him. "Tell me."

Damien's eyes roamed over her body before they landed on his own arms. Nodding to the net of black moving underneath his skin. He exhaled as he spoke, "They like you."

She blinked up at him, a look of confusion settling between her eyes. "What?"

"The shadows." He lifted a hand slightly, and one of them reacted, rippling softly near his fingertips. "They usually don't behave, not this way."

Blair studied him, unsure if it was a joke. *It wasn't.* His tone was too quiet, too careful.

"I've spent most of my life trying to control them," he continued. "They've always reacted to my emotions, especially anger, fear, and pain. If I'm not calm, they usually act out, like an involuntary defense system."

She looked down at the flickering movement along his skin. One of the shadows curved toward her like a tendril reaching for warmth, its matted darkness gently grazed her arm, then pulled back to its owner.

"Since I've been around you," he said, softer now, "they're different. Instead of just being angry, it's like they have a purpose."

Blair didn't speak right away, she just listened.

He leaned forward, resting his elbows on the counter and joining his hands together. "It's not just that they *like* you. When you're near, I don't have to fight them. I don't have to focus so hard. When I'm around you, controlling them is like breathing instead of drowning."

Her eyes stayed on his face as she gave a small smile.

"They want to be around you, to protect you," he said simply. "Like I do."

A silence fell between them then, deep and thoughtful, edged with something fragile.

"Can I know more about them? About you?" Blair asked, putting down her fork and picking up her cup. Her gaze lingered on him over the rim, as he nodded in response.

"I was a child when they first formed," he explained, "I didn't know what I was, not at first, but I knew I was born different. My father used to tell me stories about people born with these shadows and how rare it was, how powerful they could be. Unfortunately, no one ever told me what happens when the wrong people take notice."

Blair's focus was entirely on him and the vulnerability he was showing. She watched him, staying attuned to his body language.

"When I turned six, they found me and took me from my home. They wanted me to learn how to fight," Damien continued, the weight of the past pressing down on his shoulders. "I didn't understand it back then. I was just a kid. I was put through hell, and ultimately trained to be a weapon. They didn't care about who I was, only what I could do. The shadows? They were a tool to them and I was their soldier. That's how it was for anyone in those camps."

Blair tilted her head slightly. "They?"

Damien nodded, taking a drink. "The King, his kingdom."

Blair clenched her hand around the cup in front of her, her jaw setting in frustration.

She had never considered the shadows manifesting in a child. And thinking about dark, twisted operations where children were molded into weapons? Trained to kill without conscience? She didn't need to hear the rest to understand the horror of what Damien had gone through.

"Not all Shadowborn are the same," Damien added, his voice quieter now. "Each one is different. I've seen some that can slip through walls, some that can even manipulate the dark into nightmares. I knew one that could make people vanish completely into dark voids. Each ability we wield is different. I can shape my shadows into whatever I need them to be. We already touched based on the emotions factor; when I'm angry or scared, they get stronger. I can control them to a point. But if I lose control, they take over."

Blair looked at Damien with a mixture of sadness and understanding but his gaze was steady, as if he didn't want pity.

"Back then, I didn't think I could escape."

There was a silence between them as he paused, neither of them moving or breathing.

"How did you get out?" Blair asked.

Damien's eyes focused on something distant in the kitchen. "I ran the first chance I had. They hunted me for years, but I managed to stay one step ahead of them. I found SilverDawn and decided to hide there."

Blair's heart clenched, a strange mix of gratitude and guilt washing over her. Moving her hands to him, she tugged at his wrist until her fingers intertwined with his. "And now what?"

Damien's gaze flickered to their joined hands. "My whole life as a Shadowborn has been in hiding. I'm starting to wonder what other choices I have. If I stop hiding, they will find me. If they find me, they'll find you."

Blair leaned forward and kissed his arm, formulating multiple plans in her head. "You said you got out, that you ran. What happened to the others?"

Damien's eyes hardened, the shadows swirling around him in response. "The others at camp?"

"Yeah." Blair confirmed, her voice cautious but intrigued, "Was it only Shadowborn there?"

Damien sat back, his eyes moving to the ceiling as he processed her words.

After a few moments his voice filled the empty space around them. "The camp that I was in was mostly children but there were very few Shadowborn. The others there held nothing special, besides having a certain potential to wield shadows. If a child was strong and could withstand a transfer, they could be extremely useful to the King and his desire for a Shadowborn army."

"So, they trained all of you?" she asked, leaning her body into him.

Damien nodded, kissing the top of her head. "Yeah, those that had shadows were pushed harder because the goal was to forge us into the perfect weapon. We were meant to become leaders, the others were used to fill the armies, depending on their rank."

Blair nodded, her eyes following every shift small in his demeanor. She could tell this was hard for him, it was clear that he was pushing through personal barriers to have this discussion. She appreciated it all, every small glimpse he gave her.

"He slowly created an army with various skillsets, one he was able to have complete control over." Damien looked up at her then, smirking slightly. "Well, not *complete* control. There were some aspects that he didn't take into consideration, like the fact Shadowborn were never meant to be controlled." A small laugh escaped him as if he remembered something, "Oh, and the process of trying to recreate shadows isn't quite as easy as he thought it was."

Blair's shoulders went rigid.

How had she not known this existed? How are there people living a life like this?

Speaking slowly, Blair's eyes brightened with determination. "Well, what do we do now? How can you stop running?"

"Shadowborn have lived a life hiding or being hunted. The Hunters are our problem now. We'd have to take care of them first."

Blair nodded, resting her chin in her hand.

He looked up at her, his eyes darkening as he pushed his chair back and lunged toward her. Picking her up, he tossed her over his shoulder and started walking toward the bedroom. His shadows tickled her face, and she let out a giggle as her feet flailed.

Damien chuckled in approval of her playfulness. "We form a plan in the morning. I'm not done with you yet." He tightened his hold around Blair as they entered the bedroom.

This time, when they touched, it wasn't in a feral need. She wasn't bound to a wall or thrown on the bed. Her clothes weren't even torn off animalistically. Damien took his time, starting slow by kissing down her face and her neck. He pulled at the bottom of her shirt, asking permission before pulling it over her head and beginning another trail of soft kisses. Moving her hair to the side, he slowly licked the rim of her ear.

213

Blair responded in short pants, her hands lazily moving over his clothes.

"Enough about me. I want to know everything about *you*, Blair. Let's start by showing me what other sounds you can make," Damien muttered, black swirls starting to cloud his vision.

Blair nodded, reaching for his shirt and pulling it over his head. Her hands moved across the black markings that had laced up his chest and shoulders. They curled into bold, intricate swirls and then shifted to sharp, jagged lines.

The patterns never stayed still, they constantly moved as if stirred by an unseen magic beneath his skin. Some lines shimmered faintly, pulsing in time with his heartbeat, while others coiled tighter when touched by the light streaming in.

Across his collarbone, the marks branched like roots down his arms and then narrowed into delicate tendrils, wrapping around each muscle like ink caught in water.

Blair watched as the swirls occasionally rippled and when they did, she followed them with her hands.

Damien stole her attention away from his body as he slowly kissed her. Pouring himself into what restraint he had, he gripped the back of her head, deepening the kiss. Then, he moved her backward until her knees hit the side of the mattress. Slowly, he turned her around.

Kissing the side of her neck and inhaling her scent, he bent her over and kissed every scar she had on her back. The larger ones, he licked, dragging his tongue across her soft skin. With each swipe he made, more shadows released, crawling over her back to her wrists, where they bound together.

Once her wrists were secured together, the shadows tightened and moved down the side of the bed where they attached to the leg.

She raised her head and looked up at the black binds that twisted and tightened around her skin. A husky groan brought her attention back to Damien who stood behind her. Turning her head behind her, she watched him out of the corner of her eye. He stood, admiring the view of her bent over and bare. He looked up at her then, the last bit of white in his eyes turning black.

Blair shuddered at the sight, realizing just how much she liked when that happened. That dark fog of shadow meant he was losing control and that was quickly becoming her favorite thing to witness.

"Your eyes turn black, you know that?" She managed to squeak out as he slowly bent again to lick her lower back.

"Mhmm." was Damien's only reply as another shadow slid up her back to secure itself around her eyes, acting as a blindfold. Her breath seemed to quicken the moment her vision was stolen, but she trusted him, allowing him to take total control.

The blindfold began to heighten her other senses, and soon, his rough tongue and warm breath was causing goosebumps to break out along her skin. In other areas, where the cold shadows trailed, the skin felt open and exposed. The contradiction of the two pressures worked together, driving her wild.

Damien watched her body spasm before him, a smirk curving his lips. Every time his wrist flickered, his shadows moved in that direction.

The dark tendrils began a cruel dance, sliding to her throat and trailing over her collarbone before tightening just enough to make her gasp. They teased along the edges of her ribs, tracing lazy circles over her stomach, creeping even lower before retreating just as swiftly.

All Blair could do was just lay there, her body responding to every unexpected touch. Each whisper of sensation from the shadows sent shivers rippling down her spine, and as they played, she found herself panting.

"Tell me what you like Blair." Damien mused.

The shadows shifted, dragging slow and deliberate strokes over her. A whimper escaped her before she could stop it.

Damien grinned. "That? You like that?"

Blair bit her lip and nodded.

The teasing touches turned sharper. Shadows stroked, pressed, then squeezed just tight enough to make her squirm but never enough to hurt.

Every sensation built on the last, a slow, torturous ascent, winding her tighter and tighter until she was sure she would snap.

"More?" Damien questioned, voice dropping lower before the shadows completely halted.

Blair trembled in response, her pants now ragged gasps. She had not expected this; the pressure, the absence, the unrelenting tease of his power, she loved it.

"Please."

A dark chuckle filled the room and the shadows resumed as she was flipped onto her back. Her wrists stayed confined above her head as Damien's exploration continued, his fingers skimming along her jaw, and down her chest.

"Please let me see you." she whimpered, rocking her body closer to his.

The sound of pants dropping to the floor made her squeeze her thighs together.

Several seconds went by and as Blair let out an impatient groan, her vision started to return. The shadows that had masked her eyes slowly unraveled and she inhaled sharply at the sight of Damien who stood naked in front of her.

At first, it was his dark eyes that stole her attention but then her eyes flickered downward to his hands. His palm was open and his fingers were spread as he rotated his wrist, flexing his hand. Then he moved it, tantalizingly slow, across his abdomen to his thick shaft. He smiled as he wrapped a hand around himself teasing her in the most unfair way.

He *knew* she could only watch.

He *knew* this would be what drove her the most crazy.

So there she stayed, *forced* to watch as the veins in both his arm and length constricted. A low moan escaped him as he leaned his head back and swallowed.

Blair started to writhe in response, to which he stroked faster. "What's wrong, baby?" Damien cooed, as he slowed.

She whimpered one more time, the sound turning into one feral word. *Please.*

He instantly released himself and moved to her, caging her in as he laid on top of her. His eyes locked on hers and for a split second, his eyes shifted to her wrists, where the shadows disappeared. Her hands wrapped around the back of his neck as she opened her legs to him.

He shifted his weight, positioning himself. His eyes found hers as he pushed inside.

Blair moaned at the feeling, the sensation of being filled by him. He watched her face, pushing in even farther, slow and deep.

After a few more inches, she closed her eyes and winced from the pressure. He immediately responded to this, pausing for a moment before addressing her. "Keep your eyes on me, Blair. I want to see what I do to you."

She obeyed, opening her eyes to meet his gaze.

With a slight nod from her, he continued moving as she relaxed, taking him the rest of the way.

"Fuck." Damien whispered against her lips as he put his forehead to hers.

Blair moved her hands from behind his head and traced the curves of his shoulders and arms. Following the muscle, she then moved down his side, the black marks following her touch. The more he was inside of her, the more they reacted; growing and then scattering across his neck.

Damien lowered himself, grazing her ear with his lips. "You feel so good, feisty."

Those words, *that nickname*, ignited a flame in Blair's lower belly. As she moved to meet him, Damien's growls became louder and she welcomed them with her own intoxicated sounds. Wrapping her arms under his, she dug her nails into his back, relishing the sweet pressure building within her.

As her sounds rose, so did Damien's shadows. They emerged everywhere, covering him and Blair. He closed his eyes, and his nostrils flared, another growl lingering in his throat. "I can't be gentle. *I need you.* I need you in every single way I can have you Blair."

"Then take me Damien. " Blair whispered, her voice filled with need.

The nice and steady rhythm he had given her to adjust, was over. He grabbed her thighs and pulled them up, pinning her uplifted legs at her knees. Blair moaned in approval at the new angle.

Moving his hand between her legs, he began circling it with his thumb as he pushed back inside of her.

The sensation was instantly overwhelming and Blair bucked her hips, but his shadows were there, holding her in place again.

A scream broke free as the warmth in Blair's body began to build again. She tried to arch her back, but she couldn't move, once again restrained with his strength.

Damien smiled at the way she squirmed and slowed his movements, pulling out only to lower his mouth to her entrance.

She squealed as his hot breath warmed the sensitive area. He slowly licked once, pulling another moan from her lips as he focused in on one specific spot, her body winding up with every flick of his tongue.

As her muscles tightened, her climax neared and she was the one to lose control this time. Grabbing the back of his head, she moved against his mouth. A muffled groan of acceptance from him pushed her over the edge, her body convulsing as it let go.

When he pulled back, his mouth and beard glistened and he gave a content smile. Tracing her swollen clit with his finger, he forced more from her. She fought back, bringing her hands up to stop him but his shadows were faster, snapping around her wrists again.

She screamed as the intensity heightened, and his finger swirled faster. "I want another one Blair."

Lowering his mouth back down to her, his finger continued moving as he licked her thighs. Blair screamed again when his other hand moved to her opening, and he pushed two fingers inside.

She couldn't take this, it was too much.

His mouth stopped for a mere second, hovering above her skin. "Just give me one more."

Blair's body shook as he worked her, every single nerve on fire. Within a minute, another orgasm hit her head-on. Her body barely had time to recover before his hands moved to her knees and he slid back inside with one deep motion.

Screaming out, she matched his movements.

Within minutes, she was moaning out his name as waves of intense pleasure washed over her, again and again. His body tightened against hers as a shadow reached out, grabbing her jaw and making her look at him. Groaning loudly, he released into her as his shadows thrashed around him.

After both their bodies had stilled and their breathing evened out, they lay there, tangled in each other, until sleep claimed them.

21

Damien and Blair were curled together under the warmth of the blankets. The room was bathed in the soft, silvery glow of the mid-morning sun. It was late, the world outside quiet and still, and the peaceful rhythm of their breathing filled the space between them. Blair nestled closer, her head resting against his chest as she drew lazy circles on his arm, her touch gentle and comforting. Damien's fingers traced faint patterns on her arm, slow and absent, as though he was soaking in every second with her.

Blair looked up at him, sensing a quiet turmoil in his mind. She gently cupped his face, her thumb brushing across his cheek. "Top three?" she asked softly.

Damien's eyes flickered to hers, his expression distant for a moment. His fingers began lightly grazing her hips as he started to explain his thoughts, "The men hunting us? The ones that attacked you?"

She nodded, moving her hand to rest under her chin.

Damien sighed as if he was about to admit something he didn't want to. "One of them was named Alec, he trained me when I was younger."

"So, he was from your camp?" Blair asked, her fingers now drawing different shapes on his skin.

Damien nodded, watching her hand move, "Yeah. He became an Enforcer and for a while, we matched in ability."

Blair looked up at him, her hand pausing. "Explain the ranks for me one more time?

Nodding, he continued, "There are Hunters, who are the lowest of the low. They have minimal skills when it comes to fighting and training in hand-to-hand combat. They're nothing more than scouts. They can't do much except track people, follow them, and report back if they find someone who could potentially have a shadow. They don't have any shadow magic in them."

Blair looked up, shifting slightly as her legs pressed against his.

Damien brought his hand up and tucked a stray hair behind her ear. "Then, there are the Enforcers," he said, his voice taking on a darker tone. "They've been *gifted* with shadows. Not by their own doing, but through trinkets, special objects they wear that give them power. It could be a ring, necklace, or anything like that. These shadows are harder to control and angrier. They're stronger than the Hunters, but they still lack something crucial. They can fight, they can track, but their shadows don't fully belong to them. They're limited and sometimes their bodies can't handle the strain from the shadows."

Blair sat up at this, shifting the blanket to cover her exposed skin. Bringing her knees up to her chest, she crossed her arms over them. "And then what happens?" she asked quietly, her voice tinged with apprehension.

Damien's eyes grew colder, his fingers moving the blanket aside and trailing up and down her legs. His voice lowered, almost as though the memory of them was a personal threat. "It makes them deteriorate if they use the shadows longer than necessary. It's like they're burned from the inside."

He watched her closely as he explained more, "The third kind, the most dangerous ones, are the Phantoms," he said, his voice nearly a whisper. "These ones are branded and forced to take on the shadows. Their body usually rejects it, and can't handle the strain. The strong ones who survive and accept the darkness become lethal. They can manipulate the shadows, to an extent. It's possible to take them down but they're strong and the shadows they have, enhance their abilities." His hands trailed higher, moving to her arms. "Then there are people like me, who are born with the shadows. *Shadowborn*. The others were created to mimic us but we have unmatched power in the abilities we carry."

Blair felt a shiver run through her at his words. "So, Shadowborn are the strongest?" she asked, watching the way his body stayed tense. "Which means you can defeat them?"

Damien stilled, his jaw tightening. "It all comes down to potential. Shadowborn have a higher skill set but we still must train to work for it. A well-trained Phantom, or even a highly trained Enforcer, can overpower a novice Shadowborn. Like I said, I was six when my shadows awakened, and I was forced to train with all kinds of people including Hunters, Enforcers, and even a few Phantoms. The Phantoms were the worst. They were ruthless, the shadows they had brought out the darkness in them, like they were more *shadow* than person."

Damien pulled her back down into a laying position, moving her close to nestle against his chest. As he moved, something shimmered on his upper chest, right under his collarbone, a spiral made of shadows.

Blair's hands skimmed the marking."What is this?"

Damien slightly sighed, "Think of it as a birthmark. All Shadowborn should have one somewhere on their body. It's what gave them the idea for Phantoms. That's how the shadows are infused, through a brand."

Blair continued tracing the symbol. "How come I've never noticed it?" She asked, running her finger over the spot several times.

His response came fast."My shadows hide it to keep me safe. If the wrong person sees it, I can easily be identified as a Shadowborn."

Blair nodded, pulling her hand away from the mark and across Damien's chest. "What else can your shadows do?" She asked quietly.

"Well, we already know I can blindfold you and spread your-"

Blair slapped his forearm as her mouth popped open in surprise.

Damien chuckled in response and sat up, pulling her between his legs. "I've told you before. My shadows morph into things."

"But you've done other things with them? Beyond morphing them?" she asked, her eyebrows coming together in wonder.

"When I have too, yes, but it's out of instinct most of the time." he answered back, using his thumb to rub the wrinkles in her forehead.

"Is that how you survived?" she asked, her voice full of concern.

Damien's lips curled into a slight, bitter smile. "Before I got out? Yeah. I trained hard and they took notice. Once I ranked up, the Enforcers got me. When they tried to push, I pushed back, sometimes subconsciously, so, yes?"

Blair shuddered at the thought of what he must have gone through.

"What we're going up against, it's dangerous," Damien continued, his eyes locked onto hers. After a moment, his gaze softened slightly. "I just want you to understand the full picture."

Blair watched his eyes as they searched her face, probably looking for any ounce of regret. She took his hand and cradled her face with it, placing a soft kiss on the inside of his palm.

22

Blair sat at the table, wrapped in the light sheet from the bed. The fabric clung to her chest and waist, with the remainder of it laying on the floor at her feet. Her ankles were crisscrossed in her lap and her hands were folded together in front of her. A barely-put-together bun laid on top of her head, keeping her brown hair up and out of her face.

As Damien walked to his bag, he tugged at a loose strand, causing all of it to fall over her shoulders. Blair swung at him as he passed, but missed, and stuck her tongue out at him instead. He smiled in response as he grabbed a small plastic bag of jerky and offered her some. She wrinkled her nose in disapproval and crossed her arms over her chest.

The fresh moonlight poured over her from the open window, a sign that they had spent most of the evening talking and tangled in bed together.

As Damien popped a few more pieces in her mouth, Blair took a deep breath. "So, what's our next step?"

"We have a few options," he said in-between chewing, "but the Hunters are the core issue. We'll need to start there."

Blair bit down on her bottom lip as she looked down at her intertwined fingers, tapping them one by one. With a deep sigh, she looked up at him. "That means we need to find a way to take them out."

"That's awfully bold of you to assume you're coming with me." Damien taunted, lifting the bag into the air and tapping it, so the contents fell straight into his mouth.

Blair scoffed in response, her eyebrows raising as if challenging him. "That's awfully *stupid* of you to assume I'm not."

With his arm frozen mid-air, Damien looked at her from the corner of his eye and winked.

For a second, Blair glared back, and then her expression softened as she fought an intruding smile. Folding her hands over her chest, she cocked her head as if making fun of him. "What? Do you plan on taking them out all by *yourself*?"

Damien swallowed and wiped his mouth, clicking his tongue. "By myself? No. With *you*? Also no."

Blair looked at him in disbelief, her arms dropping to her sides.

Damien laughed, tossing the bag into the trash. "I know someone who can help, he's actually supposed to be around tomorrow."

Confusion filled Blair's face. "*Around*?"

Damien nodded, walking toward her, "You'll see."

Blair nodded and stood, bunching the sheet up on her chest and turning toward the clothes in her bag. Within another second, Damien was behind her, pulling the sheet off and exposing her body to the moonlight. She giggled as he began to kiss her neck, their conversation moving to the back of her mind.

As his hands began to roam over her chest, a spark of playful defiance lit inside of her.

She turned around to face him, and walked her fingers across his chest, mapping out every muscle and vein. She then looked up at him, and pushed him away with a coy smile.

Damien tilted his head in question and went to kiss her, but Blair moved faster, taking off down the dark hallway, her giggle echoing off the walls. He didn't call after her, even as she ran into the kitchen.

Crouching down behind the island, Blair inhaled deeply to control her breathing and the adrenaline flooding her body. Around her, the kitchen was cast in darkness, the only light coming from a lantern in the living room.

A flicker of a shadow formed on the wall, and Blair backed away in the opposite direction, keeping low and retreating into one of the bedrooms. She stayed low to the ground and shuffled underneath the bed, covering her mouth with her hand, to stifle the sounds of her breathing.

Within a few seconds, she sensed movement in the doorway. Straining her eyes into the black that surrounded her, she tensed and waited for the steps to come closer. There was only silence though, as she continued to hold her breath.

"Found you." Damien's dark voice boomed, as he grabbed her ankles and pulled her from beneath the bed. A scream ripped from her throat as he stood her up, her thrashing body fighting against him. He held her wrists behind her back, his shadows now entering the game.

She fought back and tried to rip away from him to run again. "No fair!" she managed to huff out as laughter escaped her in between squirms.

"Fair? You tried to hide from me in the *dark*." Damien whispered to her as he kissed her jaw and throat. She stopped fighting back and slumped against him.

Damien chuckled at her surrender, the sound seeming to bounce off the darkness around them.

Blair laughed and tried to elbow him, "You cheated."

A dark hum came from his throat. "Here, let me make it up to you." Damien whispered against her skin as he pushed her down on the bed. Using the side of his foot, he kicked her ankles open, and apologized with his tongue. Over and over again.

23

Every *part* of Blair felt weak.

Over the last two days she had been ravaged multiple times, in multiple different ways, and then last night, she spent every ounce of energy she had left, packing. They had stayed up late, going through their items and making sure they had the essentials.

Then, after spending one more morning entangled together, they had gathered their belongings and left the cottage, traveling to meet Damien's friend.

That had been three hours ago.

Now, they were passing by another small town. Blair had been walking behind Damien, watching the environment around them change from dense forest, to a green, rural area. Damien had paused many times since starting, to check-in on Blair. Without making it obvious the rest was intended for her, he would take a canteen out to drink, stretch his legs for a few minutes, or adjust the weight in the bags by setting them down and reorganizing them. Each time, he would wait for her to stand first, signaling she was ready to continue on.

Even with the extra breaks, Blair's legs were screaming as she followed his long strides.

Attempting to subdue the ache, she started talking. "So, how do you know this guy we're meeting?" Blair asked, stepping over a large rock and catching her balance quickly before having to step over another.

"He's an old friend," was Damien's only reply.

Blair paused and looked over at him. "Follow-up question: We didn't get a letter, and there's not exactly a *surplus* of runners out here. So, how do you know where to go? What time to be there?" She continued walking, waiting for a reply from him.

His body had a sheer layer of sweat covering it now, making Blair internally smile as she waited for an answer.

With each step, the forest around them came alive with different sounds and Blair looked around at the land around them. The trees lining the trail they followed were stretched high overhead, branches tangling like they were hugging each other. Sunlight filtered through the canopies in threads, not beams, lighting a patterned path ahead of them.

She stepped over another fallen log, boots crunching faintly on the bed of dead leaves, and asked again. "Are you still thinking about the answer, or is that your way of telling me you don't want me to know?"

Damien didn't slow but tilted his head slightly toward her. "It's not that. It's just not my secret to give away."

Blair straightened at his word choice, "I'm keeping *your* secret, aren't I?"

He watched her, not replying immediately. His eyes, a cool slate blue, scanned the narrow trail ahead, and for a moment, Blair thought he might ignore the question entirely. But then, he gave her a soft answer. "He came to me, in a dream."

Blair raised a brow and halted her foot, mid-step. "I'm sorry, w*hat*?"

Damien stopped walking and lowered his head with a grunt. The wind stirred his coat as he turned toward her, "I don't mean an average dream that most people have," he explained further, "It's how he communicates, it's his power. He uses his shadows and steps through the dreams of others to send messages or visit them. He came to me two nights ago, showed me an old building and the day to be there, that was all."

Blair cocked her head to the side in fascination and folded her arms. "You're saying he sends you shadow visions in your sleep?"

He nodded once. "Every Shadowborn is different, remember? His ability is to communicate through dreams. It's how we've stayed in contact through the years."

"Huh. That's a hell of a trick," she muttered.

Damien nodded in agreement but his expression darkened just a little. "It used to be more than that. When I first met him, he could reach across continents. Sometimes, he would send warnings about how Enforcers were going to train us. Other times, I would dream about a certain person being wrapped in shadows, and I would wake up to them being gone."

Blair stepped closer, voice gentler now. "He was from your camp too?"

He looked at her and nodded, turning back toward the large trees that surrounded them. "He was one of their leaders but really, he was just there to make sure the kids survived everything. They found out fast that the longer he was there, the more he got in trouble for helping us. Every time he was caught, they would hurt him. After a few months, the beatings started to affect his abilities. He was forced out before I left." Damien moved forward, eyeing the tree line like he was searching for something. "He's checked on me over the years. He can still communicate, but it's as if he's far away or the world is too loud. The visions come less clearly. Like I'm underwater."

Blair studied his face. "Why do I get the feeling you feel bad for him? Were you guys close?"

Damien's reply was short, "He's probably the reason I survived as long as I did. I owe him a lot."

They resumed walking as the trees closed in tighter and the path narrowed. Every now and then, Blair would glance at Damien, wondering how many stories lay behind those blue eyes. He didn't talk about his past easily, just fragments here and there when she asked specific questions. But this *friend*, this dream shadowspeaker, mattered to him.

That much was clear.

After a long stretch of silence, Blair spoke again. "What's his name?"

Damien glanced up at her. "He doesn't use it anymore, not the one I knew."

She clicked her tongue in understanding. "What did you call him then?"

He exhaled, not quite a sigh. "Back then, we called him Grei."

A crow called high above them, its voice harsh against the normal variety of chirping they heard. The trail curved downward, and through a break in the trees, a small building could be seen, it was disheveled and half-swallowed by decay.

Blair slowed. "Is that where we're going?"

Damien's eyes were settled on the building as he nodded and continued forward.

The usual gravel turned into soft dirt underneath their feet. The more they approached the building, the more small statues appeared in the land around it, along with large crosses and boxes that were protruding from the ground.

As Blair passed each one, she noticed names etched on them, along with weathered flowers laying next to them.

A graveyard.

It was as if the realization made her more aware of where she stepped. Applying pressure to only the tips of her toes, she dodged around patches of disturbed ground.

When they were a few feet from their destination, the structure became clear. Small and white, the building was barely standing. The roof was caved in, with small beams of exposed wood running across the top and some shingles still attached in random places. Most of the exterior paint was chipped away or weatherworn, bearing slats of wood underneath. The outside walls were covered in vines that grew up and over the foundation. Remnants of a stained-glass window adorned the front.

As they stepped inside, they were met with the same haphazard interior. The inside walls were dreary, with many holes decorating them. The wallpaper was torn in most places and where it remained, the color was stained. Broken wood was scattered, covering most of the inside. Besides that, the only recognizable things were a few pews lined in the middle.

A church.

Blair stopped and surveyed the rest of the room, following the vines that branched from the dark corners. Eventually, her eyes landed on a figure that hid in the farthest one.

From what she could make out, it was a tall, thin figure wearing a large, forest-green, stained cloak. The physique hinted that of a man, but Blair froze as she tried to strain her eyes.

Damien noticed her right away and moved his gaze to where she was focused. The shadows of the corner hid the man well, and for most people, he would have stayed out of sight.

Stepping in front of her, Damien took her hand and led them toward the stranger.

"You're late," the man said as they approached, a thick Scottish accent coating his words.

Stepping out of the shadows, Blair's eyes immediately landed on the scars that covered his face. One eye was dark, so brown, that it was almost black. The other swirled a milky blue, like he had sustained an injury or was perhaps blind in that eye.

On the same side of that eye, his skin was puckered and scarred, from his chin to his hairline. Other than that affected area, his skin was light, and his dark brown hair was secured in a small bun on the top of his head.

He eyed Blair up and down before his gaze landed on Damien who walked up and shook the man's hand. "The expected time wasn't exactly clear. Do you have it?"

Grei smirked slightly, half of his scarred mouth failing to move. He pulled a folded sheet of parchment from his coat, plain and unsealed.

"Straight to it, then." he almost laughed, handing the paper to Damien, "Six names, all real ones. Not the call signs they feed the lower ranks."

Damien moved the cream-colored sheet to the light and opened it just enough to see the contents.

Blair tensed, fighting the urge to crane her neck and read over his shoulder.

Damien's eyes wandered over the page as he began to read out loud, "Aenar Vos, Lira Vossin, Nova Scott, Kellen Smith…" He paused and looked up at the man in front of him. "All of these still active Hunters?"

Grei nodded, "Not just active. These are the assigned leaders and their stations. Mostly Enforcers but some Phantoms. Take them out and the rest will scatter."

He fumbled his hand into the pocket of his cloak and produced a cigarette and a match. He lit it, the spark illuminating the eye that shimmered like glass.

Damien folded the paper and put it into his back pocket, "When was it last updated?"

Grei took a deep inhale and let out a breath of smoke, "In the last week."

He inhaled again, the end of the cigarette blaring red against the darkness around him. "Their location isn't an exact pinpoint, but the town is accurate." He took another long inhale and then opened his palm up, creating a spiral of shadow that swallowed the cigarette. "You want to end this? You wipe out the names on that page."

Damien nodded at him, "Feel like taking them down with me?"

The swirling shadow in Grei's hand dissipated, and he shook his head, his thick, unique voice laced with a tone of sadness as he looked up at Damien. "I'm too old for that now. I'd hinder you more than I'd help. They're strong. Don't hesitate."

Footsteps echoed faintly outside, the crunching of leaves loud in the space around them.

Damien and Blair followed the sound, looking out past the door.

"Expecting company?" Blair whispered.

Grei followed her sight and looked outside too, shrugging. "Possibly, or it could just be the ghosts." He then turned away to leave, talking over his shoulder as he disappeared through the open door, "This place is full of them."

Blair took a quiet breath and looked over at Damien, "We came here for a kill list?"

Damien tightened his grip on her hand and led her out of the church, careful to step around the vines and broken debris. "No. It's a blueprint on how we tear down the Hunters," he answered emotionlessly.

The sun hit them both as they stepped out of the hazardous church and scanned their surroundings to try and find the source of the sound. They stood there for a minute, watching and waiting.

With no one in sight, Blair turned to find Damien taking the paper back out and turning it over in his hands.

Walking up to him, she saw that it wasn't so much a list but a map of Opelysk with large X's marked over certain towns, a name scribbled beside each one.

As he refolded it and placed it in his back pocket, a rustle of leaves once again filled their ears from the opposite side of the building.

Damien brought his finger up to his mouth, motioning Blair to stay silent. Her eyes flared in panic as the sound grew louder. She huddled closer to Damien, as he walked them backwards, under a large willow tree behind them. The branches around them creating a pocket of darkness to hide in.

Blair felt a pulse at her feet, and as she looked down, she noticed a veil of shadows rising from the ground.

As it grew and formed a bubble around them, they were cast into an even darker shadow.

"Everything is fine," Damien whispered into her hair, soothing her nerves. Her back was pressed to his chest, and his arms were wrapped tight around her. "Just breathe, I got you." He nuzzled into her, and her body relaxed.

The response was short-lived as a figure moved from behind the building.

Blair immediately registered that it was *not* Grei.

This stranger was taller and thicker in build, with a black cloak hiding his body and face. No skin showed, just a variety of buckles and leather. Blair searched over his body for any kind of emblem, but there was nothing besides a black leather fabric.

Damien's grip tightened on Blair as he continued to stare at the stranger who examined the building they were just in. Glancing around, his head swiveled but his hood stayed covering his face, giving no insight to who he was.

Both Blair and Damien tensed when his head turned in their direction, and he took a step toward the trees.

Damien's shadows retaliated in response, growing thicker into a black marble barrier.

The stranger suddenly stopped and paused, looking into the distance. Turning his head first, his body soon followed, and he slowly moved in another direction, away from the trees and away from them.

Blair didn't fully breathe until he was completely out of sight. Even Damien waited an extra few minutes before he released his shadows and stepped out from under the willow trees.

They walked slowly and carefully away from the church, their heads impulsively glancing around at any slight sound. Once there was enough space between them and the potential threat, Blair broke the tension that had settled around them.

"Do you think I can have another 5 questions?" she asked, her hopeful voice bright against the tension.

Damien grunted in response as he pushed a large branch out of his face and held it for Blair to walk under

She took that as a yes and thought of her first one. "What was up with his eye and the burns?"

Damien stopped and eyed the area around them, skimming over the small creek flowing next to them and the land that was covered in fallen tree limbs and medium-sized boulders. He motioned for Blair to sit on one as he took out their canteens and walked toward the creek.

"I told you already, he was punished for helping us. The eye was an extension of his ability, it used to swirl with shadows." The first canteen filled rather quickly and Damien twisted the cap on, moving the next one into the stream.

"Oh." Blair's voice was light, as if in deep thought. "His list? Can we trust it?" Blair watched as Damien contemplated this question.

"There's always a risk with everything, but I trust him."

Blair nodded at that and watched Damien cap the second bottle and walk back to her, sitting next to her on the rock.

"This is it then? This is how we take the Hunters down?" she asked, holding her hand out for water.

Damien nodded, opening the canteen for her.

"And how exactly are we going to do that?" she said, after drinking almost half the water.

Damien's shoulders tightened at this question, and he stared into the woods around them. "Well, we have locations. Now we just have to find them. If we can do that, we can figure out a way to eliminate them."

Blair sucked her top teeth, a million thoughts whirling in her mind. "Last question, are you always this broody?" She smiled at him then and nudged his shoulder.

He responded with a tight smile, "No. This is me trying to figure out a plan and a way to keep you safe at the same time." he replied, nudging her back.

"What if I also have a plan?" Blair asked, her head moving to one side.

24

"You want me to do *what*?" Damien stared at Blair with his eyebrows slightly raised.

There was a moment of silence as the wind rustled, blowing the discarded branches and loose flowers across the ground. The wind picked up again, tousling Blair's hair as she smiled, rolling her eyes and placing her hands on her hips."I want you to control them." She repeated again.

"It doesn't work like that." He sighed, lowering his eyebrows, and leaning against a tree.

Blair watched as he clearly tried to end the conversation but she *knew* he had to try. They were going to infiltrate the Hunters, but to do that, Damien would need practice with his shadows.

She blinked a few times, refocusing on the man in front of her, and looked at him thoughtfully, shrugging. "I get it, it's because you're scared."

His relaxed tone took on an edge, "that's not it."

A smile tugged the corner of Blair's mouth as she slid off the boulder she was sitting on and slowly walked up to him, stopping about a foot away. Taking a deep breath in, she laid her hands on his chest. "You control them around me," she said, walking her fingers up his neck and positioning her hands along his jaw. "I think you're just wound too tight. You bottle things up and I think it buries your ability to control them."

She stepped away again, as she reached down to her thigh and pulled out her dagger. She looked at it for a second before slowly turning it back and forth in her hand.

Damien's eyes narrowed in caution and he stood straight; his brows dipping in worry as he watched her. "Whatever you're thinking, don't."

Blair didn't answer but instead moved her eyes to the dagger. In one swift motion, she sliced it across her palm and blood immediately started to descend to the ground.

Horrified, Damien stepped up to her, his shadows cascading down his arms and wrapping around her palm. "What the hell are you doing Blair?!"

She looked at him and shrugged like she had done nothing wrong. "Testing out a suspicion." She looked down at the shadows that now cocooned her hand and slowly dragged her eyes back up to meet his. "How do you feel?" she asked, tilting her head to the side slightly.

"I feel like you are *crazy* wrapped in *chaos*," he answered, not taking his eyes off the shadows that had wrapped around her.

"Okay but do you feel anything? Adrenaline maybe? I'm willing to bet that's how you control them," Blair said, meeting his eyes.

Damien didn't speak for a few moments, his blue eyes filled with swirling thoughts. He opened his mouth just to close it a moment later as he looked back down.

Blair fought to take her hand back, but when he didn't budge, she lowered her voice and sheathed her dagger with her left hand, resting her now empty hand on his arm. "You've been taught your whole life that your shadows are bad, but there is so much good, in them and in *you*. It's time that you start seeing that too."

A silence fell as Damien's eyes softened. His breathing grew slightly heavier as he closed his eyes for a brief moment and let go of Blair, his shadows still circling her palm.

The rest of his shadows started to flicker beneath him, rippling, stretching, and moving toward Blair's hurt hand. They traveled past her hand and up her arm. She smiled at them, welcoming the soft touch as they writhed above her skin. They had just made it to her elbow, before Damien opened his eyes and realized how far they had went. His blue eyes widened as he watched them continue to climb her arm, heading towards her shoulder.

His eyes filled with concern, and he broke the connection as they grew, pulling his hand away and forcing the shadows to disconnect with it.

"Not with you. We don't ever use *you*," he said breathlessly, a look of panic buried in his eyes.

"Okay," Blair answered, watching his anxiety swell, "we'll find another way."

Damien nodded, picking up their bags and walking toward the path that led out of the clearing.

She watched him, trying to think of different ways she could help him. She flexed her hand and looked down, intending to run her finger along the fresh cut, but instead, she instantly froze at what she saw.

As she opened her hand, her breath caught at the smooth skin.

The cut was *healed*.

25

It took only a few minutes to catch up with Damien, his long legs making short work of the path they followed. As soon as she was behind him, she fell in step with him, along with the comfortable silence he carried. As they made their way along a hill, an apology hung on her lips. She hadn't meant to upset him and just as she opened up her mouth to explain further, Damien silenced her.

Grabbing her shoulders, he pushed her backwards until she was up against a tree. She went to yell, but he slid his hand over her mouth as his eyes darted around them.

Her body stilled, sensing danger.

To the left of them, a hooded figure stepped out from behind a trunk. Damien's shadows shot out in defense, creating black blades that protruded around them like a wall.

The person in front of them was the same one from the church.

Damien removed his hand from Blair's mouth and stepped in front of her instead.

Watching them closely, the stranger took a step toward them. He then stopped, and slowly put his hands up in submission, suggesting he wasn't there to hurt them. Although it was a good attempt, it did nothing to cut the thick tension rising between them. His thick black cloak, only added to the pressure, bathing his face in darkness,

Damien's eyes narrowed in on the stranger as his voice laced with authority. "What do you want?"

Blair stepped closer into Damien and peaked her head around him, looking up into his blue eyes.

The stranger paused, lowering his arms. After a few quiet moments, he took another step closer to them.

"Leave," Damien commanded, his shadows turning into jagged spikes. A moment of silence hung between them, and then Damien's shadows struck, attacking the stranger who put his arm up in defense. The shadows instantly cut into the black fabric and the muscle of his arm.

The shadows pulled back, ready to hit again when Blair stepped around Damien. "Stop!" she yelled, her eyes wide.

She wasn't sure if it was because she had noticed shadows similar to Damiens or if it was because she remembered what it was like to be shredded by the shadows but Blair raised her hand to stop it.

Damien caught her arm, trying to stop her but she just yanked it away and ignored his disgruntled sound.

Following her intuition, she took another step toward the stranger who had to attack back. Just as she lifted her foot to take another step, Damien's shadows reached across the ground and wrapped around her ankles, halting her. She looked down and then back up at the stranger who still had not moved.

"Take your hood off," Blair said, her voice strong and unwavering.

Damien stiffened behind her, a low growl in his throat, but it died down the second the stranger obeyed.

A man, around the same age as Damien, stared back. With his hood down, his features were stark. Short blonde hair shaved close on the sides with green eyes that peered at them with curiosity. An upside-down triangle cut through his left eye, connecting to black swirls that traveled down his cheek. A mischievous smile broke across his face as he eyed Damien.

Blair spoke first, drawing the man's attention. "You have shadows," she said definitively as he moved his gaze to her. With these words, Damien stepped up beside her shoulder. Blair continued to study the strange man carefully, waiting for his answer.

"I'm Blake. No last name, it's too complicated to spell. You can call me 'Your new best friend,'" the man said, touching two fingers on his head and bowing slightly. A grin covered his face as he straightened back up. "And you two must be the charming fugitives the Hunters are so pissed about. I wondered what you guys would look like. Gotta say, not what I was expecting." He said with his eyebrows raised.

Damien answered him with a slight tone of disbelief, "You were looking for us?"

Blake shrugged as he ripped a piece of fabric off the bottom of his tunic and used it to wrap his arm, staunching the bleeding. "Shadow currents are strange around this place. I'm just following the ripples. Somehow that led me to you."

This time, it was Blair who answered, "You can feel the shadows? That's your ability?"

Blake looked at her with a mock look of surprise, "How do you know our trade secrets?" and then he winked as a shadow grew above his palm and traveled up his arm, blending into the black fabric he was wearing. "Feel them, blend into them, tickle them when I'm bored. Not as flashy as your broody friend there, but I make it work."

Damien's glare sharpened, but he still didn't speak. His shadow lay low, coiling slowly around him and Blair, as she smirked at the stranger's comment.

She eyed him cautiously, "And the triangle around the eye, what is that for?"

Blake turned his back on them and sat on a nearby trunk, pulling his bag off and placing it next to him on the ground. "I tell most people it's a bad tattoo or that I lost a bet, but" he hiked one leg up on the trunk, leaning against his knee as he pointed to his eye, "I was born with it, perks of being Shadowborn."

At those words, Damien stiffened.

Blake then pointed at Damien, "Does he talk, or is the whole "walking storm cloud" thing part of his personality package?" he asked, raising his eyebrows in Blair's direction.

Blair tried to fight another smirk as Damien clenched his jaw, quickly looking at Blair before settling his gaze back on Blake,"He talks when strangers stop acting like they're friends."

Blake's eyebrows shot up as he let out a chuckle, holding his hands up in submission for the second time. "Noted. No friendship. Does that mean we can't compare dick sizes yet?"

In response, Damien took an angry step forward.

Blair put one hand out to stop him as she tried to stifle a chuckle, surprising even herself. "Great. Somehow I got stuck with broody here first," she motioned to Damien with her thumb, and then moved back to Blake, "And now what? Shadows with sarcasm?"

Blake laughed and stretched out his arms, completing small arm circles. "Sarcasm *and* good intel. I might have maybe overheard the list of names you got back at the church. What if I told you I could find out exactly where some of your friends are hiding?"

That piece of information caught both Blair's and Damien's attention, as they glanced at each other.

Damien then returned his gaze to Blake, narrowing his eyes to show suspicion. "Why would you tell us that?"

Blake stood, locking his hands behind his back and bending, stretching again."Because I hate Hunters and I'm bored, so I figured I'd show you where they are."

Blair looked at Damien, who was opening his mouth to speak. "Then walk with us but stay in front." Blair yelled at the same time Damien spat, "The hell you are."

251

Blake rested his hands on his hips and looked back and forth between Blair and Damien."So, what are you gonna do? Rock, paper, scissors? Winner gets me?" His tone was sarcastic, but a small bit of exhaustion lingered in his eyes.

When no one moved, Damien glared at Blair and stepped in front of her toward Blake. His face shifted as he analyzed the marking on Blake. "You say you were born with that?" Damien asked, eyeing the triangle on his face.

"Yup, sure did." replied Blake, tracing his finger along the shape.

Ultimately accepting him, Damien grunted, motioning with his hand for Blake to lead the way.

He smiled as he turned to Damien. "I knew I liked you, Mr-?"

Damien remained silent as they began walking and Blair let out a loud laugh at the tension unfolding between them. "He's Damien, and I'm Blair."

Damien stopped and looked at her, his eyes fueling with anger. She stopped as well and threw her hands up, shrugging. "What?! At least let us die with our real names."

Blake stopped in front of them and turned as Damien demanded his attention."Let's start on the right foot here. Her name is 'Don't fucking *think* about it.'"

Blair punched him in the shoulder as she walked past him, rolling her eyes.

Blake watched them both, his smile lighting up his eyes. "Oh yeah, this is going to be fun!"

26

The sky was painted in hues of orange and red, fading fast as the sun dipped beyond the horizon. A wind whispered through the mountains around them, and Blair's boots crunched softly against the ground as she followed the two men in front of her. A thick aura of apprehension lingered between them and she often made internal guesses at which moment they would turn and tackle each other. She was willing to bet it would only be a matter of time before they were dueling to see who would come out victorious, but Damien proved her wrong, remaining silent as he warily followed the stranger.

"This is the place," Blake said, voice low but steady as they approached a building.

Damien moved to Blair's side, his gaze sweeping the abandoned city. A black mist began to swirl in his eyes, the telltale sign that his shadows were waiting to be released. Only a couple feet away in front of them, Blake lingered in silence, a half-smile twitching at the edge of his lips.

"And you're *sure* one of them is here?" Damien asked, casting a sideways glance at Blake and then towards Blair.

Blake nodded. "At least one of them is. My bet is that this is the hideout for the North County. I'm pretty sure Nova leads them and she's on your list. There's a second one that has been in and out recently, but I don't sense them now."

Damien's jaw clenched as he eyes Blake and his carefree presence. "And how do you know that?"

Blake shrugged and moved his finger in a circle, a small shadow trailing it. "Their shadows."

The trio moved toward the entrance, a building that split into different corridors. Blake stopped at the entrance and ran his fingers over a sigil hidden deep within the brick. "This is definitely it."

Blake looked at the door and then back to them. "We won't know for sure how many are here, until we go in. It depends on who's out on patrol. I say the best plan is that Blair stays in the middle; she can even hold my hand if she gets scared." Blake said, winking at Blair.

Damien grabbed her hand and pulled her close, "She stays behind *me*." Blair stared at him for a second as Blake shrugged and turned back toward the door.

The tension in Damien only grew as they entered. Inside the corridors, the air turned colder. The only lights were small flickers from lanterns that lined the hallway.

Silence pressed in on them, no sounds filled the air around them besides their own steps. The only thing there, the only thing around them, were shadows.

This place seemed to be made for them, wielders of the dark.

They crept forward and Damien's shadow began to stir, rising like smoke. It coiled first around Blair and then moved to his feet. Another one slithered along his arm as he shaped it into a curved blade, black and whispering with dark energy.

As they continued a few paces, Blake stopped.

Damien let out a frustrated grunt as a flicker from the lights revealed that Blake was gone.

Not because he *walked* away.

And not because he *moved* behind a wall.

One blink, and he was gone, swallowed whole by the shadow beneath his feet as he stepped into it.

Blair didn't even flinch at the realization, but Damien's eyes filled with irritation at the absence. "He can hide in the shadows," Damien muttered, his voice barely loud enough for her to hear, "Or at least move between them."

"That's gotta be his ability," Blair replied as quietly as she could, scanning the corridor.

"Mhmm," Damien said back, barely audible.

From the darkness ahead, a whisper stirred and the shadows around them convulsed.

And then, they were no longer alone.

The first Hunter launched from the wall like a beast, an enforcer that was a blur of tendrils and smoke. Damien reacted instantly, a shadow-scythe arced upward, cleaving the figure in two. A second figure lunged from behind, but Damien was faster, a burst of shadow energy knocking the enemy across the corridor like a rag doll.

But then *more* came.

At first it was only three, but then four, and then five Hunters poured from the halls. Each one had a blade out, eyes glinting in the flickering light.

Damien dropped low, spreading his arms. His shadow exploded outward like a living storm, branching into sharp tendrils that snapped and lashed at their enemies. One caught a Hunter's leg and yanked, slamming them into the ceiling. Another morphed into a hammer, which Damien swung into a charging enemy's chest, sending them flying. "Now would be a good time to come out Blake." Damien barked.

Blair inhaled sharply as she tried to stay as close to the wall as she could, holding her dagger. Although she wanted to attempt to help, she was scared she would do more harm than anything else.

Suddenly, Blake emerged from the wall itself, stepping out of the shadow like it was water. His eyes shimmered pitch black, and his body wreathed in wisps of darkness. He moved like a ghost, striking and then vanishing again. He reappeared behind another Hunter, dragging a knife across their throat. Blair watched as he used his ability to move freely in the space around them.

As the last of the enemy fell, the corridor trembled and a low hum filled the air.

"Nova's close," Blake whispered.

Damien's lip pulled up in a snarled command. "We end this, *now*."

The trio burst through the reinforced door at the end of the hall and came face-to-face with her.

Nova stood in a circle of flickering sigils, her body armored in dark scales. Her hair flowed like black fire, a dark void that met Damien's with quiet contempt. Nova raised her hand slowly, and then the room erupted.

Walls peeled away into shadows that lashed like serpents. Damien dove forward, his shadow transforming into a broad shield that absorbed a blast of dark energy. Blake disappeared mid-sprint, reappearing behind Nova, but she struck first, spinning and cutting him across the chest with a blade of pure shadow

Blake cried out and vanished into the floor again.

Damien growled, shaping his shadow into twin axes and throwing them. Nova dodged one and deflected the other, but Damien moved faster, hitting her with a flurry of shadow-imbued strikes.

Nova's shrill voice echoed around them as her body absorbed the attack, "Two little shadow wielders? Ah, but what about *this* one?"

Then, Nova turned her power on *Blair*.

Shadows burst from the floor, wrapping around her limbs and crushing her to the ground. She fought back with every ounce of control, but she had no strength compared to what she was fighting against.

Just as she began to scream, Blake reappeared.

From the ceiling, he dropped like an arrow, driving his own shadow through Nova's shoulder. She screamed, her hold on Blair snapping.

She fell to her knees, gasping.

Blake stood over Nova, his body flickering between solid and smoke as he taunted her with an empty smile. His shadows coiled together and then spread, waiting for her to attack.

With her eyes on Blake, Nova didn't notice Damien come up from behind her until it was too late. A sharp cry pierced the air as her chest was impaled with a shadowed sword.

Nova collapsed, the darkness ebbing away from her form as silence fell.

Damien pulled Blair to her feet and held her close to his chest. With a staggered breath, she looked up at Blake.

"Thank you for that."

Damien nodded, looking past Blair to Blake who was watching them. Blood streaked his arm and his chest, but there was no denying it.

He *could* have left Blair to die.

Could have run.

But he hadn't.

"So, you hide and move within the shadows?" Damien asked, eyeing Blake." Any other surprises?"

Blake offered a proud smile in return, "I can also sense them."

Damien nodded in response, as if he had already guessed that. "Feel like taking some more down with us?"

Blake's face lit up at the invitation. "Damn right I do,"

They turned together as a pulse of shadow emanated from Nova's form. A small imbuement mark on the back of her hand illuminated and cracked, sending strands of faintly growing light up her arm and throughout her body. The lights expanded, breaking the skin around them and quickly causing Nova's body to flake and vanish into dust.

Blair's eyes widened, and her mouth dropped open. "What the fuck was that?"

Taking a step back, her body bumped into Damien, who brought his hands up to soothe her. "Remember how I said Enforcers burn from the inside? People who have shadows imbued into them can become unstable from the very beginning. Those with strong wills can live with them for some time, but once they are killed, the shadows release, causing this. A brand like *that* means you're a Phantom. Being a Phantom means you're a ticking time bomb." Damien explained, squeezing her arm in comfort.

"Th-this is what will eventually happen to you?" she asked, fear coating her words.

"No. Unfortunately, we were blessed with being born like *this*. That's gotta be one of the best perks, we don't have internal dynamite inside of us." Blake responds.

"I never told you *I* was a Shadowborn." Damien declared, taking a step in front of Blair in a defensive position.

Blake leaned around him, making eye contact with Blair, "Is he always so fucking *paranoid*?" Scoffing back at Damien, he continued. "I already told you I can sense the shadows. That means I can tell the difference between your strength, that of a real Shadowborn, and a Hunter. Don't get your panties in a bunch."

Damien's stance slightly relaxed, his eyes squinting in caution. "I don't like you."

Blake laughed in response, "Love you too, bud."

Blair took a deep breath as her eyes darted between the two men.

"Good. All it took was me almost dying to get you two to get along."

27

Blair hoisted the rucksack over her shoulder. They had managed to find food rations from the base they had infiltrated. Although it was a light load, it didn't help her sore body.

"Well," she exhaled, "It looks like we have food for the next few days."

"I don't know," Blake said, squinting dramatically toward the sack as he fiddled with the makeshift tourniquet around his chest. "From what we found there, I think I'd rather eat dirt."

Damien adjusted his own pack as he scanned the tree line ahead. "That can be arranged." he said, addressing Blake.

He then turned his attention back to the land in front of him. The path to their next location was narrow and uneven, but after Nova's hideout and its suffocating silence, this environment felt almost like mercy.

They walked for a while, everything quiet except for the sound of boots on packed dirt and the occasional metallic clink of canned food in Blair's bag.

A few minutes in and the silence was broken, filled with a soft hum.

Blair glanced at Blake, who was in the middle of a tuneless melody, pretending a twig was a conductor's baton. "Respectfully, why are you like this?" she asked, her eyebrows raised.

Blake's eyes widened. "Awh! Are you trying to get to know me? Could you at least wait until I'm sun-drunk and full of canned beans?"

She shook her head at him. "I'm actually serious. I watched you fight earlier. How do you go from a skilled assassin to an energetic five-year-old?"

"First of all," he said, his hand over his mouth like he was offended. "There are *many* layers to this handsome man lasagna." He said as he ran his hands from his head to his feet.

She gave him an uninterested look, and Damien snorted, herding them through a thick patch of brush.

Blake then sighed, letting the sarcasm drain a little from his voice. "Second of all, I came from a camp, probably just like the one our friend Damien was stuck in. North of the Divide. You know, beautiful skies, endless torture, Enforcers trying to pound your face in. Real trophy-worthy stuff."

Blair slowed her steps a little. "So, how are you so happy?"

Blake gave a mock bow. "Well, when you're raised to be a child soldier by day and a potential killer by night, you have to find *some* humor in the darkness, or it'll eat you alive." he shrugged nonchalantly.

Damien glanced over his shoulder, making eye contact with Blake, but said nothing as he continued to cut through the brush around them.

Blake kept talking, his tone still light, "I grew up fighting against my friends, so we would crack jokes to lighten the mood. I guess it became part of my personality."

Blair's brow furrowed as she mentally compared the differences between him and Damien. Two Shadowborn men who had the same childhood fates. "How did you get out?"

He gave a dry laugh. "Turns out my personality may have been too much. I'm all about free will and having a soul. Pretty sure they frown on both."

Blair opened her mouth, but he kept going. "They wanted machines, not people. And I, *shockingly*, didn't want to follow orders. I wanted to be an actual person. Then I figured out that I could travel through shadows, which they were not expecting."

She didn't reply at first. Just watched him as if trying to figure out which part was a joke and which part wasn't.

Blake caught her look and smirked. "Don't go giving me your tragic eyes, Blair. I'm emotionally drained but not broken."

"You could've fooled me," Damien muttered under his breath.

"Look who speaks," Blake shot back. "I was wondering if your voice box *actually* worked or if you had traded it for another one of those brooding stares you love so much."

Damien didn't respond, but the faintest smile tugged at the corner of his mouth.

Blair shook her head and kept walking. "It's interesting to know that you use humor to cope."

Blake let out a mock gasp at her assumption. "I cope by using my charm and devilish good looks. There's a difference, thank you very much."

But there was something quieter in his steps after that. Something heavier in the way he adjusted his bag like she had seen through him, and he wasn't comfortable being vulnerable.

After that, they walked in silence for a while, the wind picking up and threading through the trees, a slight chill beginning to form.

Eventually, Blair glanced back at him. "I'm guessing eliminating the Hunters would benefit you too, then? Whether it's a personal vendetta or whatever else, thank you for helping us. Well, helping Damien. I can't do much for the team."

"Not true, you're pretty to look at." Blake replied, blowing her a kiss.

Within the next second, Damien had turned and punched him in the stomach, his hand wrapped in a glove of shadow for extra power. "I told you already, don't fucking think about it." Damien snarled.

Blake immediately bent over, wheezing and holding his stomach. As he knelt, Damien grabbed the back of his neck and pushed him down.

"Okay. okay!" he responded in short breaths, trying to suck in as much air as he could. "I get it. O-off limits."

Damien released his hold, and Blake dropped, inhaling rapidly as he hit the ground. Blair huffed at the childish behavior and turned sharply, leading them down a small path to a medium-sized patch of grass. Damien followed her, with Blake catching up shortly after.

Coming up to a tree, Damien sat on the ground next to it. Blair followed next, sitting to his right, and Blake watched farther back, rubbing the back of his neck as he approached.

Damien moved swiftly, taking out the piece of paper that had been secured firmly in his pocket. He laid down the map of Opelysk and pointed to an area just outside of Togar. He then moved his fingers to the other surrounding areas showcasing the Xs where the leaders would be.

Blake stepped up next to him then, and followed Damien's hands as he pointed to Togar, the closest area that contained an X.

As Damien lifted his finger off the map, Blake brought his hand up to his chin, stroking it with one finger. "I think something's off." Blake brought his finger to an area labeled Kaythorn Pines and let his finger hover over an X there before moving it to the city of Keithston, "They joined together here."

Damien didn't move as he double-checked the names and locations. "How *sure* are you about that?"

Blake made a small sound like Damien's question had been a dumb one. "Pretty sure. Call it a gut feeling."

"Good, hopefully I won't have to hunt you down in the afterlife because you got us killed." Damien replied, rolling up the map and standing up.

"Is that all it takes for you to joke with me? I just need to be beat up a little bit?! That means we can definitely have dick-measuring contests soon." Blake excitedly yelled as he fist-pumped the air next to Damien.

Blair rose up last, pushing her shoulder into Blake and knocking him off balance. "Could it be a trap?" she asked, shifting her pack off her back and setting it down on a broken tree next to her.

"A trap or a coincidence? Who wants to bet money that it's the first one?" Blake asked as he looked up at Blair and waggled his eyebrows, "...we could bet clothes. Whoever loses takes theirs off."

Just like before, Damien attacked. A wall of black shadows moved toward Blake, who disappeared a fraction of a second before impact. He reappeared behind Blair and stepped around her, "Just checking if you were still awake!"

Damien rubbed his temples and looked at Blair, "I'm going to kill him."

Blair laughed out loud as she stepped up to Damien and placed her hands on his shoulders, rubbing the tension from his neck. He exhaled loudly and closed his eyes.

Blair looked over at Blake, "Why don't you find somewhere for us to set up camp for the night?"

His mouth popped open in surprise. "I don't know anything about-" he started to say but Blair held up her hand. "I don't want to hear it. Go find somewhere before I let Damien have you," she said with a smile.

He snapped his mouth shut and looked at Damien. Turning around and stomping away, his voice faded as muttered broken words made their way back to Blair and Damien. The phrases "...my neck still hurts..." and "I definitely have the bigger dick" echoed off the trees around them.

Blair moved in front of Damien, kissing his lips lightly. "I think we should keep him." She said with a wink. "Now I understand why you like that face I make so much.

Damien smiled at her and wrapped his arms around her, pulling her into his lap." That's different. Besides, I can barely deal with you, Feisty. I don't know if I'll survive two." He said, lowering his lips to hers.

"You'll just have to find a way to handle it." she replied with a sweet tone, batting her eyelashes.

"I'll handle *something*, alright." he murmured as their lips touched. She wrapped her arms around his neck and pushed into him, his torso barely moving as he squeezed her tighter, nestling his hands in her hair. The kiss became more passionate as they rocked back and forth, consuming each other and the raw emotions that had come with the last few days.

A twig snapping caught Blair's attention, and she pulled away, licking her puffy lips and eyeing Blake as he dropped a variety of sticks and wood. His jaw was open in surprise. "Of *course* you like the tall, dark, and broody ones."

She giggled, nuzzling Damien's nose with her own. "I sure do. Turns out the broody ones are also the ones who have anger issues. I would *hate* for you to be a victim of that." she said cloyingly.

Blake rolled his shoulders in response and blew a raspberry in her direction. He then turned his attention to Damien. "I was thinking. I think we should take on the two closest ones. They have the strongest leaders. If we do that, bigger targets are gone."

Damien nodded, threading his fingers with Blair's. "I agree. We can make a plan in the morning." Damien said, pulling Blair behind him toward the open spot in the grass. "Oh, and Blake?" Damien said slowly as he passed, rearing up his fist and pulling it back. Blake tensed and blocked his face, squealing with dramatic effect. "Two for flinching." Damien laughed, punching him squarely in the shoulder twice, his muscles bulging from the force.

Blake winced as a small smile broke on his face.

Damien bent and quickly grabbed the sack that held the tent as his shadows slowly unfurled. Working together to stretch the fabric and anchor the poles into the ground, Blair watched as the job was done within a couple minutes. She gathered the wood Blake had found and created a fire.

Soon, flickering shapes began to dance across the stretched fabric behind them.

Blair crouched near the fire pit, stirring a battered pot of beans suspended above the flames. It wasn't much of a dinner, but it was the substance their bodies needed. The only other items retrieved were different cans of vegetables and dehydrated meat.

As dinner warmed fully, Blake finished hammering down the last stake for his tent, dusted off his hands, and dropped beside Damien on a fallen log near the fire. "You know," Blake said, glancing toward the forest, "it's been a while since I sat around a fire without someone trying to kill me."

Damien snorted. "There's still time."

Blair smiled, pulling the spoon out of the pot and tasting the beans. Damien watched her and gave a small smile as she lined up makeshift bowls. Ladling scoops of beans into each one, she methodically measured equal portions into the three dented metal containers.

"This is what we're eating?" Blake asked, raising an eyebrow. Blair gave him an annoyed look in response. "You're welcome to chew tree bark instead."

He grinned up at her. "Eh, No complaints here, really. It smells better than half the things I've eaten before."

They ate in silence for a few minutes, the sound of the fire and the occasional crack of a twig breaking the stillness. Then Blake leaned back and stretched out his legs, letting the heat warm his boots.

"So," he began, eyeing Damien, "*you've* got shadows," his eyes then shifted to Blair, "but you don't?"

Damien didn't respond, but Blair nodded, taking another bite of beans. Blake didn't seem bothered by their lack of enthusiasm. He took another bite as well, and then swallowed, continuing to talk through bites.

"As you saw, I can move through them," he swallowed, spooning another mouthful in, "it's like stepping through a door, and the distance can go pretty far. Although," he spooned more in, almost gagging at how big of a bite it was, "I've never tested how far I can go."

Blair looked down at her bowl, her dinner almost gone. "It almost seems like second nature for you."

Blake nodded. "I call it Shadowstepping." He paused, wiping his mouth with the back of his hand before continuing, "Feels like falling sideways. Cold, but fast. You learn not to puke after the first dozen times."

Blair watched him, her eyebrows raising in surprise. "And your other ability? You said you can sense others?"

"Yeah. Everyone who wields shadows carries a kind of hum," Blake explained, tapping his temple. "It's not sound, but I feel it like pressure in the air. I can't tell exactly where they are, but I get an internal warning if they are nearby. It's like my insides vibrate."

He turned his attention to Damien. "What can you do?"

Damien didn't look at him but finished his last few bites, only raising his eyes to meet Blair's. The fire popped, casting sudden sparks skyward. Blake waited, then looked at Blair.

She set down her tin with a small sigh. "He's not the bragging type," she said. "But I've seen him do things with shadows I didn't think were possible."

Blake leaned in, intrigued. "Like what?"

"Well," Blair said, holding up her fingers as if ticking off a list, " he can build things out of them, he can do barriers, he's even ripped the ground open."

Blake raised his brows but said nothing.

"My favorite thing he does is when he makes different objects," she continued. "Daggers, hammers, anything he might need. The first time I ever saw his shadows, they were being used to cover parts of his skin like gloves, protecting his hands from fire." She looked up in thought, recalling other moments she had witnessed, "I think he can do more, too." she murmured, squeezing her hand where a scar should have been. We just haven't tested other things out yet."

Blake stared at Damien, slack-jawed for a moment. "That's really something, and really not normal."

Blair blinked. "Excuse me?"

Damien finally looked up but didn't speak.

Blake sat forward, voice low but firm. "Every Shadowborn I've ever met, myself included, has one or two gifts. That's it. One specialization, maybe a side trick."

Blair frowned, looking at Damien, who had returned his eyes to the fire. "Damien's shadows seem different, even from yours. They react instinctively." Blair said defensively.

"That's exactly what I mean." Blake's eyes didn't leave Damien. "You're not supposed to be able to do that much. Barriers? Constructs? Splitting the ground? That's three or four talents minimum, and every one of those would take someone years to master on its own. But one person having that many, it's unheard of."

Damien was still, firelight flickering across his face.

Blake leaned back slowly, thoughtful now. "There are old stories about Shadowborn like that. People who weren't bound by the usual limits. They were the first of our kind."

Blair's voice dropped. "What does that have to do with him?"

"Well, he's definitely not normal, as far as our normal goes," Blake said, almost with awe. "Out of all the people I could have found, of course, I found you guys."

Damien didn't respond. He just sat, staring into the fire with his shoulders tight.. He looked up then, casting his eyes in Blair's direction.

Damien set his bowl down next to the fire. "Well, *he* is tired of people talking around him like he's invisible." He then turned to Blair. "Let's go to bed."

He stood, walking over to her and helping her up by her hand. Damien then turned and addressed Blake. "Do not wake us up unless you're dying or things are on fire." Damien said.

Blake eagerly straightened at that and brought his fingers to his forehead in salute. "Sir, yes sir!" he replied with a mocking voice.

Damien opened the tent flap and ushered Blair inside.

Questions flickered in Blair's eyes, and as she opened her mouth, Damien spoke over her. "I don't want to talk. I just want to feel your skin."

She nodded, feeling the uneasiness rolling off of him.

They laid down on the cold earth, with only a thick blanket separating them and the ground. Damien moved to his back, pulling Blair on his chest and breathing in her scent.

"I'm sorry if I shared too much. It wasn't my story to tell. I understand why you didn't want to tell me about Grei's," she said quietly, wrapping her arms around his torso.

"I know your heart was in the right place, but if the wrong people knew about me, it would end badly. So, maybe next time, let me at least give you a thumbs up or something," he replied, his hand roaming her back.

"Deal." she yawned.

Both closed their eyes for a brief second before falling asleep to the sounds of Blake muttering to himself outside of their tent.

28

The sun was rising, its light casting fractured shadows across the map that was once again in between the three of them. Blair crouched over it, her fingertip tracing the two x-marked locations like they might spring to life and bite her. "The next one is Keithston." Blair stated, tapping on the map.

Damien nodded where he sat across from her, one knee up, a hard line drawn across his brow. "If they learn of any sign of an attack, they'll be expecting a full assault."

"Good," Blake said, from where he was lying on his back, arms behind his head. "We'll disappoint them with our underwhelming numbers."

Blair ignored him. "If Blake is right and there's more than one, we don't need to fight all of them. We need to outthink them. Pick the right time and hit hard."

Damien nodded. "It worked last time."

Blair looked up at him, an idea sprouting. "What if we train as we travel? Anything to help us in fights? Speed drills. Endurance. Reflex skills. Shadow work. That way, we can be ready for anything we can come across."

"Why *endurance*?" Blake sighed, rolling to his side. "Can't I try to be the morally complex one who stays hot and mysterious but doesn't have to run laps?"

"You're already morally complex," Damien said dryly. "Now, be useful."

Blair looked between them, then added, "We'll rotate sparring, too. I want both of you to push each other. No holding back."

Blake raised a brow. "So, we beat each other senseless and call it progress. Love this plan."

"Harder to kill you if you're harder to hit," Damien said simply."And what about you, Blair?" Blake asked suddenly, his voice lighter than his eyes. "All this scheduling for us, but what happens when the shadows start swinging? Are you just gonna duck and hope for the best?"

Blair blinked at him. "I'm not helpless."

"Didn't say you were. But you're not a fighter, not like us, and these aren't petty thieves, they're trained killers." Blake relented.

Blair shifted so she could access her sheath. "I'll be fine, I have-" She went to pull out the dagger, but a shadow moved over her hand and stopped her, urging her to release it and move back into a sitting position. Her eyes glanced in Damien's direction as a look of confusion passed her face.

Damien straightened next to her, "She has me, and she won't be in the front line."

"I'm not saying she should be," Blake said, sitting up now,"but she shouldn't be a liability either and I don't think she has to be."

275

Blair's eyes lit up as an idea formed in her head, "What if I didn't have to be?"

"Meaning?" Both men said in unison, a cautious glare in Damien's eyes.

"Have you ever tried shadowstepping with more than one person?" Blair asked, a genuine smile spreading across her face. "What if you could take me with you? Through the shadows?"

"No," Damien said immediately, dismissing the idea before it even had a chance to become concrete.

Blair frowned, tearing her eyes from Blake's hopeful face and landing on Damien. "Why not?"

"Because I don't like it," Damien said, shrugging. "We don't know how it could affect your body."

"It's *my* body, and I want to learn," Blair interrupted, turning her attention back to Blake and sitting up straighter. "Besides, I won't be the one actively using the shadows. I'll just be tagging along." Her eyes then bounced between them, a sadness lurking in the connection. "You've both had training since you could walk and if there's something I can do now that can help me to survive this, I'm not going to turn away because it's risky."

Damien's jaw tightened. His shoulders coiled like he wanted to shield her with his entire frame. "I still don't like it."

"Well, You don't have to," she said softly. "But I do, and I hope you would respect that."

A tense silence hung between Damien and Blair as they held each other's gaze, both of them rooted in stubbornness.

Blake broke it with a sigh, leaning into Damien. "Look, big guy, I get the protective thing. Really. She's smarter than both of us combined, maybe more reckless, but still, they won't think twice."

Damien didn't answer.

Blake stood, brushing off his cloak, and gave Blair a nod. "I can try it. Take you in short jumps. This would be a controlled environment, allowing us to assess the risks as we proceed *before* getting to any of the dangerous places. Just enough to let you feel what it's like." He then looked over at Damien. "You can monitor her the whole time, oh fearless guardian."

After a long moment where his eyes never left Blair, Damien clenched his jaw, his voice firm as he spoke to her, "I told you I wouldn't take away any more of your free will. This is your choice. I won't fight you on it." His expression softened in the last few words. "With that being said, if it hurts or is uncomfortable in any way, we stop. I can find another way for you to help."

Blair met his gaze, her expression grateful as she nodded.

Blake grinned. "Look at us, compromising like one big, happy family."

Damien exhaled through his nose. "You talk too much."

Blake winked. "Just compensating for your brooding silence."

Damien sighed. "It's smartest to move at dawn. Travel as much as we can during the day and take timed breaks to train when the sun is the highest."

Blake scoffed at that, his reply laced with a thick layer of sarcasm, "You do know we want to be stronger, right? Training when there's barely any shadows sounds like a big fat no thank you to me."

Damien ignored his tone, yet again. "That's *exactly* why we do it in daylight. Shadows are weaker then, thinner and less willing to bend. If you can shape and command them at their weakest, you'll be twice as effective when night falls, and that's when we'll attack."

Blake opened his mouth, paused, and then actually looked impressed. "Huh. That's... not a bad point."

Damien continued, "The first bunker falls within six days. We should get plenty of practice before then."

"Sounds good to me," Blake said.

Blair looked up at him, eyes hard with purpose.

"They won't even know what hit them," she said with an encouraging smile.

29

The next morning began before the sun rose. Blake groaned his way out of his bedroll like a man personally offended by physical effort, while Damien stood already stretched by the fire, a silent wall of focus and frustration. Blair created a quick breakfast to fortify everyone before they began their journey.

Once nourished, they moved with the winding roads and sometimes hidden pathways. Their pace was steady, unyielding, and silent. The path they followed wound through the dense forest and then into grassy plains.

Overhead, the sun tracked them like a watchful eye, its heat intensifying with each hour as Damien led the way. Behind him, Blair matched his pace and Blake trailed just a few steps behind them both, muttering occasionally about sunburn, dust, and the tragic absence of snacks.

They didn't speak much as they traveled, not out of tension but because the road demanded their full attention. The three of them had agreed on a method: walk for four hours, train, rest, and repeat.

By the time the sun was almost halfway to its peak, they had passed the four-hour mark. They came to a cracked stone worn smooth by years of wind and weather.

Just beyond it, tucked between a small ridge and a line of boulders, was an extensive clearing perfect for the day's first training site.

"Here," Damien said, bringing his hand up to signal them. The others stopped beside him. The area was mostly flat and open, with enough stone and brush nearby to offer obstacles.

Blair dropped her bag and exhaled. She rolled her shoulders and stepped back, eyes already scanning the terrain. Blake followed suit, dropping his bag to the ground next to him. "Four hours down. Time to punch each other!"

Damien ignored him and moved into position on the flattened patch of dirt, raising a hand. His own shadow stretched long and jagged beneath him, coiling ever so slightly despite the noon sun. Blake mirrored him, shedding his cloak and stepping forward with a grin that was part challenge, part complaint.

Blair stayed back, settling onto a nearby rock. She pulled out a flask of water and drank slowly, eyes never leaving the makeshift ring where the two Shadowborn faced off.

It started simple. Damien and his shadow tendrils, whipping low and fast. Blake, constantly shifting as he popped in and out of shadow, trying to get the upper hand on Damien. The sunlight weakened their edges, making the dark shapes flicker, harder to control. Both boys strained, working in concentration as they pulled their shadows into different shapes and controlled them, each in a unique but similar way.

Blair could see the effort in their movements. The way Damien's jaw tightened as he forced a barrier into existence, a wall of darkness only half-formed before it wavered in the harsh light and shattered into strands. Blake ducked into a shadow, reappearing behind Damien.

Neither of them spoke. The space around them filled with low grunts as they deflected each other.

Damien's technique was precise and controlled. Every movement was deliberate, even under the most intense strain.

Blake was erratic but creative, using speed to make up for power and adapting in bursts. They moved in a dance of flickering shadows, forcing their abilities to obey even when the sun tried to burn the power out of them.

Eventually, Blake's breathing grew labored. Sweat shimmered on his forehead, and dust clung to their clothes. He eventually dropped to one knee, panting. "Can I wave my white flag now?" he wheezed.

Damien answered him by giving a slight nod and letting his shadow retract fully. They napped to his feet with a final flicker before going still.

Blair rose and walked over, handing each of them a canteen without a word, fighting down the pride she had for both of them. "Still think this method is a good idea?" she asked, nudging Blake.

He drank deeply, then held up a finger. "Yes, he's just aggressively unpleasant, a freaking monster," Pausing mid-sentence, he was still trying to catch his breath, "Does he ever get tired?"

A small laugh escaped her. "No, I've tried to tire him out on multiple occasions, but I have yet to win that battle." She responded with a wink.

"Oh. Ew." Blake said with a grimace as he disappeared into the shadow below him and shadowstepped away from the conversation.

They sat in the shade for half an hour, taking a rest as Blair jotted quick notes in a small leather-bound journal. She had decided that when she wasn't actively helping with training, her form of help would be tracking information to help them improve.

Today, she noticed Damien's formations, Blake's recovery speed, and even the light's effect on their control. She never commented on anything during their training, but she watched everything, writing down each of her thoughts.

Then, as the sun began its slow descent toward early afternoon, they stood again, packed up camp, and resumed their march. Four hours forward. Another site. Another battle. The last one was about power and fighting through the draining sun. This one was about control and precision.

Having an idea for both, Blair instructed Blake to come stand next to her on a big tree stump. With arms full of various items, such as rocks, pinecones, and sticks. Blair announced, "Okay, Damien, you are going to have to use your shadows to catch or smash these items. Do not let them touch the ground."

"And what do I get when none of them touch the ground?" Damien questioned.

"Me." Blair teased.

"But if even one touches the ground, you get *me*." Blake said with a smirk.

Damien's face paled, and he looked as though he was going to be sick. "I never know when you're joking or when you're actually serious." His expression lightened as he turned to Blair, "Let's get started."

They both took turns throwing them in the air. Starting with a rock, they slowly progressed to two items, and then by the end of it, it was three. Damien moved effortlessly, his shadows either slicing or grabbing each time something was thrown. After running out of all the items and him not missing one, Damien approached with a smug look on his face.

Blake, however, began to pout, stomping his foot as he jumped down from the stump.

"Not so fast, you're up next." Blair said, stopping Blake from slipping away.

"Uh. I can't do *that* with my shadows." Blake retorted, walking back towards the group.

"I have a different game for you. Go stand over there." Blair pointed. "You are going to have to be quick. Remember, the goal is speed and precision. We are going to throw one thing at a time, you need to shadowstep to that shadow and stop the item from landing. If we go too fast, just let us know. I'm not yet familiar with your abilities. This will help me practice my aim as well."

"Ooh, I like this game! What do I get when I win?" Blake said, wiggling his eyebrows.

"How about for every item you catch, I *won't* punch you in the dick." Damien threatened as he threw the first object.

Blake immediately shadowstepped to a nearby tree, catching the pinecone. "Don't tease me with a good time. I like it when daddy is rough." He disappeared again, as a stone came hurtling toward him and lodged into the tree behind him.

Holding her side in a fit of laughter, Blair looked at Damien's stone-cold face. "Okay, enough messing around," she managed to get out in between snorts. "Let's do this."

For the next fifteen minutes, they proceeded to toss various things in different directions for Blake to catch. At first, the movements were quick and well-executed, but toward the end, he began showing signs of fatigue. Fumbling on a tree branch, and then again on a ball of cloth, he held his hands up, motioning for them to stop. "I guess my endurance isn't what I thought it was." Blake gasped, breathing heavily.

Granting him time to recharge, they all agreed to rest a bit before continuing.

By day three, the routine was almost ritual. Breakfast. Hiking. Training. Today, they were focusing again on endurance.

"Alright," Blake yawned, running a hand through his mess of blonde hair. "Ready to make me cry again with your stoic superiority?"

Damien didn't even glance at him in response."Five laps. Then sparring."

"You forgot the part where I nearly die from exhaustion. It's rude to leave out how hard I try." Blake whined.

They ran through a narrow path skirting the forest, feet crunching on packed dirt and dew-slick grass. Damien ran with the efficient grace of someone who had been trained since birth. Blake, while less polished, had the grit of someone too stubborn to stay down.

After the laps, the training began in earnest.

They moved through forms, knives, hand-to-hand, shadow control. Each time that Blake's focus slipped or his jokes dragged too long, Damien punished him with a jab to the ribs, or a leg sweep that planted him flat on his back. Sometimes, Blair would keep score, cheering on one or the other to stir their energy.

"Okay, that was unfair," Blake wheezed after a particularly brutal fall. "You have a shadow advantage and a moral superiority complex. It's like fighting a rage-induced thunderstorm."

"Round two." Damien said, already resetting his stance and motioning for Blake to get off the ground.

Blake rolled to his feet and grinned. "At least buy me dinner first."

The most intense sessions they had tried were those involving reflex and emotional shadow work. These moments were when Damien had to trigger his shadows without thinking, without calling them.

Blake threw stones, slashed close to him with dulled blades, and whispered things Damien didn't expect. Most of the time, nothing happened, unless Blair was involved, that always initiated the shadows.

"What is it about Blair that makes your shadows react like that?" Blake muttered during one drill.

Damien's hands flared dark, a reflexive burst of shadow spearing up to deflect Blake's lunge. "Because," he said, breathing hard. "She's mine."

Blake didn't respond. He just nodded.

They could at least use that to their advantage.

On the fourth afternoon, the sun broke through the trees in a rare, golden streak. They set up by a shallow stretch of calm and clear river, just off the training site.

Blair had left early that morning after making breakfast, bound and determined to find somewhere to wash their clothes. "Try not to destroy each other while I'm gone," she had said, kissing Damien and winking at Blake.

Blake gave a two-finger salute. "Can't promise anything."

Training resumed shortly after. Kicks and dodges. Shadow strikes. Blake ducked low, then threw a palmful of dirt up, grinning like a devil. "Think fast!"

Damien blocked, grimacing. "You fight like a drunk raccoon."

"Only when I'm winning."

They kept at it until Blake until Blake bowed out, panting. Wiping the sweat from his brow, he staggered toward the riverbank to refill his flask. Just as he stepped through the brush, a movement made him pause. Looking up, he caught sight of a very naked Blair who dove beneath the surface with a quiet splash. Her bare skin gleamed as her back arched, the setting sun catching her tanned skin.

Blake froze.

"Damien's gonna kill me." he groaned under his breath, turning quickly back towards camp. As he took his first step, he sensed Damien's shadows moving at him

Jumping backward, Blake tried to explain himself. But Damien glanced past him, up the river and caught a glimpse of Blair.

"She's-look, it was accidental, I swear! Uh, and I," Blake stammered, catching on his own words.

Damien stepped out of the shadow and pushed him.

Blake stumbled back, half-laughing. "You can't be mad at me! I was just getting water!"

The whites of Damien's eyes darkened, leaving just the icy blue circles of his irises. The shadows curled along his jawline, his arms tense, fists twitching with reined-in fury.

Blake raised both hands. "Whoa, whoa, easy. I'm not writing poetry about her spine. I'm telling you; I accidentally got flashed."

Damien stepped forward, a spear of shadow materialized, directly aimed at Blake.

"DAMIEN!" Blake shrieked.

Another splash from the river caught the attention of both the men. "Blake? Damien? Is that you?" Blair's voice rang out cautiously.

In one swift motion, Damien kicked the back of Blake's leg, causing him to fall to his knees. He then used his shadows to push Blake's face deeper into the mud as Blair popped her head up. Blake flailed his arms, but his muffled complaints were quickly stifled.

"Yeah, just passing through. We're almost done with training." Damien then winked, as Blair smiled and dove back into the water.

As soon as she was far enough away, Damien released Blake. He immediately spat mud out of his mouth and wiped his eyes with the back of his hands. "You are ruthless, and that was disgusting."

"I want you to burn that mental image of her." Damien said, his voice thick with annoyance.

"Well, considering mud is now *burned* into my retinas, that won't be a problem." Blake joked back but as he opened his eyes to Damien, his face was still full of anger. Blake took that moment to Shadowstep behind Damien, taking off in a mad dash back to camp.

Within minutes, Blair appeared back at camp, wearing dry clothes and a towel around her neck. Her eyes quickly found Damien and she moved next to his side, kissing his cheek. "Where's Blake?"

"He was a little dirty from training, he chose to wash off in another part of the river." Damien responded, wrapping his arm around her.

"Was it dirt or blood because I don't have the necessary tools to heal him if the damage is too bad." Blair joked, nudging Damien with her shoulder.

"No blood," Blake said, walking up behind them, his voice, an octave too high. "Just training-induced hallucinations and possibly a near-death experience."

Damien pulled Blair closer, his shadows trailing at his back like loyal wolves. "Don't forget about the mud you ate."

Blair choked, looking at Blake. "You already make some questionable decisions but *mud*?! That's too far."

Blake's eyes narrowed at Damien but then softened as he looked back at Blair, "It wasn't my fault. I slipped and fell face-first. Lesson lewarned."

She sighed, then smirked. "Maybe you should train with just me tomorrow. Less injuries. More focus."

"Honestly?" Blake said, crouching down on the floor next to them to start a fire, "That sounds suspiciously like mercy. I accept."

After starting a small fire and sitting next to it for a few minutes, Blake tossed a twig into the flames and watched it shrivel into ash. "We should play a game."

Blair looked up from where she stood with Damien. "A game?"

"Yeah," he said with a smirk. "To keep us from going completely dead-eyed and hollow. Or is that just my coping mechanism showing?"

Damien exhaled loudly in annoyance at the idea, and Blair just smiled in the firelight.

Blake leaned back, "It's simple. One question. You answer it honestly or I get a free day from training. No pressure."

"You're insufferable," Blair said, though her lips twitched with the hint of a smile.

"And you're deflecting. Go on then," he waved his hand dramatically. "What's your biggest fear?"

Blair's smile faltered as her gaze dropped to the fire. "That's really what we're starting with?"

"Straight to the soul, babe. We don't have time for icebreakers in our world."

Blair took a breath, then another. The flames reflected in her eyes as she finally answered. "Losing the people I love, or worse, being right there and still not being able to protect them."

The words hung in the air like smoke. Damien's hand moved to her leg, and he squeezed her thigh.

Blake didn't joke immediately. He watched her, eyes softer now. "That's fair."

She nodded and met his gaze. "What about you?"

He laughed, short and humorless. "Thought you'd never ask." Then he looked back at the fire, suddenly quiet. "Being left behind. I act like I don't care, but I do. I always end up being the one watching people walk away. Sometimes without a word."

Blair reached across and placed a hand over his for a moment. Blake didn't look at her, but he didn't pull away either.

After a pause, they both turned to Damien who didn't look up, he just kept staring into the fire.

"Well?" Blake prodded, back to his sardonic tone. "Mighty, brooding Damien. What keeps you up at night? Spiders? Commitment?"

Damien remained silent as the fire cracked again and sparks danced into the air, but the quiet was louder than before.

"Seriously?" Blake asked. "You don't get to skip just because you're the dark, mysterious one."

Still nothing.

Blake opened his mouth, probably to make another snarky retort, but the look in Damien's eyes shut him up for once.

No one spoke for a while as the fire burned lower, and the night grew colder.

Blake broke the silence first, his voice low but not unkind. "Well. That wasn't emotionally scarring at all."

Blair gave a small huff of laughter.

Soon, dinner was served and eaten. The canned beans slightly burnt at the edge of the pot. Blair passed plates out and they ate quickly. As she finished, Blair let her plate rest in her lap. Her eyes went from Blake's silhouette to Damien, who hadn't moved and hadn't blinked.

After a long pause, Damien stepped forward. He took Blair's plate from her hands, his fingers brushing hers. She blinked up at him in surprise.

"Come on," Damien said, voice low. "You need rest."

She nodded, letting him help her up, pausing slightly as she eyed Blake out of the corner of her eye.

"I'll be there in just a minute. I'm going to clean up really fast." Damien nodded and kissed her on the forehead as he headed into the tent.

As soon as Damien was out of sight, she turned her attention to Blake. "I just want to make it clear that we won't leave you."

Blake looked up at her as many emotions crossed over his face. "I wouldn't say that just yet. I have yet to annoy Damien to the maximum level," he said quietly, a sad smile resting on his face.

"You can hide behind the humor all you want, but I wanted you to hear it from me," Blair said sternly as she stood and brushed off the dirt that clung to her legs. "Do me a favor and clean up dinner?"

Inside the tent, the air was warmer.

As Blair crouched in, Damien was already laying on his back, waiting for her. He was shirtless, with his hands resting behind his head and his feet crossed. She lay next to him, laying her back gently on the padded bedroll next to him. She started to speak, but he brought a finger to her cheek and trailed it to her lips. He then rolled over, straddling her. Using his hands to push her arms above her head, he motioned for her to grab onto the seam of the tent.

"Shhh," he said, and the shadows at his fingertips darkened, curling softly over her mouth. They then formed across the back of her head, creating a gag.

His face hovered close, a whisper away, as he lifted his body up and moved between her legs. "I don't want him to hear you." he murmured, tracing his hands down her stomach and stopping at the waistband of her shorts. She nodded, watching his eyes as he slipped his fingers in and pulled them down. "I missed you."

Blair cocked her head to the side and furrowed her eyebrows, nodding again as if she was trying to say the same thing.

Her eyes began to roll as his mouth traveled lower, his hands spreading her thighs as he lowered his lips to her center. He rolled his tongue slowly over her, and she bucked and lowered her arms. He looked up and shook his head, willing her arms back up. This time, a small tether of shadow bound them. She arched her back, silently pleading with him to return to the spot he left.

His tongue returned, savoring every inch of her. He started with elongated movements and then centered on her clit. The sensitivity made Blair's body shake, her moans muffled by the makeshift gag. As the feeling intensified and pressure began to build, her legs started to close. Damien looked up, his mouth still on her as he winked, and two shadows curled up her thighs, pulling them to the ground. This act was enough to seal her orgasm, sending her into an oblivion of pleasure. Damien continued eating as she exploded and then convulsed, coming down from the intensity.

He smiled at her and kissed her lower stomach. He then grabbed her thighs and flipped her onto her stomach.

Using his hands, he lifted his body weight up, pressing his chest against her back. "You might want to bite onto this." Blair's eyes widened as the shadows pulled away from her mouth, just long enough for Damien to slide in a folded piece of fabric. She studied him as she complied, biting down as the shadows once again covered her mouth.

He moved back down her body, kissing her back and hovering above her ass. "The next time you bathe in the creek, you cover *this*." He bit down lightly, and her eyes rolled. "Do you understand?"

She nodded, the side of her face pushing into the floor.

His hands gripped her hips, and he pulled her up, so she was on her knees, her chest still flat on the floor. "Bite down, Blair."

She listened, bracing herself for whatever was coming. "And know that the next time *this* is out, it'll have my teeth marks."

His warm breath hit her skin, concentrating on the area he was hovering above, "Nod, if you understand."

Blair didn't even have time to process his words before her head was nodding, and his teeth sank into the soft skin of her ass. She bit down, concealing a scream. His hands held her in place as he bit harder, fully intending to bruise her.

Blair squeezed her eyes shut until he pulled away, smacking the sensitive area with his hand and rubbing his fingers in the saliva left behind. He then took his fingers and placed them at her entrance, pushing inside as he licked the imprint of his teeth, which was already swelling.

Shadows raced up the walls of the tent, creating a barrier between them and the outside world. The obsidian shield blocked out all light and sound.

She tried to moan as she rocked her hips, but he shushed her again and began thrusting his fingers in and out before positioning himself behind her, his knees between her legs. The sound of a buckle coming undone had Blair trying to turn around, but Damien spanked her again, and she straightened, looking forward but biting down on the material again.

As he lined himself up, he bent over slightly. Fisting her hair, he drove himself inside with one thrust.

Her mind wanted to apologize, but as she tried, no words came out, just muffled sounds around her gag. She pushed back on Damien as he took her from behind. Every time he pushed in, she felt a deeper understanding of his need for her and his frustration.

The force of him amplified as his grip turned to stone, and Blair squeezed her legs together, reveling in the resounding grunt of approval from Damien. The sound of smacking skin became louder, and Damien tensed, finishing inside of her. He slid in and out until his legs shook. One his shadows released her, he pulled her into him, kissing her forehead.

"How come you didn't answer the question earlier?" Blair asked as he started to kiss her, rolled on his back, "Are you not scared of anything?"

"Of course, I am." Damien sighed, lifting his fingers to her cheekbone and tracing the curve of her face. "It's *you*. I don't want to lose you."

"I think you're kind of stuck with me." Blair answered as she yawned, poking his chest.

"I sure am, Feisty," Damien replied with a small smile.

She murmured a small 'mhmm' as her mind became drowsy, and she fell asleep in his arms.

30

The morning crept in slowly, casting light across the top of the tent. The forest outside was quiet; only the faint chirp of birds and the occasional creak of swaying branches that hinted at awakening life outside.

Inside the tent, the warmth still clung to the sleeping bodies nestled under layers of patched wool.

Blair was the first to stir, noticing they slept past the time they had intended to be awake. Her breath fogged lightly in the cold air as she blinked sleep from her eyes. She shifted slightly, careful not to wake Damien whose arm was slung over her waist, heavy and unmoving. His body curled protectively around hers.

She let herself stay there a moment longer, watching his face in the early light. Her eyes traced over his sharp cheekbones, his scruffy auburn hair, and a scar leading from behind his ear down his neck that she hadn't noticed before.

Even at rest, his expression was tense.

Blair reached up and brushed her fingertips against his temple. "Hey," she whispered. "You awake?"

A slow inhale was her answer. Damien's eyes opened, one by one. His deep-set eyes, encased in a piercing blue, had speckles of a paler shade around his irises. "Yeah," he murmured, voice thick with sleep.

She smiled softly, lowering her volume."You didn't move at all last night. I think that's a new record for you."

"I was tired. All the training is catching up to me," he explained, pulling her body into him.

Blair pulled back just enough to study him, her hand trailing down his chest. "How about we switch it up today? We need to stop in town for some supplies anyway. I am not eating beans again." Her face contorted into a look of disgust.

"Sounds good," Damien agreed as he yawned, stretching.

They sat like that in silence, the cold creeping in beneath the tent flap as the world outside came to life. Finally, Blair sat up a little, propping herself on one elbow.

"Also," she began, observing his face as she walked her fingers up his chest. "Before we head to town, I want to do some new type of training with Blake."

Damien, who was watching her fingers, blinked once. His face didn't change as she continued,"What do you think?"

His jaw tensed. "If you insist."

"Can I insist on something else too?" she asked, her head slightly cocking to the side as she moved her fingers up his throat and along his beard.

"And what would that be?" Damien replied suspiciously, holding her hand against his face.

Blair pulled her fingers away and sat all the way up, letting the blanket fall to her waist. "You telling me why I couldn't show Blake the dagger?"

He looked at her, taking a deep breath. "If I'm being honest, I don't know the real answer. I don't know a lot about it, but I know it's different, and I'm just more comfortable keeping it hidden right now."

"What do you mean different?" Blair asked, her expression concerned.

Damien kept his gaze steady, "I've always been able to sense it, like it's alive. I've been researching it for the last few years, and there's a lot of old stories that fit its description." He paused a moment before bringing his hand back to scratch his head, "The sheath I made for you? The one I gave you when we left SilverDawn? It's special. When sheathed, it hides the dagger, making it so no one can sense it."

She looked down, clutching the blanket to her chest. "Why would you give it to me in the first place then?"

He repositioned himself, moving his body to sit in front of her. "I've always been able to sense the dagger and not in the same way Blake senses shadows. I feel it on a deeper level, and I knew if you had the dagger, no matter where you were, I could find you. I felt like it *belonged* with you, but I wasn't sure how it would affect you. It's part of the reason I've been wanting you to keep it sheathed. I don't know exactly who can sense it."

"Don't you think that's something we need to find out?" Blair blurted out, bringing her eyes to him as she clutched the blanket tighter. "Blake is right here. He is on our side. There probably isn't a better person to test it out on, especially with his enhanced abilities."

"Fair," he said, softer now, eyes searching hers. "You know, as much as I regret dragging you into this mess, I'm glad it was you. You help me in more ways than you can ever know." He leaned in with those words, kissing her on the cheek.

Blair smiled up at him before moving close to his side. "Same, actually. I always thought I had a good life. I loved everything about it, especially teaching, but these last few weeks, I've felt more alive than I ever have before."

"Good," Damien said proudly. "So, about this training, should I be worried about anything?" he asks, his eyebrows rising slightly.

Blair let out a short laugh, "No, if anything, I would pull up a seat and enjoy the show." She laughed again as he buried his face into her neck. "Actually, I think I might know the perfect way to see if he can sense the dagger!" she squealed as his teeth bit into her earlobe. She pushed his face away from her, trying to move to get away but failed immediately. "And when he *doesn't* sense it, I get to openly wield it. Deal?!"

Damien's eyes narrowed in response as he began to full-on attack her, making her squirm in a fit of laughter.

"Deal," he said in between squeezes.

After a few more minutes of laughter, kissing, and uninterrupted bliss, the two made their way out of the tent hand-in-hand.

Blake eyed Damien as he packed his gear, moving slowly and with caution. Blair caught sight as she rolled the tent linens up and paused, letting out a sigh. "He's not going to kill you. You're fine," she breathed out as she continued to roll the cloth.

"Are you sure? He still hasn't said one word to me. Is that his play, psychological warfare?" Blake asked, putting the last of the items in his bag and raising his eyebrows. Blair stood, giving him a bright smile.

"I promise, we're good." Throwing her bag over her shoulder, she shrugged at him, "Just give him time. Besides, I need you to have a clear head going into training today."

Blake's shoulders slumped as he peered into the sky above them,"Isn't it a little late? I thought maybe we were taking the day off."

Blair's smile grew as she nodded to him, "We are, kind of. We're going to do some light training and then go into town for some supplies. Did you think I was kidding yesterday?" she smirked at him as his face started to light up. "Damien can be stealthy, but he uses raw power and his fists. I want to test you on something else. Unless, of course, you're not up for the challenge?" she finished, raising her eyebrows in a challenge.

Blake's dimples popped as he answered with a ferocious smile."Oh, bring it on!" Blake yelled in response, pounding a fist into his open palm.

Damien scoffed as he walked across the site, his own bag at his back. Looking back at Blake, he smacked his left shoulder. "I got money on Feisty," he said, as he continued walking past him and up behind Blair, putting his arm around her waist and pulling her close. Blake laughed out loud at that and gestured to the path that led to their training area.

They walked away with half of their supplies packed and in bags, and the rest left at camp. Once in place, Blake shuffled back and forth on his feet in preparation and rapidly blew in and out several times. Blair looked at Damien but pointed to Blake, rolling her eyes at his choices and blew out a deep breath.

"Eyes closed, Blake, no peeking." Blair said as Blake's body stilled, a look of confusion on his face.

After realizing she was serious, Blake sighed dramatically, folding his arms. Blair moved behind him, pulling his shoulder down so he leaned over. She tied a piece of cloth around his eyes, blinding him. As she did so, Damien turned and started to walk away.

Muffled footsteps moved around Blake as he tried turning in the direction of the sounds. "We're going to test out your ability. I want you to find me. It'll be harder than finding someone with shadows, that comes easy to you. I don't have any shadows to sense, and Damien won't be around. So, close your eyes and try to hit me, and as you try, tell me if you feel any changes around you." Blair stomped a few times and then quietly snuck to one side of the field.

Blake threw his head up, "You blindfold me, tell me to sense you, and now you want me to just trust that you won't make me look like an idiot?!"

A soft chuckle echoed from somewhere to his left or maybe his right as she took out her sheathed dagger and secured it to her thigh.

"Great," he muttered. "He was definitely right about you being feisty."

The air was quiet except for the faint rustling of the trees around them. Blair silently slipped off her shoes and felt the grass with her bare feet. Blake strained to hear it, focusing. No sight. No crutch of visual cues. Just the whisper of air and the sound of her breath when she let him hear it.

He pivoted toward the sound of a weight shift and jabbed forward. Nothing. Just empty air.

"Missed," Blair said sweetly from behind him.

He spun with his fists up. "Stop teleporting, witch."

Another quiet laugh escaped her. "No magic. Just skill."

A second later, two fingers pinched his nipple."Ow! Hey!" Blake recoiled. "What kind of training involves sexual assault?"

"Consider it an incentive to sharpen your instincts." Blair was moving again, light as the shadows that Blake harbored, already gone from where she'd spoken.

"Great. Because nothing enhances warrior focus like fear of an ambush titty twist."

She smacked the back of his head lightly at his comment and moved her hand to her dagger, pulling it out slowly.

"Okay! See, now that, that was rude," he said dramatically, rubbing the back of his head and then freezing.

"No fair, Damien, you can't be in the ring!"

What?

Blair paused, her dagger now in the air. "What makes you think he's here?"

"Don't be coy. I can sense him, remember? His shadow has a certain 'dark and angry' vibe. So if you guys were planning on ganging up on me," He continued, rubbing the back of his skull and frowning. ",there's probably no way I'll win, but it kind of makes me want to try harder."

Blake closed his mouth and breathed in slowly. The air moved as he shifted left and kicked, almost making contact.

It's like Damien. He senses the same thing for both.

"Ooh," Blair said, breaking her train of thought and moving her attention back to the task at hand as his foot grazed her. "Close."

"Close doesn't feed the ego," Blake muttered. "Close gets my nipple pinched."

She circled again, keeping her dagger out, and this time, he caught the faintest tickle of movement around his left shoulder. He dropped low and swept his leg, catching her ankle.

"If you guys stay next to each other like that, it will be easy."

Okay. So, let's move it away.

Blair let out a surprised "Hmph!" and leaped back, regaining her balance. "Progress!" he cheered, arms raised in blind victory.

"Mark it down, Damien. I'm winning."

A moment passed. Then, whap, another light smack to the back of his head. "Or you're *losing*." Blair said as she giggled.

"Damn it!" he shouted, bringing up his hands in karate motions, chopping the air around him. Blake scowled under the blindfold. "You know what else makes me sloppy? Blunt force head trauma," he yelled.

Blair laughed again, moving back to her bag and sheathing the dagger to hide its presence. *Now let's see what happens.*

"Focus. You're starting to anticipate. That's good. Now, do it without talking so much." She slipped back into her movements, circling around him.

"Hey, where did Damien go?" Blake paused, moving his head from side to side as if he could see anything in front of him. "I don't like this."

I knew it.

She didn't answer but moved again, soundless now. Blake's brow furrowed. He steadied his breath, pushing out the noise of his thoughts. He felt for the absence. The void. The part of the air around him that wasn't quite right.

He struck out with a palm… and felt his hand brush cloth.

Contact.

Then came another smack, this time square to his forehead. He froze, a grin slowly spreading across his face. He put one hand on his hip, then popped it out and twirled his finger in a circle."You're just mad because I'm improving."

Blair laughed, exposing her location for a brief second. "You're just mad you can't beat me *or* Damien," she countered as she continued to move.

"Fair. I concede. I admit, I need more practice." he admitted, clasping his hands together and dropping to his knees.

Blair scoffed and removed the blindfold which left Blake blinking into the sunlight. He rose as Damien entered through a thicket of trees.

"Hey," Blake yelled, pointing a glare at Damien as he continued to walk toward them. "Next time, don't join in. You already fight unfairly; at least let Blair learn correctly."

Damien looked at Blair as he approached and nodded slowly.

Blake moved his gaze to Blair, "What's up with that? What's going on?"

Blair reached for her thigh, unlatching the sheath and stepping up close to Blake. His eyes narrowed on the concealed dagger and then moved to Damien as he walked up beside them. "Why are you giving me this?" He asked as he picked up the sheath and turned it around, eyeing the fabric that covered most of the blade.

"We thought we would ask for your input," Blair answered, taking a slow breath in and exhaling loudly. "It's my dagger but it's *different* and I wanted to ask you what you sensed about it."

Blake slowly raised his eyes to Damien, "Okay?" Well.." he started, drawing out the first word as he continued to analyze the item. "I don't sense anything. It seems like any other piece of metal."

"Good." Blair whispered, raising her voice as she continued, "Now, take it out of the sheath."

Blake looked at her as if she were delusional, but he obeyed the request. Slipping the dagger out, he laid it flat in his hand as he tilted his wrist around in a circular motion, his eyes widening with every second that passed. After a few more seconds, he looked at Damien. "It's like you... It's the same exact signature. Dark. It's so strange."

His eyes then moved to Blair, "Did you have this in the ring?" On his last word, he offered the dagger and the sheath back to her.

Blair nodded, reaching for it. "Not to use on you, obviously, but just to see if you picked up on it."

"First of all, your doubt wounds me. Second, I didn't at first. When I did sense something, I thought it was Damien. But this..." he implied as he pointed to the dagger in her hands, "It has a strong energy source of some kind. Everything I sense is based on the strength of the shadow within it. That's why I can't sense Hunters. They have nothing there to sense but the more shadow, the more I can feel it."

He leaned into her then, lowering his voice and pulling his hand up as in secret, "Don't tell him I said this, but Damien's energy has been one of the strongest I have ever felt, if not the strongest." He then pulled away as he noticed Damien narrowing his eyes and cocking his head in their direction.

"Your dagger gives off the same exact amount or level. However, you want to word it. Put him and that thing behind two different doors, and I wouldn't know which is which. Which makes me think-" he said, wrinkling his forehead and bringing his hand up to his chin in thought, "I would be willing to bet it was forged using some sort of Shadowborn ability."

"You think?" Blair inquired as she ran a finger along the design on the blade.

"Yeah, that's what I figured. I guess you just confirmed it." Damien commented as he stepped up beside them, talking to both but then addressing Blair directly, "It's why we have the same signature. It's like we're made from the same DNA."

"Yeah, I'd put money on it. You don't come across those kinds of things. I'd be careful with it. Hunters get a whiff of that," he motioned to the dagger as he moved a couple feet away and sat down, "and they'll be on you faster than Damien finishes. Well, I guess not if you keep it sheathed."

Blair rolled her eyes and sheathed the small blade. "Right about the Hunters, wrong about the Damien part."

Damien followed her movement and then scowled at Blake. "More like as fast as it takes for you to give up." he taunted with a smile, "your nipples a little sore?"

"Like you could do any better, Mr. Fancypants." Without hesitation, Damien looked over and raised one eyebrow at Blair. He then looked at Blake and nodded, signaling that he needed a blindfold. Blake obliged, scoffing as he kicked his feet out and stretched.

Damien became still, dropping his hands to his sides and placing them in his pockets. Blair immediately turned up the stealth, giving small smiles in his direction. She moved constantly, her bare feet gliding across the floor. Damien was patient, waiting until he could pinpoint her exact location.

A knowing grin spread across his face as she moved to his left, and he struck out his arm, catching Blair by the neck. She made a startled noise as the wind knocked out of her, and he pulled her close, grabbing her face and kissing her passionately. He then raised his other arm, directing his middle finger at Blake.

"Joke's on you. I like it when Mommy and Daddy kiss." Blake replied, clapping his hands. Both Damien and Blair pulled away at that comment, giving him a disgruntled look.

Blake fell on the floor in a fit of laughter.

Damien kissed Blair one more time, pulling her under his arm. "I think that was a successful session. Let's go get you some supplies."

31

Within twenty minutes, they were face-to-face with the city of Togar's market. Not exactly what they were expecting, this town exhibited significant differences from the ones they had journeyed through. The streets were littered with trash, a dark demeanor claiming the area.

The first thing Blair had noticed as they crossed into the new town, was the sky. It was the middle of the day, and the clouds were heavy, casting the streets in an overcast light. The buildings here were separated with lots of space, tall and narrow, with crooked chimneys and soot-darkened stone.

All colors were in muted grays and tans, from the cloaks to the linen that perched over the stalls. Most carts were small, offering a few items, and those that stood had a lot of space in between.

As she continued to look around, Blake mumbled about finding a possible place to update his weapons.

Squinting past a group of hunched townsfolk dragging carts of what looked like dried herbs and cracked pottery, Damien and Blair spotted a shop. Blake's eyesight followed, and his body immediately went toward it.

Halting him, Damien motioned silently to a slanted wooden sign half-hanging by rusted chains. "This area is small enough that we can still split up and keep tabs on each other. Do you sense anything unusual?" he asked Blake.

After a second, Blake shook his head in answer, and Damien continued, "Grab what you need and meet back here in an hour."

"Or sooner, if possible?" Blair said softly, watching as the townspeople walked around them, eyeing them suspiciously and talking in their native tongue.

Damien stepped forward to kiss her forehead, slipping a small bag into her back pocket. He stalled at her ear, "I'm gonna go with him and make sure he doesn't break anything. Will you be okay?"

She nodded as he pulled away.

Blake gave a mock salute as he turned away toward the store. Damien mumbled a quick "Be safe." and then followed him.

Blair turned the opposite way, eyeing the options to replenish their food source. As she walked, she found the only fruit stand.

Observing the contents, a bright red fruit was waved in her face that smelled of iron and citrus. She politely declined and walked a few feet to the next vendor, a woman offering her hard cheese-wrapped salted meat with cloves and pepper. Blair weighed the options and politely declined again.

As she continued across the path, a merchant pushed dried nuts into her hands, insisting that she taste them. She popped some into her mouth and smiled at the vendor, who had different nuts she had across her table.

Recalling the bag Damien had slipped her, she reached into her pocket and produced the small silk bag with various coins. Comparing how many she had with what she needed, she counted out enough for a large bag of mixed nuts and turned toward the next opportunity.

Finding carts full of corn and eggs, she moved across the way to a table of chicken jerky. She was almost there when she came across a small table with two chairs. It was bare except for a wooden sign that lay upside down in the middle of the table. She turned it, reading "Fortune Teller," and rolled her eyes. Taking another step, an elderly woman dressed in a tan cloak grabbed her hand and pulled her close.

Blair's body was yanked down to a hunched form, sitting on a third chair to the side. As she focused her attention, her eyes zeroed in on an elderly woman with white hair wrapped in a bun and covered by her hood. She wore dangly earrings, and her skin was wrinkled with age.

Blair tried to pull back, but the woman's grip was abnormally strong. Brown eyes looked up at her, their inner glow tinged with a purple hue. An eerie voice floated around them, "I have a message for you."

Blair looked around and then stared at her, confused, unable to answer. The voice continued as if three voices were stacked on top of each other, "The blade will not protect you, child, not until it turns inward. When shadows rise, and all is lost, only blood will wake the power."

Startled, Blair yanked her arm back and fell from the force, landing on her butt. She winced, grabbing the things she dropped and standing, bringing her eyes back up to the woman.

What?

Her mouth froze.

As she looked back toward the fortune teller, she was not the same. No purple hint to her eyes, no cryptic voice. Her figure was even straight, with no arch in her back.

The woman smiled at her; her face bathed in happiness."Would you like your fortune told? I do palms and cards!"

Blair blinked rapidly, no words escaping her open mouth. She cleared her throat before speaking, "You just-" she lifted her arms up, pointing to the woman, "There was-" she shook her head, lowering her hands back down. "No, thank you." Her words came out in a rush.

"Okay, my dear, just come on back if you change your mind." the woman responded, turning to grab the attention of others who were passing by.

Willing her body to move, she turned around and led herself to the last cart she needed, bearing the dried meat. Every couple of steps, she would look back at the woman who now sat with another customer, shuffling her cards and laying them on the table.

32

A short way down the path, Blake and Damien had just reached their destination, when the sharper sounds of metal and leatherwork echoed from an ironmonger's quarter.

They stopped before a stone building with a slanted roof and an anvil sign hanging from a thick iron chain. Inside, the walls were lined with blades: curved, straight, and jagged.

Blake ran his fingers along a row of short swords. "I wish I could just magically shape things like you can. It would mean I wouldn't have to buy my weapons."

"Yeah, it is a bonus," Damien replied, watching him inspect another small sword. "Hey, thanks for helping us."

Blake picked up a dagger with a blackened hilt. "No biggie."

After an exchange of coins and a firm handshake with the smith, Blake strapped a new blade to his back. It was slightly curved, with a dark steel sheen and a grip wrapped in midnight-blue leather, accompanied by a pair of knives made for speed and precision to match his shadows.

Walking back to Blair, the town square appeared more of a broken circle. The few vendors there curving in front of the dark, soot-covered buildings behind them. A crooked fountain gurgled weakly in the center close to the sign Damien had pointed out earlier. Blair was already there, leaning against the edge with her bag of food at her feet.

"Score anything good?" Damien asked, walking up and kissing her cheek.

"Yeah, enough to feed us for two weeks if we ration." her eyes moved to Blake, "Maybe one if Blake's really hungry."

Blake grinned and winked. "Food and weapons. Check and check," he said, drawing his new addition halfway from its sheath.

"Nice," Blair nodded, impressed. "That's going to make some Hunters very nervous."

Just then, there was a soft shuffle brushed against Damien's side. He turned sharply and caught a small wrist in mid-motion.

A child, no older than seven, stared up at him, wide-eyed and filthy. His fingers wrapped around the small coin pouch from Damien's pocket. The boy's face was streaked with soot, his clothes too big and riddled with holes.

Blake reached instinctively for his weapon, but Damien held up a hand, addressing the child. "I believe that belongs to me."

The child tensed at his words, ripping his hand away and straightening his body. "I'll fight you for it," the boy yelled, pushing his chest out. "I'll bet that I can take you down."

Damien watched with raised eyebrows as the child raised his fists and started punching the air. "Come on, let's go."

Blake scoffed, resulting in the boy quickly moving and punching him right between the legs. He dropped instantly, grabbing his groin and groaning, "You... little... shit."

Blair's mouth dropped open with a suppressed smile, and she stepped in front of Blake on the ground, "Hey there, bud, what's your name?"

The child eyed her suspiciously as he regained his fighting stance. "Ollie."

"Hi, Ollie. I'm Blair, and I'm gonna have to ask you to take it easy on my friend here. That one may be a better opponent," she said, pointing to Damien.

The boy turned, his body now facing Damien as he began to shift from side to side, pounding his right fist into his open left hand.

Damien watched the child move, a small smile breaking across his face. He kneeled as the boy braced, expecting to be hit. Instead, Damien used his hand to take out the pouch. He opened it, counted out five silver coins, and pressed them gently into the child's palm.

The boy stared, frozen.

"I guess you already won then," Damien said softly, voice stern but not unkind. "But keep your hands out of strangers' pockets, Ollie. Not all of them make bets."

The boy's mouth opened, then closed. He gave a stiff nod, then vanished into the alley behind them. Blair watched the exchange silently, her eyes brimming with tears as Damien pulled her beside him and wrapped his arm around her shoulder, beginning the walk back to their site.

As Damien led them, Blair's mind replayed the scene that had just unfolded, and soon, memories of her past students began to play in her mind. She blinked away tears as she stepped. Damien paused, looking back at her, noticing the shift in her demeanor. Walking up to her, he took the bag of supplies and slung it over his shoulder, grabbing her hand and squeezing it as he pulled her up next to him.

The next few moments were silent until Damien spoke, "Tell me about them?" he said, nudging into Blair's shoulder.

"Tell you about what?" she answered, kicking a large rock in her path.

"Your kids. Did you have any like that sticky-handed fighter back there?" Damien asked, raising his eyebrows.

"I mean, yeah, the ones who tested their strength in your forge?" she said, a smile forming on her face as she watched the ground where she stepped. "I actually had quite a few boys who thought they were bigger than everyone. Nothing could touch them, and they weren't scared of anything. They were the best. Each one had a different personality, but they all had hearts of gold." She recalled each one of them then, stepping over a pile of rocks. "And I loved all of them. I guess I miss them more than I thought." Her voice quieted in the last few words.

"I bet they miss you, too. When this is all done, we'll go see them." Damien promised as they came across a turn in the road. "Yeah, I'd love to meet- Blake shifted, his eyes scanning the area around them. The two others looked back, watching his sudden change.

A beat of silence passed, too long.

Snap.

A twig cracked behind them, and all three froze.

Damien moved first, rapidly turning his body toward the sound and pushing Blair behind him in one swift motion. Blair reached instinctively for her dagger and Blake vanished into the underbrush like smoke.

Then the shadows peeled back, and a figure emerged from the tree line, tall and cloaked in midnight leathers. A dark hood shadowed the face, but the shadows at his feet writhed around him unnaturally.

The Enforcer lunged fast, impossibly fast. A blur of motion. His blade gleamed silver as he came down toward Damien. Blake intercepted, appearing next to Damien and colliding with the attacker. The impact sent them both tumbling toward the ground, a whirlwind of shadows and skin.

Damien thrust his hands forward, and a wall of shadow erupted between him and Blair. "Go! Move!" Blair nodded, then sprinted uphill, back toward camp.

The duel continued and moved closer into the forest, where the ground sloped back toward the town's river, slick with moss and roots. Blake ducked a swing, spun low, and sliced across the Hunter's ribs. The man didn't flinch, but he retaliated with a vicious elbow to Blake's temple, sending him sprawling.

Damien was already moving, shadows spiraling around his arms like smoke made solid. He extended his hands, and tendrils lashed forward, binding the figure's ankles for just a heartbeat.

That was all Blake needed.

The Enforcer roared in pain as Blake blinked out of sight and then materialized in front of him, slicing a dagger at his throat.

"Blake! Move!" Damien shouted.

Blake rolled as his opponent unleashed a burst of raw force, cracking the earth near the river's edge.

Damien stepped in, hands raised. He drew the shadows from the surrounding trees and the Hunter's own form, twisting them into spears of pure darkness. Then, he thrust his arms forward.

The spears struck, piercing the Hunter's torso. The man staggered, then dropped to his knees, breath wheezing in his throat. Blair appeared at the top of the hill, sliding down to join them, her dagger drawn and eyes sharp.

The Hunter collapsed in the mud by the river, lifeless.

A long silence followed.

Blake exhaled, looking around and wiping blood from his brow. "He wasn't supposed to be here."

"No," Damien agreed grimly. "I'm willing to bet he's looking for us. Normally, it's just a normal Hunter as a scout, not an Enforcer. We must be closer than we realize."

"We have to move. Now." Blake stated, staring at the lifeless form. Damien nodded in agreement, already turning and stepping away from the scene.

Blair stayed still, clutching the food bag, minus a couple of items that had fallen during the fight. As the two men continued to walk, Blair's heart began to race. "What if they sent him because they know we're coming?" Blair continued, chest heaving. "What if we don't know what we're walking into?"

"We'll handle it," Damien replied, looking at Blake, who wiped his new sword and sheathed it behind his back.

33

Returning to their camp, they quickly changed and gathered the essentials. Blair's fingers worked fast, but without precision. She grabbed extra throwing knives and placed them in the scabbards lining her leather. Her mind wouldn't stay still long enough to remember what else was needed. Her heartbeat was uneven and not from rushing, but from something else.

When shadows rise and all is lost.

The fortune teller's voice echoed in her memory, gravelly and sure. Blair had brushed it off then, like she always did with cryptic omens. But now, something inside her twisted.

Could this be it?

She wondered about that, pausing to look at the men around her. She clenched her jaw and bent down, shoving her bags against the large rock meant to hide their belongings.

"You're moving like you're angry," came a voice from behind her.

Blair jerked her head up finding Damien standing behind her with his arms crossed and his brow raised in concern. His shadows stretched long across the floor, reaching toward her.

"Just double-checking I have everything," she said quickly, *too quickly.*

"You sure?" he asked, taking a step closer to her. "Something tells me that's not it."

Blair didn't answer him; instead, she looked down at her hand, which lay frozen over her satchel. Damien's boots thudded softly as he knelt beside her. Grabbing her chin and guiding her gaze to him, he didn't need her to speak; he could see it in her eyes and the way her shoulders were too tight.

"You're shaking," he said gently.

Blair looked down.

So, she was.

"I'm scared," she admitted, voice low. "I just feel… like we're walking into something bigger than we thought."

Damien was quiet for a moment. Then, with careful movements, he reached out and took her hand.

"We got this," he said softly.

Her eyes flicked up to meet him. "And if we don't?"

Damien didn't laugh. Didn't dismiss her with logic or comfort disguised as reason. Instead, he simply nodded, grounding her. "You said before you trusted me," he said. "I need you to do it one more time. Follow and listen and we'll get through whatever comes our way."

Blair's breath slowed. The tightness in her chest didn't vanish, but it eased. Just enough.

"Whatever's coming," Damien continued, his thumb brushing her knuckles, "we'll face it together. I'm not going anywhere."

She nodded slowly.

Together.

With that, they stood and grabbed the last remaining weapons. Their movements were fast, knowing every second wasted was a second more they could be in danger.

The forest around them seemed too still, any sound or movement putting them on edge. Within a few minutes, armor was on, weapons were hidden, and their gear was strapped. Damien turned, pulling the shadows from the trees around them and using them to conceal their belongings, which were all now hidden in a small crevice in the rocky terrain.

They silently began walking the short hike to the fort alongside the river. Much like the one they had just fought at, it would be at another riverbank. They traveled on their toes, calling no attention to themselves as they walked in silence. They dodged in between trees, and as they drew nearer, they looked at each other and nodded.

Arriving, they paused at the top, before the land sloped toward the riverbank. Blake crouched low in the grass, eyes scanning the broken towers. "Charming place," he muttered. "Smells like the tomb that something clawed its way out of."

It wasn't a strong, towering structure of stone and banners. Being the exact opposite, it was sunk into the ground. Partially devoured by time and water, what remained above ground was crumbling stone. An archway marked the opening, half of it covered by the earth. Vines clung to every inch, dripping with dew as if the land below it was trying to swallow it whole.

Blair slid her dagger out, pointing at the decayed structure. "That doesn't *look* like a fortified base."

"It's not," Damien said. "Not anymore, at least."

They descended slowly down the hill, their boots sinking into the soft riverbank. The ground became stone as they reached the mouth of the sunken building.

Blake stepped forward, peering inside. "If we make it out of here, I better be the best man at your wedding."

Blair let out a nervous laugh, and Damien showed no emotional response as they took a step inside. The building immediately split into a variety of tunnels, sloping down beneath the surface. The air was dense and muggy, smelling of salt water and mold.

Blake motioned, his hand signals barely visible in the darkness. He moved first, with the other two walking behind him down the long, narrow, uneven corridors. The deeper they walked, the darker it grew. The little light that filtered from vents and old grates barely reached the lower levels.

Every few minutes, the trio would pause then Blake would sense for any shadows. Blair took a deep breath during these moments, trying to focus on her surroundings. At their feet, the floor was uneven with broken flagstones and mud. The walls were carved, with some sections featuring specific designs.

"We're close to them," Blake murmured, touching the wall."There's definitely going to be a few friends joining the party, I sense multiple shadows."

"Of course you do." Blair muttered, breathing in to steady her nerves.

They continued to move cautiously, weaving through low halls and collapsed arches. Blake still led, pausing with any inkling of others around them. Blair was in the middle of them, gripping her dagger tightly. Damien was the last, his arms free and his shadows at the ready.

The more they walked, the more Damien's presence seemed to ripple with tension. His shadows coiled tighter and tighter around his arms like bracing ropes.

They paused next to a tall, dome-like chamber with fractured columns and a sunken floor. This time, when Blake focused, he brought both his hands up, turning his head. Blair spun, but it was too late. Two men dropped from above. One slammed into her, driving her to the ground, which caused her dagger to fall from her hands. A knife sliced across the side, tearing through her jacket and into her flesh.

Damien flung a dagger into one of their throats, then grabbed Blair by the arm and yanked her behind a column. "Breathe. Stay low. Don't die."

He then moved back to the battle, his shadows wrapping around his arms like living armor. He struck fast and hard, blades of blackened energy slicing through the narrow space between him and the Hunter.

Blake tried to help, but an Enforcer arose before him, forming himself out of the shadows. Before his body was complete, he was already swinging towards him, forcing Blake to duck and vanish into the shadows. Three more attackers emerged from the dark, all masked in defensive dark shadows. Damien growled in response as his shadows exploded outward, driving two of them back. He moved with an aggressive precision, pushing into the enemy, blades of darkness slicing through anything and everything around him.

But just as they started to gain an advantage, another form stepped into the corridor from the long hallway. He was massive, armored in deep obsidian, a burned symbol showcased on his shoulder. His weapon was a long, bladeshaped scythe covered in flowing shadows. It whistled as he circled it around him, through the air.

Blair barely had time to register what was happening before the gleaming edge of the scythe sliced the air toward Damien. She screamed, gaining the attention of the Phantom. Just as he moved toward her, a burst of black light exploded beside her, and suddenly, she wasn't standing behind the column anymore.

She hit the damp ground of a side passage, heart hammering in her throat. She could just make out a blurry profile of Blake as she felt a dagger being placed in her hand, and then movement flashed in her peripheral vision. He was gone before she fully turned her head. She looked back toward the fight as Blake reappeared behind a Hunter and quickly impaled him before vanishing again. Blair clung to the wall, her head spinning.

Through the tunnel's broken stone arches, Blair watched as her vision cleared. Blake and Damien moved together as they danced around the enemies surrounding them. The opening and closing of Blake's shadow stepping created a field of black circles on the ground as he materialized in and out of them, striking Hunters and Enforcers alike. Awestruck, she noticed how the two men fought alongside each other, their skills enhanced by their training.

Damien's focus was on the Phantom. His shadow sword clanged hard against the scythe, sparks cascading in the dark. Shadow tendrils shot from the Phantom's body, slicing across Damien's arm. He winced but didn't slow.

Blake was across the room, intent on taking down the Enforcer, and appeared behind him in a blink. The blade in his hands broke into twin swords that slashed upward, catching the creature in its side. For a moment, Blair thought it was over until the shadows reformed, knitting the Enforcer's body back together as if nothing had touched it.

Then, the tunnel darkened further.

Without being directly there, she could feel it. Another presence seeped into the cavern. She didn't have to look at Blake to know his demeanor had shifted, his body in a defensive stance. From the crevice behind the first Phantom, a second one emerged. This one was leaner, almost skeletal, with black veins glowing beneath the skin that was stretched too tight. Its eyes were voids. Its grin was that of a nightmare. A burned symbol underneath his right eye.

"Great, another one." Blake bit out, blood on his lips.

The second Phantom raised his lips in a snarl, extending both arms as his shadows erupted outward toward Damien. The second Phantom raised his arms, black wisps pouring from his wrists, creating a web of thick, dense shadows that moved and spread around them. The shadows settled, creating fog that thickened the air around the dome. Moving together, the Phantoms stepped toward Damien, who braced for impact and was thrown against the stone wall. Blake tried to shadowstep around the Enforcer to help, but the air was so thick he struggled to conjure his shadows. Tendrils spilled out from the Enforcer's back, sliding across the floor and crawling up Blake's legs. He quickly swung his sword, but it only swiped through the black mist as it locked on him.

Blair tensed as she watched them continue to fight. Damien had recovered quickly, a black array of swirls pulsing down his face, neck, and chest. He swung a variety of raised weapons forged from his shadows. They seemed to move in every direction, but ultimately not inflicting any damage on the monstrosities around him. Blake's shadows stopped opening beneath him as he fought to free the shadow claw clamped around his calf. A piercing cry filled the air as the claw protruded spikes, puncturing Blake's leg.

Blood began to pool around him as the attack continued, and Blair watched it all, helpless.

Blake was the first to fall. The shadow tendril that had impaled his leg dragged him forward and hung him upside down. Blake roared in pain as he finally managed to cut the shadow holding him, causing him to fall to the ground with a sickening thud. Shadows from the floor rushed over him, and his screams intensified as they carved into his body.

Within a mere second, a soundless roar filled the tunnel. The sound was not heard but felt. A pulse of shadow erupted from Damien's chest, sending a ripple of energy through the entire corridor. The force smacked into everything it touched. The torches blew out. The air crackled, producing a darker black haze that took the place of the one that had lingered. Damien's form twisted, cloaked in the void. Wings of darkness unfolded from his back, lashing the walls. Multiple silver runes seared into his arms. His shadow engulfed everything around him.

The Phantoms faltered.

Damien descended upon them, a god of ruin, his shadows wrapping around their form and pushing them together. Then, in one swift motion, he tore into both the figure's chest, bleeding them of the shadows he controlled. A deformed cry made of multiple voices ripped from their throat. As the shadows were pulled out, they rapidly swirled high above the scene before surging into Damien. His head snapped back, and his body tensed as he absorbed them. His eyes opened, the darkness starting to leak out, creating black tears rimmed in silver. As the last bit of black smoke was forced out, the bodies disintegrated into a pile below Damien.

More Hunters who had entered the corridor watched in horror, the Phantom's dehydrated body in a ruined pile.

Immediately, they tried to run, but Damien's shadows surged, his wings lifting him to the center of the room, above Blake. Each shadow acted as a spear, driving into each body and lifting them into the air as their screams filled the room. As he unleashed his power, the movement appeared in the dark, different sigils of glowing light illuminating and identifying the new Phantoms that had just entered the room.

"There's too many!" Blake screamed. "Damien, We need to leave!" he yelled again, mustering up what energy he had to try and make himself stand. He then turned to Blair, still hidden, "Run, Blair, get out of here!"

Damien landed in front of Blake in a defensive stance as the shapes circled in, three in total. The largest one, well over eight feet and wrapped in coiling shadows, opened his mouth, his voice thick and full of menace. "The King sends us with his warmest regards."

Damien narrowed his eyes, anticipating their next move. Throwing a barrage of shadows at him and moving in closer, Damien moved around Blake to protect him

Soon, the Phantoms worked together, simultaneously hitting from different angles. Lifting himself back up into the air, Damien had managed to impale one with blades of darkness, killing him on the spot.

As he moved to the next, his wings were clipped by a shadowed tomahawk. His eyes shifted to Blair as he careened to the floor. Shadows instantly formed, creating a protection bubble around him and Blake, who was kneeling on the ground next to him, clutching his leg. Damien's face was solemn as the Phantoms bombarded his shield. His eyes shone with regret, and his voice boomed toward Blair, amplified by the shadows. "Get out of here!"

At that moment, one Phantom sickle struck through the barrier, hitting his chest and cleaving through the dark armor that had formed on his chest. He collapsed to his knees, coughing thick red blood.

Blair couldn't breathe.

Her heartbeat thundered in her chest, and as their eyes turned to her, her mind reeled back to that memory in the market. The face of a fortune teller, her booth, and the message she gave. The crone's words echoed in her mind: *".. turn it inward.."*

Tears blurred her vision as she took a step and looked down at the dagger in her hands. With trembling hands, she gripped the hilt and raised it. With no hesitation, she drove it into her own stomach. On impact, the dagger shattered, and the pieces turned into dark threads, weaving into her body.

Agony tore through her like lightning as she heard Damien scream for her, but then her mind went black, a smoke screen of shadows blurring her vision.

A wave of darkness erupted from her body, swallowing the mounded room in pitch black. When it cleared, she stood in the center, next to Damien, a pillar of obsidian fire. Her eyes glowed a bright violet. Her hair whipped around her like a living thing. Lavender cracks raced across her skin, glowing from within as if molten power now ran through her veins.

She raised her hands, and the shadows obeyed. Not just the ones around her but every dark fragment, even the shadows controlled by the Phantoms. They turned, betraying their hosts, and moved toward her.

The Phantom next to her lunged, but Blair didn't flinch.

With a flick of her fingers, the scythe turned to ash in his hand. She clenched her fist, and his body folded in on itself, crumpling into a pile of steam. The second Phantom tried to finish the job and went after Damien, but she was there before he blinked. Her hand plunged into his chest, fingers wrapping around the thing where his heart should've been.

"You will not harm them," she whispered, her voice deepening as her arms ripped back. A black film sprayed across the walls. The Phantom shrieked one last time before falling silent, a hollow husk.

And then the tunnel was quiet.

Blair stood still, her chest heaving. A mixture of blood and shadow streaming from her wound, running down her hip.

Her skin began to crack in multiple places along her body, peeling and flaking like burnt paper. The glow in her eyes flickered and started to dim as she fumbled backward and coughed.

"Blair?" Blake's voice was hoarse, his hands pushing against the floor as he crawled toward her.

She looked up slowly, her body trembling. "It's okay," she whispered with a small smile. "I found a way to help." With that, she collapsed.

"No!" Damien shouted, moving to catch her just before she hit the ground. Her skin was disintegrating in his hands, softening to ash. Damien, bleeding and staggering in and out of consciousness, dragged himself into a sitting position. "Her body is rejecting it," he murmured. His voice cracking, "It's fighting the shadows."

Blake's voice was void of his usual humor as he started to wheeze. "I don't care what's happening. Fix it."

Damien gripped Blair's waist, pulling her weight into him. Her breath was coming in shallow gasps, the wound in her abdomen gaping.

Damien closed his eyes, his body becoming unnaturally still. Then, he moved, lifting his hand to Blair's forehead. A pulse of energy shot into her skull. He repeated the process at her heart and stomach, anywhere that an open injury lay. His shadows acted as a bandage, wrapping around the injuries.

He then moved lower, drawing a line with his finger on her thigh, just above another open wound. His mouth opened, and whispers of something ancient poured out, his fingers tracing a design on her thigh over and over again. A ripple of shadow bled from his palm, curling into her skin.

The shadow fed into her, willingly transferring from him to her, and then, with a dark neon light, it seared itself into her skin. A black, dagger-shaped mark pulsated once with illuminated light.

Laying Blair down and sitting up on his knees, Damien continued chanting, and then his words turned to mumbling and then something even quieter. The energy dissipated from him as it finished funneling into her. Blake watched as the black aura that had swarmed around him, retreated back into his body. The shadowed black webs receded from his face and eyes, highlighting the crystal blue that now bore into Blair as his chest slowed, and hers picked up speed. As the shadows riled around her, inside and out, the physical injuries hindering her body slowly started to heal themselves. Her stomach closed as tremors continued to wrack her body. Damien's voice echoed around her, chanting words in a foreign language.

Finally, Blair stirred. Her fingers, twitching in response to something. Then her body stopped, and she stilled. After a few moments, she started to completely convulse, her mouth slightly opened, a black ooze trickling out. As the shadows from Damien's body filled her, a black mist entered through her eyes, ears, mouth, and nose. It shrouded her skin, laying a thin veil of glistening black webs that sunk in and absorbed themselves. Underneath her skin, it weaved through her veins, stitching her wounds from the inside.

His own life force poured into her as her chest continued to rise. The cracks slowed, forming together and moving to the dagger shape on her thigh. A natural color returned to her skin, but Damien's dimmed. His eyes rolled back as blood seeped from his nose.

"Enough!" Blake cried, reaching up and grabbing Damien's shoulder, yanking him back.

Damien collapsed, slumping over while Blair lay still, her breathing steady.

Blake's attention shifted back and forth as his body began to turn cold. Just as his vision started to fade, Damien opened his eyes.

"Is she gonna be okay?" Blake asked, his throat dry, his eyes closing.

Damien straightened and put her hand into his, leaning to skim his lips over her fingers. "Yes. She'll be better than okay, " he answered, tracing the dagger mark that was now seared into her skin; an exact replica of the one that she had carried, the one that had fractured apart. As he moved his fingers, a visible, black static electricity rose from her skin and followed his movement.

"H-how do you know that?" Blake asked, his eyelids lowering.

Setting Blair's hands down, Damien turned his attention to Blake. He willed his last remaining shadows to cover Blake's body.

They obeyed, wrapping around the injuries and healing him.

"Because, she's been marked," was Damien's only reply.

Blair's eyes opened on his last word, an abyss of swirling black and purple.

DAMIEN

Bonus Chapter

The hammer came down on the metal hard, a flash of sparks igniting the area around it. I watched the light dissipate as the reverberation traveled through my hand, then my arm. *That* feeling was one of my favorites, an advantage of working with my hands in the forge- A place where I could be alone, and not have to worry about people bothering me.

For the most part, it worked well. There were a few regulars who came in for orders, but other than that, I lived in solitude with my shadows.

As I started to finish my last commission of the day, I realized I was just short on materials. *Damn it.* As much as I hated it, I would have to go into town. My body reacted to the spike in annoyance, and small shadows started circling my feet.

Shaking my head, I took a breath and willed them to return as I grabbed my cloak.

Soon enough, the sun-soaked town square was in front of me, along with the bustle of everyone who lived here. People roamed in every direction and conversations carried through the aisles.

I was quick to find what I needed at a specific stall, one I had visited often over the years. He knew me, knew that I didn't do small talk.

Don't get me wrong, I liked some people.. for the most part. I couldn't always manage the noise or the stares, but I could deal with them.

As I walked away, I spotted a group of elderly women who sat in a loose circle beneath a flowering tree. One tossed crumbs to a fat bird and another laughed so hard she slapped her own knee. Their faces were soft with age and sun, their voices drifting in and out amid the morning chaos. None of them seemed to have a care in the world.

No masks, no shields.

Just existing.

I envied that. *Gods, how I envied that.*

My body paused but my eyes kept moving, half out of habit and half out of awareness.

That's when I saw her.

Blair.

The damn school teacher that I always seemed to run into. Despite my best efforts, my journey here always led to her in some way. I wasn't afraid to admit that the last few times I was here, I had even found myself following her.

She made me feel something *different*, something I hadn't quite figured out.

Today, she was sitting on a bench near the fountain, one leg tucked under the other, a book balanced between her and a child beside her. Her chestnut hair was tied in a bun, wisps catching the light like threads of burned copper. There was nothing curated or contained about her, and it was intoxicating.

That was what had drawn me in. She just didn't care and was always entirely unconcerned with who might be watching. I admired that. It was like it came easy to her, being seen without apology.

The child beside her, maybe five or six, huffed and shoved the book away with both hands. Frustration danced across his face like a storm cloud. In the next moment, he kicked off his shoes with a force that could've launched them into orbit. One sailed directly into the crowd, earning a startled shout from a passerby.

I tensed out of instinct, expecting her to snap at him. But she surprised me instead. Her lips curved into a slow and amused smile as she set the book down beside her. Slipping her own shoes off like it was a game, she picked one up and brought it to her nose with theatrical flair, then recoiled in mock horror. The child giggled.

"Ugh, will you tell me if this smells?" she teased, grinning.

The child laughed harder, his earlier frustration already forgotten. She leaned toward him, wagging the shoe like a weapon as he squealed in protest, dodging it with delighted shrieks.

There, on a simple wooden bench, two people created a world of their own. No rules, and no judgement, just joy as I stood in shadow, watching it unfold like a page from a story I'd never been written into.

Eventually, she chased him over to his thrown shoes and they picked them up together. The woman slipped hers back on, then helped the boy with his as he fumbled in a clumsy manner. They rose together with their fingers entwined and walked away through the square, laughing about something I couldn't hear.

How could someone live like that? So full of light? No armor to protect them, no shadow to hide behind.

They walked around the corner to a house that was nestled behind a broken fence. Passing through the busted wire, they approached the door. After a few knocks, a man answered with a warm smile on his face. Blair waved goodbye before turning away and walking back down the path.

I instantly followed her, hidden by the shadows between the buildings. Once again, I found myself invested in the way she saw the world. My footsteps mimicked hers as she walked down the winding path through the trees. It was like she owned the woods, whistling to the birds around her and lighting up when they whistled back. There was something about the way she walked, like she never had a reason to fear the dark.

Like it belonged *to her*, not me.

I stayed close, now cloaked in the long shadows casted by the surrounding trees. It wasn't long before she settled, finding a bench. As she sat, she pulled out another book, this one with a well worn cover.

I moved closer, slipping under some heavy branches across from her. Crouching there, I stayed silent, my hand aimlessly toying with the dagger that hung from my belt- an item that had always brought me a certain sense of comfort and belonging.

Did she have something like that?

Suddenly, my brain was yelling at me to give it to her and my hand gripped the hilt in agreement.

Shaking my head, I scoffed at my stupidity and refocused on her.

She would read for a few minutes and then look up at the world around her, her hazel eyes illuminated by the sun. Every time she looked back down, more soft strands fell over her face. It took everything in me to stay still, and not expose myself just to be able to tuck them back behind her ear.

I pushed through the adrenaline that internal fight somehow activated. As I inhaled deeply, I forced a sense of calm to wash over my body.

She laid on her stomach now, across the bench, holding her chin in her hands. It was only a few moments before she shifted again, as something from the book made her laugh. It was a quick, bright sound that did something strange to my chest.

That's what always happened when I was around her. The quiet didn't seem to matter and I felt... *alive*.

My shadows agreed, coming out to curl around me. They layered over each other as I shifted my position to a standing one, readying myself for them to misbehave. Weirdly enough, they also seemed at ease.

My shadow magic had always been strong, but that didn't exactly matter when it always seemed to be in a volatile state. I had grown accustomed to them fighting back but recently, I had come to find that around her, they calmed. *Fucking traitors*.

My chest filled with an emotion I wasn't familiar with and I stepped back, uncomfortable. My shadows hissed quietly at my retreat as I looked up at Blair one more time.

Gods, she was beautiful.

Turning away, I faded back into the darkness where it was comfortable. Here, I knew what to expect. Here, I was in control.

Walking back to the forge, I tried everything I could to *not* think about her. The biggest irritation of all was that I could feel it, a need to protect her, to keep her safe… and I had no idea why.

My mind retaliated, envisioning her hazel eyes, her freckles and her lips.

Fuck.

She's gonna ruin me.

Acknowledgements

I have no words to express my gratitude to every single person who encouraged me to write this. Not only did you believe in me, but you pushed me to pour my heart into it.

To my friends who listened to me rant about it until my brain bled and received midnight text messages about updates- I see you and I appreciate you.

To the readers who took a chance on a new author, your faith means more to me than you'll ever know.

Lastly, to my husband who literally held my hand every step of this journey, I owe you everything. Thank you for loving every dark shadow I carry and being the reason my light shines so bright.

Want to see what happens next
for the Shadowborn?..

BOUND

Book Two

Some bonds protect.
Others destroy.

1/25/2026

www.ingramcontent.com/pod-product-compliance
Lightning Source LLC
Chambersburg PA
CBHW030238120726
47903CB00005B/1536